GRAVITY
The Alex Cave Series Book 4.

Written by James M. Corkill.

I0589805

Chapter 1

BUFORD GLACIER, ICELAND:

A distant noise caused Baltistan Nilsson to look up from his equipment on the northern edge of the ice sheet. There had been a larger than normal amount of ice breaking away from the face, so he was taking readings on the rate of calving, using a small quad copter with a built-in video camera.

He knelt down to check the chopper when he heard a strange hissing noise. He stood and stared in the direction of the sound, but all he could see on the other side of an ice ridge was a large, vertical white cloud against the sky blue background.

He carried the copter up to the top of the ridge separating him from the steam plumes, where an ominous glow reflected sporadically from his sunglasses. As he pulled them off to get a better look, his eyes widened and his jaw sagged in disbelief.

"What in God's name is that?"

He realized no one would believe this without a video recording and quickly flipped the switch to power up the chopper. He stared at the screen and began recording, then turned the helicopter toward the steam cloud.

***

MONTANA STATE COLLEGE, BOZEMAN:

Alex Cave sat on the edge of his old wooden desk, gazing out over his second year geophysics students, all feverishly trying to finish final exams on the last day of class. The faces changed, yet the material remained much the same. Year after year, it was the same lectures, the same tests, and the same student performance.

He grimaced, wondering silently about his chosen profession at the college. He loved the subject, and teaching paid the bills, but even with the occasional field trip to interesting formations, the work was becoming all too boring. He felt like a caged animal required to perform the same trick repeatedly for a tiny bit of a reward.

Since the highly classified Red Energy Operation last year, he would do the occasional investigation of extraordinary circumstances for his friend, Martin Donner, the Director of National Security. However, occasional was the optimal word, and it wasn't enough to get him out of his monotonous rut.

He looked up at the clock and felt a sense of relief. In a few more minutes, his classes would end for the summer. When he heard a knock on the door, he turned to look at a man in a US Postal Service uniform standing on the other side and strolled over to find out what he wanted. "Can I help you?"

The man held out an envelope. "Sorry to bother you, Professor Cave, but I need your signature."

Alex signed for the letter and read the return address as the man walked away. It was from Reykjavík, Iceland, with Urgent written in red letters. The bell rang, and he looked at his students. "Have a great summer, everyone."

He stepped aside while they left his classroom and then sat at his desk to grab a letter opener. Inside the envelope were a round-trip airline ticket from New York to Iceland, and a single page note.

'Hello Alex. I am Jeffery Sliven, the Director of the Nordic Volcanological Center, and I need your help with an unusual geological discovery and Director Martin Donner said this might interest you. Below you will find the time, date, and location of the symposium we will hold with other top professionals in your field. I know this is short notice, but your expertise would be greatly appreciated. Sincerely, Jeffery.'

Alex felt a small adrenalin rush, thinking about the potential for a new challenge. He called the local airport and got a connecting flight to New York, but it would leave in two hours. As exhilarated as he was at the prospect of a new adventure, he knew his girlfriend, Fala, would not be happy about his having to leave again.

He tucked the envelope into his briefcase and headed out the door. When he reached the parking lot, he climbed into his SUV and headed home.

***

Alex drove into the driveway on his small ranch and parked next to his girlfriend's SUV. When he climbed out, he heard a familiar giggle and smiled. Halona, Fala's nine-year-old daughter, was playing tug-of-war with his dog, Barney, a mixed-breed he had rescued from an animal shelter as a pup, who had grown up to look more like a brown bear than a dog.

When Alex knelt down, Barney let go of the thick rope to run to him, causing Halona to fall on her butt. She laughed and jumped up, running after the dog. They both stopped in front of him, and he ran his hand through Barney's thick fur. "How you doing, big fella?"

Halona smiled and held the rope out for her friend to see. "I won, Alex."

Alex grinned, swept her up onto his arm, and stood up. "I saw that. You're getting stronger every day. Has your mom been giving you some kind of magic Native American growing medicine?"

Halona laughed. "No, silly. I'm just growing tall, like her."

"You sure are, so it's time you do your own walking." He set her on the grass. "See if you can beat Barney again, while I go talk to your mom."

Halona looked up at Alex and frowned. "You're leaving again, aren't you?"

Alex knelt down in front of her. "I'm afraid so."

"Will you be back for my birthday party on Sunday?"

Alex loved Halona as much as he loved her mother, who had planned the party several weeks ago, and he dare not miss it. "I promise I'll do my best to be here."

Her lower lip fell into a pout. "All right."

Alex stood and climbed the steps onto the back porch. When he looked back, Halona and Barney were playing again, so he went into the house.

***

Alex set his briefcase near the hallway and found Fala sitting in a chair in the living room. Because of her raven black hair, her parents had named her for the Native American word for crow. Fala.

Fala looked up from her laptop when she heard the door open, then saw Alex, and smiled. "Somebody sure looks excited. I bet you're happy to be done with classes for the summer."

"Definitely, but that's not why I'm excited. I've been asked to attend an urgent geological meeting in Iceland."

Fala's smile was replaced with a scowl. Nearly slamming her laptop on the coffee table, she stood. "Iceland? Are you kidding me, Alex?"

"What?"

"You just got out for the summer and I thought we might finally do some traveling together. All three of us, or maybe you and I could go somewhere. Between classes and your mysterious rock excursions, I feel like we don't see you enough. Hell, I don't see you enough."

Alex walked over, grabbing her around the waist and pulling her close to him. "Fala, you know I love you."

Fala smirked slightly and rolled her eyes, "You have a funny way of showing it, traveling around the world, leaving me here to feed your dog and bring in your mail."

"How about this? When I get back, we'll make time for us. We'll take Halona to your parents, and then we'll go on a little trip. Just the two of us."

"You promise?"

He kissed her on the lips. "Of course."

"Why wait, Alex? There are thousands of perfectly qualified geologists in the world that can handle a little rock crisis in Iceland. Let one of them deal with it."

"I can't. Not this time. I *have* to go."

Fala pulled out of his grasp. "No, Alex. You *want* to go. There's a big difference."

When she stormed into the kitchen to start dinner, he stared after her. He knew she was right, but he still wanted to go to Iceland. Something about the urgency of the message gnawed at him.

Fala slammed cupboard doors closed and tossed silverware into drawers. "Will you be joining us for dinner, or will you be leaving right away?"

Alex stood in the kitchen doorway, watching her slam the oven door closed and toss a pot of water on the stove to boil. "My flight leaves in less than an hour, so I'll leave as soon as I finish packing."

Fala stopped in her tracks, folded her arms across her chest, and stared at him. "Well, when do you plan on being back? You know Halona's birthday party is on Sunday. She'll be crushed if you're not here."

"I know, and I promise I'll try to be back on time."

"Don't make promises you don't intend to keep, Alex. The last time you went off on one of your geological symposiums or digs or whatever it is you keep running off to do, you said the exact same thing. You know, my parents went to a lot of trouble arranging the ceremony with the Cherokee leaders to welcome you into our tribe."

"I know, and I apologized to them, but this time it's different. They just need my opinion about a geology problem."

Fala uncrossed her arms and went back to fixing dinner. She searched through the cupboards, slamming the doors as she went. "Yeah, right. The last time you came back from one of your 'geology' trips, your face was all bruised and you had three broken ribs. Since when did studying rocks become so dangerous?"

Alex stepped into the kitchen and smiled as he grabbed Fala's hands. "This time, I'll be in an auditorium on a university campus." He felt Fala's hands relax slightly in his and looked into her dark brown eyes. "Are we okay?"

When Fala nodded, he kissed her on the cheek. He strolled down the hallway to his office to grab a suitcase from the closet and his passport from the desk drawer, and continued to the master bedroom and packed for a short trip. When he entered the bathroom, he opened the only drawer out of six that was his, and grabbed his shaving bag, then went back and added it into his suitcase. He returned to the living room, where Fala was in the kitchen. "I'm all set."

Fala moved to the kitchen doorway, her disposition having softened considerably since he had packed. "Do you need a ride?"

"No thanks. Actually, I don't think I'll be gone more than one night, and I'm not sure what time I'll be getting back. I'll take my truck so you don't have to leave your veterinary clinic to pick me up."

"All right. Just call me when you get back."

"I will."

When he turned and headed for the back door, Fala followed him outside. She just hoped he was telling the truth about staying in an auditorium.

She followed him to his car and waited while he said goodbye to Halona, then wrapped her arms around his neck. "Be careful, Alex."

He kissed her lips. "I will. I'll call when I'm headed back."

When Alex drove away, Fala climbed the steps up to the deck and sat in a chair. She knew about Alex's past working for the CIA, and he had promised never to work for them again, but for the last four months, she suspected that on some of his supposed field trips, he was really doing some kind of secret mission for the Director of National Security. Whatever he was doing on those occasions, it wasn't studying rock formations.

She wanted a comfortable family life, with a husband who doted on her, a father who adored her daughter, and family dinners together every night. She wanted a chance to travel across the country on summer vacation like a normal family, not stuck here alone for weeks at a time while Alex ran off on some adventure.

This new trip to Iceland didn't sit well with her, and she had a bad feeling this excursion was some type of secret mission, and that Alex would wind up getting hurt again, or worse, killed.

Fala looked away from the pasture when she felt a small hand on her shoulder, then turned to see her daughter's troubled expression. "What's on your mind, sweetie?"

"You looked sad, Mom, so I came over to cheer you up."

Fala smiled. "Well, thank you, baby. You did. Shall we have some supper?"

"Is Alex going to get hurt again?"

Fala's smile slipped away when she realized she wasn't the only one worried about Alex's safety on this new trip. "We'll ask the Spirits to watch over him after we eat, okay?"

"All right."

Chapter 2

ICELAND:

NordVulC, (Nordic Volcanological Center), in Reykjavík, was on the campus of the College of Iceland, which was on the Southern Peninsula of the island. When Alex entered the small auditorium, he recognized several of the most prominent figures in the geophysics community, and knew whatever was going on must be of great significance for all of them to arrive on such short notice. He nodded to the familiar faces and sat down in the front row.

A small man with wavy white hair stepped up to the podium and adjusted the microphone. "Thank you for coming. For those of you who may not know me, my name is Jeffery Sliven, the director of this facility. I'll get right to the point. Two weeks ago, a student discovered a strange event on the north side of the Buford glacier, and if he had not been there, it is doubtful anyone would have noticed this strange event. Rather than my trying to explain it to you, here is the video from his remotely operated aircraft."

Sliven looked at the projectionist, the lights dimmed, and an image appeared on the screen. The motion picture showed the aircraft approaching a billowing cloud of steam rising above a glacier. When it pierced through the haze, the image caused everyone to gasp. Massive globules of glowing molten rock appeared to be floating up out of the glacier. Suddenly, they all slammed down onto the ice, sending plumes of steam hissing into the air. An instant later, the camera lens shattered, and the movie ended.

The picture on the screen vanished, and then lights in the auditorium blinked on as Sliven stepped up to the podium. "Even stranger is the complete lack of seismic activity to account for lava movement. Now, this next video was taken by the same student four days ago." He nodded to the projectionist.

Once again, the picture was from a drone flying over the glacier. The camera focused on the smooth walls of a black tunnel, and showed it was not straight down, but like a corkscrew. The drone dropped inside, showing darkness for a few moments, and then the picture blinked off.

The lights came on and Sliven went back up to the podium. "That, ladies and gentlemen, is the exact spot where the magma floated up out of the glacier. My colleagues and I are at a loss to explain either of these events." Sliven held his palms up. "I am open to suggestions."

Muffled conversations quickly filled the room, and Alex sat quietly listening to the ideas offered to the Director, but none of them appeared confident in their theories. Doctor Leo Bernstein theorized a slow-moving pocket of super-heated gas forced the magma up through an ancient lava tube until Sergey Outremer reminded him that the Atlantic rift through Iceland results from recent volcanic activity, not ancient.

Alex leaned back in his chair and looked up at the Director. He knew about Sliven's reputation as the world's leading volcanologist, but he had never met him in person. If Sliven didn't know the cause of the strange volcanic tunnel, he doubted the other volcanologists would know, either. The only way to get definitive answers would be to get inside and take a good look around, so he raised his hand.

"Yes, Mister Cave?"

The room became quiet, and Alex noticed everyone staring at him. "Excuse me for interrupting, Director, but have you sent a team down into the tunnel?"

"No, but the student who went inside to retrieve his drone said it continued down much farther than he wanted to go without proper equipment. We all know your reputation for dealing with strange situations, so I was hoping you would like to lead the first team."

Alex grinned. "Yes, thank you. I would love to. I'll need a couple of days to get organized though, if that's all right? I have an idea, and it will let us know what we might be up against."

"Of course." He looked at the other hands being raised and pointed to a woman. "Yes, Ms. Stafford?"

"I'd like to go on the expedition with Mister Cave."

Sliven looked at Alex. "Mister Cave?"

Alex already knew this development was unusually odd, and he did not want to jeopardize anyone else's life before he understood the situation. "My partner and I will assess the area first to make sure it is safe. Once the preliminary findings verify there is no imminent danger, I'll organize a larger expedition and Ms. Stafford can join us."

Sliven turned to the audience. "Are there any more questions? All right. Those who wish to be included in the second expedition, please add your name to the list for Mister Cave. Thank you all for coming."

Sliven walked down to talk to Alex face-to-face. "I'm glad you came. You were at the top of my list of people who needed to be in on this discovery."

"Well, thanks for allowing me to do this. I'll head back to the States and let you know when I'm ready."

"All right. It is your expedition, so just let me know if there is anything I can do to help."

"I will. Thank you."

When Sliven walked over to join a small group of people, Alex noticed the Ms. Stafford speaking into her phone. He headed over to talk to her, but when she noticed he was moving in her direction, she quickly hung up and hurried out of the auditorium. He followed her out to the parking lot, wondering if she wanted to talk outside, but she climbed into a car and drove away. "That was strange."

***

Stacy Stafford drove off campus to a small Internet café and hurried inside to a vacant table. She brought out her smartphone, took a quick look around, and pressed one contact. "Hey Janice, you're not going to believe this. I'm sending you a recording showing you why I was called to this meeting. I think your legend might be true."

"When are you coming home?"

"I'm not sure. Sliven put some geologist named Alex Cave in charge of forming an expedition, but he insists on doing a preliminary assessment by himself. If he finds what you're after before anyone else, you'll never get your hands on it."

Janice Sloan knew a little about Cave's reputation and his connection with the CIA, and he would have all the resources he would need to go down the tunnel and take her prize. "When is he starting?"

"He didn't say, but he's headed back to the States right away. He'll call Sliven when he's ready, so use your contacts to tap into the Director's phone service."

"I will."

"Okay, I'll call if I learn anything new. I love you."

"Yeah, back at you."

***

When Alex boarded the airplane back to the States, he felt the familiar adrenalin rush of being on the hunt again. He sat down next to the window and thought about the best way to survey the tunnel before he entered, but what he couldn't figure out was the smooth surface. It reminded him of black volcanic glass called obsidian, but that would be impossible. The material needed to make the glass was silicate sand, and it was not native to that region of Iceland.

He leaned back, closed his eyes, and tried to sleep, but couldn't stop thinking about the tunnel. The flight seemed to take forever before the pilot finally announced they were on final approach to LaGuardia International Airport. As the plane taxied to the air terminal, he had an idea about how he could survey the tunnel before going down. The only problem was he didn't have the resources to make it happen, and then he smiled and brought out his phone to ask for Director Donner's assistance.

***

WASHINGTON, DC:

When Alex walked into his office, Director Donner stood from behind his desk and held out his hand. "Welcome back. Have a seat and tell me more about this unusual lava tube."

Alex sat down. "You didn't have to send your private plane to pick me up, Martin. We could have done this over the phone."

"I know, but this sounds important. Just like the missing oil in the Dead Energy Operation, and the sudden polar vortex issue in the Cold Energy mission, you seem to have a knack for discovering and solving problems never heard of before. I just want to make sure you get everything you need."

Alex told him what he saw in the movie. "I'm not positive it was created by lava, but for the moment, I don't have an alternate theory. I think I know how to check the interior before I go down, but I need your help to procure these items." He slid a sheet of paper across the desk. "Here's what I need to make this work."

Donner's eyes went wide when he learned what he had in mind. "Good grief, Alex. I've never heard of one being used for that purpose, but I'm sure it can be arranged. Where are you going to build it?"

"The Naval Test Facility in Keyport, Washington, but I need to return home first. It's Halona's birthday tomorrow."

"Of course. Fala sounds like a wonderful woman. One of these days, I'd like to meet your new family."

Alex smiled. "She is wonderful. Amazing, actually. You'll have to come out sometime. For leisure, of course, not business." He stood. "I'd better get going or I'll miss my flight."

Donner stood and walked him to the door. "I'll set everything up for when you're ready. Just let me know if there is anything else I can do to help."

"Thanks, Martin."

When Alex headed down the hall and out of the building, his thoughts immediately went to Fala. In all the excitement of the floating lava, he had completely forgotten about his promise to her, and wondered how he could explain this, knowing she would probably wring his neck.

***

FALLON, NEVADA:

Janice Sloan stepped through the open doorway of a small private jet airplane and stared out across the desert, then looked around the complex. On the other side of the runway was a pyramid-shaped building with three glass spires. She saw several aircraft hangars on other parts of the compound, and the one alongside the runway had an odd-looking railing protruding from one side. When she climbed down the steps, a five foot tall man with thinning hair greeted her. "Hello, Essex. I'm glad you accepted my offer."

John Essex smiled. "Hello, Janice. I just hope it's worth the trouble. Are you certain about this? Because if you're correct, it would solve my problems for inexpensive space travel."

"I'm certain. We'll need to have a jet ready to take us to Iceland on a moment's notice."

Essex smiled. "I have the right connections to get us anywhere, anytime."

"Good. Now, take me to your living quarters. I need a drink."

Essex indicated the car was parked a short distance from the plane. He knew a little about Sloan's illegal operation. He also knew she was a ruthless woman and had some deep-seated psychological need to be in charge of her situations. He would just have to trust her about this opportunity if he wanted a viable means for launching his space vehicles.

The car stopped in front of the building with the spires, and they climbed out. As they headed for the entrance into his office and living quarters, they passed several polished green granite blocks with ESSEX SPACE RESEARCH AND DEVELOPMENT CORPORATION carved into them.

Chapter 3

MONTANA:

Halona was waiting on the porch as an SUV parked in the driveway, and when she recognized the tall man with black hair getting out, she smiled and jumped out of her chair. "Alex!"

Alex smiled and swept her up into his arms. "Hello, birthday girl. Did you miss me?"

"Yes, but Barney kept me company."

When the woman he loved stepped out onto the porch, Alex set Halona down, wrapped his arms around Fala's waist, and then gave her a kiss. "See, I told you I'd be okay. And I'd like the record to show that I am also back in time for the party."

Fala smiled and kissed him back, holding him close, and breathing him in. "I'll make a note in my diary."

"Have you heard from your cousin?"

"He's on his way here as we speak."

When Alex felt Halona pulling on his shirtsleeve, he looked down at her. "You're in a big hurry."

"Mom said I had to wait until you got here before I got my surprise present. So can I open it? Please!"

Alex smiled. "Not until your Uncle Okawna gets here."

Seeing Halona and Alex getting along so well made Fala smile. Halona's real father was a mean bastard who considered women subservient, hitting them occasionally to show his dominance. Alex was the complete opposite, treating women as if they were precious gems to be protected at any cost. It was one of the many qualities she loved about him.

As Halona ran off to play with Barney, Alex and Fala sat down in green plastic deck chairs. He reached into the ice chest, grabbed two beers, and opened one before handing it to Fala. As they sat watching Halona and Barney, Alex gave her the dull highlights of his trip to Iceland; how long and boring the plane ride was, how much he enjoyed talking with his fellow geologists, and all the different foods no one could pronounce in the hotel buffet. He talked about everything, except the true meaning behind the urgent meeting. All he mentioned about the geological discovery was there was an unusual tunnel below a glacier.

Recalling how she reacted to his sudden trip to Iceland, he dreaded having to tell her about needing to turn around and leave again to go to Seattle. "I've got something to tell you, Fala. Now, before you get upset, please hear me out."

Fala sighed in resignation. "Why am I not going to like what I am about to hear?"

"I have to fly into Seattle tomorrow morning to make the arrangements for surveying the tunnel."

Fala slammed her beer can on the table, and foam erupted from the top. "You promised, Alex! You said when you got back, we'd go on a trip. Just the two of us."

"I know, and I plan on keeping my promise, but the job isn't done and they still need my help. Let me finish what I've started and I'll take you wherever you want to go."

"No, Alex. For once, can't you just let someone else take care of it?"

"No, Fala. This is my job."

"No, Alex. Your job is teaching geology. You're a college professor, not Indiana Jones, who gets to traipse all over the world on some epic adventure. We're a family, Alex, and we're supposed to be together. At least, that's what I thought when you asked us to move in with you."

"I know, but you have to understand, this is very important to me."

Fala stared at the ground, nodding her head. "Important to you, huh? More important than me and Halona?"

"Fala, you know that's not what I meant."

"It's what you said though, Alex, isn't it? Sit there and tell me that's not what you just said."

When he didn't reply, tears blurred her vision, and then rolled down her cheeks. She turned away from him to stare at Halona and Barney, knowing she made a big mistake moving in with him.

Alex set his beer down and knelt in front of her, wiping her tears away with his fingers. "Fala, you know you and Halona mean the world to me. I would kill for you. That's how much you mean to me. Now tell me, why are you getting so worked up about this job? I'm just going to explore a tunnel. Pretty standard stuff."

"I just have a bad feeling about this trip. It sounds dangerous, Alex. The last time you went somewhere, you came back all battered and bruised. What if this time you come back in a body bag?"

Alex stood up and kissed her on the lips. "I love that you worry about me so much, but you have nothing to worry about. I'll be fine. It's not like I'm going by myself. I'll have company."

She wiped the rest of her tears away. "Who's going with you?"

"Your cousin, if he agrees."

Halona suddenly ran up the steps, smiling. "Uncle Okawna is here!"

Alex and Fala stood up and turned to look at the white pickup coming up the driveway. When Okawna stopped and climbed out, they all walked over to greet the tall man with shaggy blond hair.

Okawna smiled and picked Halona up. "You're getting big, and you're as pretty as your mom."

"Thanks, Uncle Okawna. What's my surprise?"

Okawna gave Fala a questioning look. When she gave him a nod, he opened the passenger door and grabbed something inside, then knelt down to give Halona a puppy. "Happy birthday."

Halona smiled and cradled the little ball of fur in her arms, giggling when it licked her nose, then she kissed Okawna on the cheek. "Thank you, Uncle Okawna. What's his name?"

"He's a she, and that's up to you. She's a golden retriever, and she needs someone to care for and play with her."

Halona held the puppy at arm's length and studied its face. "I think she looks like a Trixie."

Fala smiled at Alex. "So, what do you think?"

Alex wrapped his arm around her waist. "I think she makes a nice addition to the family. Is the pup from your clinic?"

"Yes, the mother was hit by a car and I couldn't save her. This one was the runt of the litter, and the only puppy nobody wanted. The poor little thing is so affectionate I just couldn't put her down."

Alex watched as three more cars parked in the driveway, and suddenly several of Halona's little friends climbed out and ran up to see the puppy. Fala moved out of his grasp and went over to talk to the other mothers.

When Okawna walked up, Alex reached into the ice chest and held out a beer. "Have a seat and tell me about your work in Alaska."

Okawna accepted the beer and sat down. "Mike is taking his research ship, the *Mystic*, to the location of that cylinder you told us about. Tomorrow I'll fly back to help him with the search."

"Do you think Mike can spare you for a few days?"

"I can ask. What have you got in mind?"

Alex explained what had happened in Iceland. "I'll do the first exploratory survey, and I'd like you to join me."

Okawna grinned. "I'm sure Mike won't mind. In fact, I think he'd love to join us."

"I'd prefer it just be you and me for the moment."

"All right. When are you planning to go down the tunnel?"

"I'll need some time in Keyport to get organized, so let's meet in Iceland in four days."

"Four days? Didn't you just get back?"

"Yeah, today."

"I bet Fala wasn't happy when you told her you were leaving again."

"She was pretty upset."

"Take it from someone who has been with his fair share of women, my friend. Unless you like sleeping on the sofa, don't piss off the woman you're sleeping with. Trust me, it's sound advice. A sofa doesn't hold a candle to a soft warm woman lying beside you, so you best keep her happy. But as for your question, we've been through a lot of tough situations together, so I'm in."

"I appreciate it."

Okawna stuck around until Halona cut her birthday cake and had one piece before heading for his truck. As he strolled over to say goodbye, he noticed Alex's serene expression. And held his hand out to him. "It's nice to see you happy again, my friend."

Alex smiled. "I've never been happier."

"Remember what I said. Sofa city."

Alex glanced at Fala. "Got it. I'll see you in Iceland."

When Okawna drove away, Alex walked up onto the porch, grabbed his beer, and sat down in a chair. He had a family he loved, and an adventure to go on with his best friend. Things just couldn't get any better.

Chapter 4

KEYPORT, WASHINGTON:

Alex looked down at the six-foot long by twenty-four-inch diameter rear section of a submarine torpedo mounted onto a four-wheeled cart. The front of the deadly device had been removed, replaced by a small metal rack, which supported the lights, camera, and atmosphere sensing equipment needed to determine if the tunnel was safe to enter.

A one-mile length of optical cable was coiled inside the torpedo, and Alex grabbed the end to plug it in to a laptop computer and turned it on. When the face of the civilian woman standing in front of his creation appeared on the monitor, he knew this part of the system was working and looked over the top of the torpedo at her. "Ready to test the atmosphere sensors, Susan."

"All right. We'll start with methane."

Susan opened a valve on a small cylinder, allowing the gas to escape in front of the small plastic tube. "It's on."

Alex studied the digital numbers along one side of the small monitor. "I have a positive reading for methane, at three-thousand parts per million. Ready for the next gas."

Thirty minutes later, Alex turned the computer off and smiled. "All systems are functioning as promised. Thanks for your help, Susan."

She smiled. "You're welcome. Mind if I ask where you plan on using this thing?"

"A tunnel in Iceland. It's deep, and this will let us know if we need special equipment before we begin our descent."

"Well, you'll have to donate this to the Smithsonian when you're through. It's definitely one of a kind."

"I'm afraid it will be a one-way trip."

"That's too bad. I doubt there will ever be another one like this. If you're a geophysics instructor, how do you know so much about engineering?"

"I almost got my master's degree in mechanical engineering, and then I realized I would be stuck in an office all day."

"True. How are you planning on getting it to Iceland?"

"I have a rental van waiting outside. I'll take it to the Whidbey Island Naval Air Station and load it into a military transport plane and we should arrive in Iceland tomorrow afternoon."

"Good luck, Alex."

"Thank you."

Chapter 5

ICELAND:

Alex stared out through the window of the air terminal in Reykjavík as a private jet rolled to a stop. When the side door opened, he recognized Okawna walking down the steps with an attractive brunette woman clinging to his arm. He grinned and shook his head in wonder. That was just like Okawna. He had a way with women. Another couple exiting the airplane caught his attention, and the tall woman made the man beside her look extremely small.

Okawna brought his companion through the doorway and then stopped in front of his best friend. "Alex, this is Brenda Tillman, a photographer I met at the airport. She offered me a ride on this private plane, so I couldn't refuse."

Alex reached out and shook her hand. "My pleasure."

Okawna kissed the woman on the cheek. "Thanks for the ride."

Alex stared past Okawna at the two people he had seen getting out of the airplane. He was about to look away when the woman stared in his direction, and the look in her eyes was one of recognition, but he could not remember meeting her.

Okawna noticed Alex's wary expression and turned to see what had his attention, but didn't notice anything unusual. "I've seen that look before. What's on your mind?"

"Did you talk with those two on the flight here?"

"No, they sat alone in the back corner. Besides, I was too preoccupied to pay much attention, if you know what I mean."

"When are you going to settle down with a nice girl?"

"Settle down? When I get applications in the mail for AARP and the Hair Club for Men, then I might find me a good woman to marry. Until then, I'm going to get my kicks whenever I can."

"Okay. Let's get your gear loaded into the helicopter. Everything else is already on board."

"Any idea how deep this tunnel is?"

"No, but we have enough food and water for seven days. If we don't reach the bottom after three, we'll have to come back to the surface."

"Maybe we'll find a strange world of topless women in the center of the Earth."

"You need to start thinking with your mind, not what's between your legs."

"Not until I'm toothless and bald."

***

BUFORD GLACIER:

The helicopter approached from the Arctic Ocean as Alex stared down at the cracked white face of the massive glacier below. Directly ahead, the large ice field stretched off like a wrinkled white sheet toward the top of the volcano. Ten minutes later, they arrived at the black hole in the planet, and their pilot, Ron Crowder, set down a short distance away.

Alex and Okawna climbed out and walked over to the edge of the tunnel to assess the situation. The ice had melted and refroze back nearly twenty-feet from the dark opening, forming a smooth surface. They carefully followed the gentle slope down to the exposed flat basaltic rock surrounding the rim of the twelve-foot diameter tunnel.

Alex knelt close to the entrance to satisfy his curiosity, and it was just as he thought. The surface was smooth, as if covered in glass, with no loose gravel or dirt. As far as he could see, the inside diameter of the tunnel remained the same size as the opening, and curved around and down like a corkscrew.

Alex got up. "It looks like a fifteen percent down grade. A little on the steep side, but walkable. The odd part is the surface appears to be melted."

Okawna grinned. "Let's get your contraption unpacked, and then we'll see what we're up against."

They returned to the helicopter, and Alex walked up to Ron. "It looks promising, so shut her down."

Ron flipped a few switches, the jet engines stopped whining, and he climbed out to lend a hand. He moved over next to the cargo door to learn more about what they were doing.

Okawna opened the door on the cargo compartment and stared at Alex. "How did you come up with this crazy invention? The rear end of a torpedo as a drone?"

Alex grinned and spun one of the four small tires mounted to a metal frame. "A friend of mine in Washington gave me the idea. The newer torpedoes already have a trailing cable with optical fibers, so whoever launched it could maintain control. I'm using the cables to send us data and digital video from the equipment on the nose."

Okawna slid the two ramps out of the compartment and set them in place. "I'm an engineer, and I would never have thought up something like this."

Alex turned to Ron. "Could you operate the hoist?"

Ron grabbed the push button control pad on the end of a small electrical cord. "Ready when you are."

"Go ahead."

The winch whined under the strain of lifting the heavy device, and Alex grabbed the front end of the torpedo, careful not to let the camera and sensor equipment bump into the side of the helicopter. He swung it most of the way out of the compartment, and when Okawna grabbed the back end, Ron lowered it onto the ramps and they walked on either side to guide it down onto the hard ice.

Alex grabbed the trailing cable from the back of the torpedo, secured it to the helicopter, and then carried the end up into the helicopter and sat down. When he plugged the end into a laptop computer, the camera image and sensor information appeared on the screen, then he set the computer on the floor of the helicopter and stepped out. "We're all set here, so let's roll it to the opening."

Ron continued releasing the steel hoist cable while keeping a close eye on their progress. On several occasions, he thought both men would fall on the slippery surface, but somehow, they kept their balance and continued down to the tunnel. When Alex gave him a signal to stop, he released the button and waited. A moment later, he noticed the cable jiggle, and then Alex and Okawna were hurrying as carefully as possible in his direction.

When Alex reached the helicopter, he jumped inside and held the computer monitor so everyone could watch the progress. The data from the sensors appeared as varying shades of color down the left side of the screen, and they were all in the green area. The light from the headlamp on the drone glistened off the smooth surface, and staring at the screen was like being in the front row of a roller coaster ride.

The altimeter indicated the torpedo had just passed the one-thousand-foot mark when the screen went dark. Alex reversed the recording back to the last few moments and then played it forward one frame at a time, but the glare from the headlamp made it impossible to see anything unusual until it went dark. "The sensor reading shows the atmosphere is fine, so let's find out what caused this."

Ron watched them put on their backpacks and found their eagerness a little odd. "Aren't you going to wait for the rest of your team?"

Okawna grinned. "We *are* the team."

Alex noticed Ron's perplexed expression. "We'll be fine, but thanks for asking. I'll call when we're ready to be picked up."

"That works for me. I just got a call from another customer. Be careful down there."

With one last wave to Ron, Alex turned on his headlamp, then he and Okawna began their journey into the planet. The thin cable from the torpedo was wrapped around the inner wall, held taut by the weight of the rest of the cable further down the tunnel. They continued down the steep incline in comfortable silence, with the illumination from their headlamps guiding the way, and it was just as Alex suspected. The tunnel kept curving down and around to the right, like a corkscrew.

An hour later, Alex suddenly stopped to listen, then heard a sharp tapping sound and muffled voices echoing off the walls from somewhere back up the tunnel. "It seems we have company."

Okawna slid his backpack to the ground, then reached into his front pocket and brought out a .38 caliber pistol. "Just in case they're not the friendly type."

Alex took off his backpack, and then they headed uphill toward the noise. The tapping sound slowly grew louder, then around the curve up ahead, they saw a beam of light moving across the shiny walls of the tunnel. They came around the curve and recognized the two people from the airport, and the tapping was created by the man beating a metal spike into the wall. Alex thought he recognized the small man from somewhere other than the airport, but could not remember where. He had not realized how tall the woman was until she stood near Okawna, and they were both three inches taller than he was. "Would you mind telling me what you're doing down here?"

The woman turned to put her hand down on the man's shoulder, and he stopped. "I'm Doctor Janice Sloan, this is John Essex, and you're Alex Cave."

"That's correct, so back to my question. What are you doing here?"

Sloan smiled and extended her hand as she stepped forward. "I hope you'll excuse the intrusion. I'm an archaeologist, and I'm not here to interfere with your expedition. I'm following a lead from a reliable source that was in the meeting at the Nordic Volcanological Center several days ago. It's an ancient legend from Norse mythology about a place called Edda's Chimney."

Alex's eyebrow rose. "Perhaps you're not aware, but this tunnel is recent. I doubt it's the source of your Nordic myth."

"I wouldn't be so quick to jump to conclusions, Mister Cave. This may not be the original tunnel from the legend, but I'm hoping this one will be similar. I won't get in your way."

"What do you expect to find down here?"

"Whatever caused the magma to float out of this tunnel."

Okawna tilted his head away, and Alex followed him a few feet from their visitors. "I'm getting a funny vibe from those two, Alex. I don't enjoy looking over my shoulder all the time, so I'd just as soon have them come with us."

Alex looked over at their new acquaintances. "I agree."

Alex moved back to Sloan. "Why don't you join us?"

Sloan looked at Essex, who nodded his agreement. "We accept your offer, but I insist we continue setting our anchors along the way."

"All right. What are they for, Doctor?"

Sloan smiled. "If we're going to be traveling together, call me Janice. They're just a precaution, Alex. Can I call you Alex?"

"Of course."

Okawna had a feeling she was holding back some important information. "A precaution for what?"

"None of us knows how steep this tunnel will become further down, and we may need places to tie off our ropes."

Alex didn't believe her. No archeologist would be interested in something so recent. They waited for Essex to re-pack his hammer, and then they began the trek back down the tunnel.

Even though Okawna thought Sloan was several years older than he was, and at six foot one, just as tall, he found her quite attractive and moved up to walk beside her. "Since you didn't ask, my name is Okawna." He held out his hand. When she didn't take it, he wondered if he was losing his charm.

Sloan didn't bother to look over at him. "I saw you on the plane, Mister Okawna, and I know your type."

"Oh, that? No, I was just being polite because she was giving me a free ride. I'm totally single."

Sloan stopped and stared evenly at Okawna. "And I'm totally gay, so drop the charm."

When Sloan turned and continued down the tunnel, Alex grinned at Okawna, who looked over at him and shrugged. A smile of determination spread across Okawna's face, and then he hurried to catch up to Sloan, causing Alex to grin. That's the one consistent thing about his friend. Okawna never gives up.

On the way, listening to Okawna and Sloan's mostly one-sided conversation, Alex learned she was from New York, but not much else. From the way she talked, he was sure she was not an archeologist.

Essex remained quiet, so Alex moved up beside him. "Are you an archeologist as well?"

"No, I'm not."

"So, what's your stake in this exploration?"

Essex smiled. "If Janice is correct, and the legend is true, I'll be the first person to accomplish viable transportation between here and the moon. The entire planet will know my name for generations to come."

Alex grinned at the man's ego. "What is it you do for a living?"

"I'm an engineer, and I design living accommodations for surviving in space. Once I have a viable and inexpensive launch vehicle, I plan to mine the moon. My name will be a part of history, and I'll be immortalized. "

Now Alex's curiosity was piqued, as was Okawna's, who moved closer to listen. "And you expect to find the answer down here?"

"Yes, I do."

Alex got Sloan's attention. "Why don't we take a break, and you tell us about Edda's Chimney."

Sloan followed Alex's lead and shrugged off her backpack. "All right. The legend tells of three Viking warriors who set out to find the center of the earth, down a tunnel such as this one, with smooth sides, bare of fractures. After three days, one warrior returned, claiming the God, Edda, the destructor of worlds, crushed the others under his invisible foot, before casting him out of Valhalla and back to the surface."

"So, what? You were thinking it could have been a change in gravity that crushed the others?"

"Something like that."

She knew about Alex's history of dealing with unusual situations, and wasn't surprised when she learned he and his friend were coming down here. She also knew about his time in the CIA, and had to be careful what she told him, including the fact she was a smuggler of stolen high-tech and experimental equipment. She stared evenly at Alex. "The video of the floating magma is proof that something in this tunnel is affecting gravity, and I want it."

Alex stared back. He had seen that same expression on another woman not too long ago, and it was very disconcerting. Her name was Rita Harrow, and during the Red Energy Operation, she would have killed him and his friends just to get rich. He knew if there really were a device capable of controlling gravity, in the wrong hands, it could be extremely destructive.

Okawna suddenly stopped walking. "Something isn't right. I feel a lot lighter." He smiled and bounced on his toes, but then he didn't come down. "Oh, hell no! Alex? What's going on?"

Everyone was suddenly weightless and floating up the tunnel, desperately trying to find something to grab. Even their gear started floating upward without being touched.

Each time Alex bumped against the sides, his fingers slid across the smooth surface, so he kept moving up the dark void. The only illumination was the light from their headlamps sweeping around the interior in all directions as they rotated in the air.

Just as quickly as it started, everyone suddenly slammed down onto the floor. Alex landed face down, sliding head first deeper into the tunnel, then the thin cable from the torpedo zipped past above their heads. He felt as if something was dragging him across the smooth surface, like on a sled sliding down the ice with no brakes. The pressure building in his ears became painful, and just when it felt like his head would explode, the force dragging him down the tunnel suddenly ceased, and he slid to a stop. He rolled over and stood up, sighing with relief when his ears popped, then looked around at the others, still on the ground. "Is everyone all right?"

Okawna, Sloan, and Essex sat up, each pinching their nose to relieve the pressure, and then Okawna smiled with relief when his ears popped. "That was an interesting ride. How deep are we?"

Alex checked the altimeter strapped to his wrist. "Damn! I must have smashed it during the ride. Grab your gear and let's get moving. We have a long walk back to the surface."

When Alex bent down and slung his backpack onto his shoulders, Okawna stood up and grabbed his pack. "You're damn right, Alex. Let's get out of here."

Sloan stood and stared at Alex. "Leave if you wish, but John and I are continuing down."

"That would be foolish, and you know it. It's as you said earlier, we have no idea how steep this tunnel might become further down, and if the gravity changes again, we may not stop. We have a long hike ahead of us, and it's all uphill."

Sloan bent down and grabbed her gear. "No, Alex. Whatever is manipulating gravity will be worth a fortune, and I won't leave without it."

Alex stared at Sloan for a moment. "Is it really worth your life?"

"You bet it is."

Alex knew greed had that effect on some people, and it would be impossible to reason with her. "I can't let you have it. When I reach the surface, I'll contact the authorities and we'll be waiting to take you into custody."

Sloan grinned. "On what grounds? I'm not doing anything illegal."

Alex knew she had a valid point. Even so, he could not let her keep something so potentially destructive.

When Okawna reached into his pocket for his pistol, Alex moved closer to stop him. "They're not going anywhere except down. We need to get back to the surface and let Donner know about this. Let's go."

Okawna reluctantly brought out his empty hand. "All right."

Alex turned to Sloan. "I'll be waiting for you."

When Sloan ignored him and headed down the tunnel with Essex, Alex and Okawna started the long trek back to the surface. A few moments later, they heard sharp tapping sounds echoing up the tunnel.

Chapter 6

THE TUNNEL:

After hours of walking uphill without a break, the men stopped for a moment, and Alex looked over at Okawna. "Sloan is correct about something below changing the gravity in this tunnel."

Okawna grinned. "You wanted to go with them, didn't you? Yeah, me too."

"I'll get my chance, but right now, my first responsibility is to return to the surface and let Sliven know what happened down here. We'll come back with the proper equipment for an extended stay."

Alex and Okawna continued the trek toward the surface and made good time, but it still took another hour to reach the last anchor Essex had set right before they were dragged down the tunnel. During the entire hike, Okawna kept worrying about being dragged back down the tunnel, and he sighed with relief when he saw the anchor. "How do you want to do this, Alex?"

"Do what?"

"Use the anchors on the way up, of course. What if the gravity comes on again?"

"I suppose there's no sense taking the chance. How about this? We'll attach your rope to this anchor, and you wait here hanging on to the end of my rope while I continue on to the next one. Once it's attached, you can unhook and use my rope to follow me up. We'll keep repeating the process the rest of the way to the surface, that way, if the change in gravity should happen again, we'll be tethered to at least one anchor."

"I was thinking the same thing. How about we trade off from anchor to anchor?"

"Sure."

As Okawna clipped the carabineer to the steel loop of the anchor, he noticed several fracture lines spreading out like spider webs where the spike was driven into the rock. He yanked on the rope with all his strength and the anchor felt solid, so he held the end of Alex's rope and waited while he continued the trek up the tunnel.

***

Sloan and Essex continued down the steep incline, frequently stopping to rest while he hammered another spike into the rock. When they reached the next anchor point, Essex held up the last spike. "It's deeper than we thought, and it's getting steeper, too. You didn't tell me I'd be risking my life."

"Don't blame me. How was I to know something like this would happen?"

Essex grabbed his hammer and drove the last stake into the wall, then clipped his carabineer onto the rope. "How come I have to do all the work?"

"Stop whining. You wouldn't know about this if it wasn't for me."

A sudden change in gravity jerked them off their feet, and they began sliding down the tunnel. Sloan reached out, barely managing to grab Essex's belt. When his rope jerked them both to a stop, she barely hung on. She stared at Essex's tortured expression as the gravity threatened to rip her away. "Help me, damn it!"

The rope was tangled around Essex's throat, and he struggled to hang on above his head with both hands. He knew if he let go, he would be strangled.

"Damn it, John! Help me!"

Essex's hands were slipping because of the extra weight, and her violent thrashing around. "Get off me!"

"No!"

The noose tightened around his throat, and Essex decided he wasn't going to let her kill him. He brought his knee up to knock her away and then watched her headlight disappear into the darkness.

Sloan screamed, as she dragged her hands along the surface with no effect. Even the centrifugal force against the outside surface wasn't slowing her down.

***

It was Okawna's turn, and he was hiking up to the next anchor when he had to stop to holler down the tunnel. "Hang on a minute. We just ran out of rope."

Alex felt the jerk on the line in his hand and heard Okawna's voice echoing from far away. "Essex must have changed the spacing on the way down."

The sudden change in gravity caught Alex off guard and he slid feet first down the tunnel until his rope snapped taut. The fierce pull from the gravity caused his harness to dig painfully into his stomach and crotch, then the end of Okawna's rope shot past his head and was torn from his grasp.

He looked up the tunnel in time to see Okawna sliding down, feet first, so he desperately clawed at the slick surface to reach the center of the tunnel. He barely managing to grasp Okawna's wrist, but when Okawna jerked to a stop, Alex's arm felt like it was being ripped out of the socket, and the pain from his harness also increased because of the extra weight.

He gritted his teeth as he struggled to hang on and Okawna's wrist started slipping through his grasp, but Alex was not going to lose his best friend. He squeezed Okawna's wrist with all his strength, then suddenly Okawna's other arm reached across his waist. The strain on his arm was gone, as Okawna grabbed the carabineer attached to his belt. He grabbed Okawna's coat collar and helped pull him up to where his belt clip slipped over the taut line, and then sighed with relief when the extra weight was gone and they were still alive, even though he was still in pain from the pain from the pressure of his own weight. "Sweet mother of Pearl, this hurts! Are you okay?"

Okawna turned his head to where his headlamp was illuminating Alex's face. "Yeah. That was close."

Alex was about to agree when they heard a sharp cracking sound echo down to the tunnel. The anchor tore loose from the rock, and they both began the bobsled ride down into the planet.

***

Sloan slid down into the darkness, helpless to stop. She tilted her head so her headlamp would illuminate the tunnel below, but it was ripped off her head, and she watched the beam of light tumbled around the sides of the walls. It suddenly stopped moving, then she hit what she thought was a wall. She thought her legs would break, and then she fell forward and lay prone on the ground, face down beneath her backpack. A moment later, Essex slammed into the ground a short distance away.

She rolled over and could see the light from her headlamp reflecting off something silver, then realized the gravity wasn't affecting her anymore.

She removed her backpack, careful not to get any closer to the reflection. She stayed on her hands and knees, slowly approaching her headlamp, only a few inches from the device. When she reached out and touched the strap, nothing happened, so she grabbed it and slipped it over her head, then leaned back and stood to check out her situation.

She turned in a circle, realizing she was in a much larger area, nearly forty-feet across. When she tilted her head back to look up into the tunnel, the room appeared to be shaped like an egg, pointing straight up. On the other side of the strange device was an odd-looking torpedo.

She suddenly remembered Essex and found him lying on his side a few feet away, but he appeared to be dead. "We'll, shit!"

She rushed over and knelt beside him, feeling his neck for a pulse. When she felt a steady thumping, she stood and went back to the device. The top appeared to be emitting neon blue light, and she could see amber and ruby colors on the side. She realized nothing was being affected by the gravity, except directly above it. She moved closer, and then the colored lights went dark.

***

The gravity suddenly ceased and Alex and Okawna slid to a stop, then Okawna chuckled. "What a rush."

Alex slowly stood, trying to ignore the deep throbbing pain in his crotch. "My balls feel like they got caught in a pair of vice grips. We didn't slide too far this time, and we're close to the surface, so let's leave our gear and head back up."

"What if the gravity changes again? I hate what that thing is doing to me, Alex. I hate it!"

"We'll have to take the chance. It was a long time between events, and my money is on us. If we hurry, we just might make it out before the next event."

Okawna slid his backpack to the ground. "Right. Let's get going."

They jogged up the steep grade, and Okawna set an unusually fast pace. At first, Alex struggled to keep up because of his pain, but it finally abated enough to catch up with him. When Okawna jogged faster, Alex saw another side of his friend. He had never seen Okawna afraid of anything before, but this gravity device appeared to scare the hell out of him.

He thought about Sloan and Essex, wondering how they might have been affected after this last incident with the gravity. They would have been much closer to what was causing the anomaly, so perhaps they were killed. Now the problem would be getting to the bottom with the right equipment.

***

Sloan looked up at the steep sides of the tunnel and realized they didn't stand a chance in hell of getting out on their own. "Shit!"

She stared at the shiny pinpoint of light reflecting off the small block in the center of the room. It was ten inches square, with four inches sticking out of the ground, and a concave surface on the top.

She knelt down for a closer look at the side and saw something distorting her reflection. "What the hell?"

Three colored pads were barely visible just beneath the silver surface. The amber, turquoise, and ruby-colored lights formed the tips of a three-inch triangle, and she thought they must be the control buttons. When she noticed the ragged edge of lava around the bottom of the device, she was amazed it had survived in molten rock. "Not even a scratch. You're one tough son of a bitch."

She wondered how much deeper it was buried and carefully grabbed the outer edges away from the touchpads. When it slid out with very little effort, she smiled. Now fully exposed, it was only six inches thick.

When she turned it around, she noticed a small square crystal protruding slightly on the opposite side from the pads, and it was still emitting a soft blue glow. Her first instinct was to grab it, but then she decided not to take the chance it would activate again. She buried it inside her backpack, using a drinking cup to protect the colored pads.

With the gravity device safely in her possession, Sloan breathed a sigh of relief. Now all she needed to do was find a buyer for it, preferably an extremely wealthy buyer. She smiled at the idea of how rich she was going to become off this little gem, and then her eyes drifted to the semi-lifeless lump on the ground that was Essex. As she stared at him, her thoughts drifted to what had happened on the way down the tunnel, and remembered how adamant he was about not reaching down to help her. When she remembered how his knee had pushed her away, a seething rage coursed through her body, then with fury burning in her eyes, she kicked him as hard as she could in the stomach. "You tried to kill me, you son of a bitch! If I had a gun, you'd be a dead man!"

After several moments, she relaxed and stared up at the walls of the chamber, realizing even standing on Essex's shoulders, she could never get out. They had enough food and water for six days, but she hoped Cave and Okawna would return to get them before they ran out. She crinkled her nose in disgust when she thought about what it would be like when they had to relieve themselves. No privacy and no way to get rid of it.

Essex groaned and tried to sit up, but cringed at the pain in his stomach and stayed on the ground. "What happened?"

Sloan saw the spike still attached to the end of the rope so grabbed it to show him. "The anchor didn't hold you idiot, and we hit the floor."

"I feel like I've been sucker punched in the gut."

She looked up so her headlamp illuminated the tunnel. "Suck it up, would you? We have bigger problems to worry about. We can't get out."

***

When they finally reached the surface, Alex and Okawna both dropped to their hands and knees on the glacier. Neither one spoke as they took in deep gasps of cold air, which burned their lungs with each breath.

Okawna rolled onto his back, but Alex slowly sat up, squinting from the glare off the ice. He reached into his coat pocket and grabbed his sunglasses, then his phone. When he turned it on, he heard the chimes and selected the number for the helicopter service. While he waited, Alex stood up and slowly turned around to stare across the white ice, blue sky, and the top of the volcano on the horizon. A few moments later, the dispatcher answered, and he explained his situation, then put his phone away and sat down next to Okawna. "A helicopter should be here in about fifteen minutes."

"I think you should call the director at NordVulC and let him know what's happened. I doubt he even knows about Sloan."

Alex thought about it for a moment. "She's correct in not having any legal grounds to detain her. Even if they find a gravity machine, they could never get it out on their own. When our pilot arrives, we'll go back to Reykjavík and make sure they don't get a ride back until we're ready. Donner will find out if Sloan or Essex has a criminal background, and maybe he can find something we can use to arrest them."

"Yeah, well, let's hope so. I've got a bad feeling about those two."

***

Sloan felt a strange tingling sensation on her skin, then was suddenly weightless and she and Essex floated up out of the chamber. She tensed her muscles, waiting for the gravity to reverse, but she kept going up.

***

Okawna reached over to get Alex's attention. "You're not going to believe this. Look!"

Alex turned to see what he meant, then stared at their backpacks floating up out of the tunnel and hanging in the air. A moment later, Essex came up out of the tunnel, and then Sloan appeared, struggling with her backpack as they floated above the tunnel. Sloan was thrashing wildly, but Essex was face down with his arms and legs hanging limply.

When Alex realized they were moving in his direction, he grabbed Okawna's arm, then suddenly, everything was falling down toward the glacier, just like the globules in the movie. They ran over to catch Sloan and Essex, trying to judge where they would fall before they slammed onto the ice.

Sloan glimpsed black hair as she plummeted toward the ground. Just when she expected to land hard on the ice, she heard a deep whoosh as she landed on something soft instead.

Okawna looked up at Essex, dropping through the air with his arms and legs still pointed down and still wearing his backpack. To his surprise, Essex was looking at him, his eyes wide with fear, before slamming into him. The weight drove Okawna onto the glacier, and then he pushed Essex off his body and stood to check on Alex.

Alex lay on his back, trying to catch his breath, and then Sloan was standing over him, concern in her eyes. "I'll be all right. I just need a second."

"I could have broken my neck. Thank you."

When Okawna knelt down beside him, Alex sat up. "How is Essex?"

Okawna glanced over his shoulder, and Essex was sitting up, holding a spot on his head. "He'll be fine."

Sloan looked over at Essex. "He was knocked out when we hit the bottom. I'd better check on him."

When they heard the word bottom, Alex and Okawna looked at each other, and then Alex jumped up and knelt beside Sloan. "Did you say you reached the bottom?"

Sloan parted the bloody hair on the side of Essex's head to study his wound, but also to keep from looking at Alex. "That's right. It's a dead end. Whatever is controlling gravity must be deeper than the tunnel. The only way to get it out is to blast, and I'm not going to waste my time trying to get permits for something they will never let me keep."

Alex stood to look at Okawna. "This just became a diplomatic issue, so I'll have to call this in to Donner."

The deep thumping of the approaching helicopter interrupted their conversation, and a few moments later, it set down a few yards away. Once everyone was inside, the different pilot took off from the glacier and headed back toward the Reykjavik Airport.

Alex had noticed the look of surprise in Essex's eyes when Sloan had said the tunnel was a dead end, so he sat across from him and leaned forward to judge his reactions. "What was it like at the bottom? Is there enough room for some mining equipment?"

Essex glanced at Sloan before he answered. "I don't know. I must've been unconscious."

Okawna heard Alex and put his face within inches of Sloan's. "Tell us what it was like at the bottom."

Sloan smiled at his attempt to intimidate her. She had dealt with more threatening men than Okawna. "What more do you want me to say? It levels out and ends at a rock wall."

Okawna realized Sloan was tougher than he had thought, so he leaned back in his seat. "I don't suppose your name is really Janice Sloan, is it?"

Sloan just smiled and looked out the window while she thought about the device. By the time Alex and Okawna figured out her deception, she would be long gone.

Alex leaned back in his seat and gently eased his smart phone out from his coat pocket. He secretly took several pictures of their guests and then slid it back in without them knowing. He leaned his head back against the headrest and stared out the window, hoping he gets selected for the recovery operation. Suddenly he thought about Fala, wondering how he was going to explain he wasn't finished in Iceland.

***

REYKJAVIK AIRPORT:

When they entered the terminal, Okawna noticed his photographer friend and smiled at Alex. "I might get us a private ride back to the States."

"No. This is too important. No, I call Donner and let him know what's going on and he's letting us borrow his jet."

"All right. I'll prod her for information instead. Maybe she knows something about our new acquaintances. I'll be right back."

Brenda stood and smiled as Okawna approached. "Hey, you."

When Okawna stopped in front of her, she stood on her toes to give him a kiss on the cheek. "How was your trip?"

"Much better now."

"Did you find what you were looking for?"

"More or less. Do you know the couple who flew here with us?"

"No, but they must know somebody important if my dad let them use his private jet."

Okawna gave her a quizzical stare. "Who's your father?"

Brenda grinned. "He owns a big record company."

"I see. So, when are you leaving?"

Brenda looked across the room at Sloan and Essex. "Whenever they feel like it. I've never been to Iceland before, so I just came along for the free ride, like you."

Okawna looked over at Sloan and Essex, hurrying in his direction. "Looks like we're about to find out."

Sloan stopped in front of Brenda. "We're not taking them with us."

Brenda stared back at her. "Actually, we are. This is my father's plane, and I just invited them."

The bitterness in Sloan's eyes caused Alex to grin as he turned to Brenda. "Thank you anyway, but we have made other arrangements."

Sloan glared at Brenda. "We're leaving, so if you're going with us, get your butt on the plane."

Brenda glared at Sloan's back as she walked away and then smiled up at Okawna. "Can I get a ride with you? It's a long trip back to the States, and I'd much rather be on a plane with you than Miss stick-Up-Her-Butt."

Alex shook his head no. "I'm sorry, but we have urgent business."

Okawna focused back on Brenda, took her hand, and gave it a kiss. "Thank you again for a lovely time."

He let go and received a quick kiss on the lips before she turned and hurried to catch up with Sloan. He smiled as he stared after her, glad she had given him her phone number. His smile disappeared when Sloan glanced back at him before she turned the corner to the boarding station.

Alex noticed Okawna's concerned expression. "What's the matter?"

"I've got a bad feeling about those two."

Alex turned in time to see Sloan glance back at him before she walked out of the terminal. "I agree, and I don't think that's the last we'll see of those two. Donner wants to see me right away, and his private jet will be here in three hours."

"Great. I'm starving, and I saw this interesting restaurant not too far from here. Oh, by the way. You're buying this time."

Chapter 7

WASHINGTON, D.C. DIRECTOR DONNER'S OFFICE:

Donner listened to Alex's account of what happened, and just like with his other discoveries, the Director could only smile and shake his head in amazement. "I can tell you're anxious about this operation. Mister Sliven cleared the way, and you have permission to get started."

"Okawna and I will work together on this one."

"I thought he was working for Mike Tanner?"

"Mike's just as curious as we are, and loaned Okawna to me for a while. He flew out to recover the cylinder, so you should get it in a few days. Once he's done, we'll meet up in Iceland."

"I'll have it delivered to Groom Lake and send Mister Tanner a nice bottle of wine. I've got the information on Sloan and Essex, and those are their real names. Essex has a company in Nevada competing for private space exploration, so I can see why he would want a way to control gravity."

"I thought I recognized him from a magazine article. And Sloan?"

"She's an opportunist, and an unscrupulous one. No convictions, but she's a person of interest in several murders, both here and in Western Europe. The authorities haven't been able to find any substantial evidence to convict her, but they're still looking. Inside is a list of known associates. I've notified the authorities in Iceland about Sloan, and they'll stop her if she shows up again."

"Thanks. The first thing I need to do is get down that tunnel to see what I'm up against."

Donner saw the corners of Alex's mouth rise slightly. "You've already figured out a way to do it, haven't you?"

"I just need your approval and a government credit card."

"I'll see you get what you need. David and Henry are deciphering the logs from the spaceship you found. Maybe they can help."

Alex stood to leave. "That's good. I'll call you when we're ready to go back to Iceland."

"Be careful, Alex."

With a nod, Alex left the room. Now it was time to face Fala.

***

MONTANA:

When Alex approached his ranch, the thought of having to explain another trip to Fala made his stomach turn, and reminded him of the tunnel, where the harness had squeezed his crotch. Right now, he would prefer the crotch strap to having to tell Fala about returning to Iceland.

When he drove into the driveway, he saw Halona playing with her puppy, Trixie, and Barney, sitting nearby, casually observing his new friend. He parked and got out, then walked up and knelt beside Halona. "Did you miss me?"

She smiled. "Yes, I did. Are you staying this time?"

Alex stood and grabbed her hand, and then they walked up onto the porch to the door. "I'm sorry, sweetie, but no. I can't."

***

Fala was tending the flower bed around the corner of the house and heard Alex talking to Halona, saying he was leaving again, and she stood and took off her gardening gloves. When she heard the door close, she leaned back against the side of the house, now sure she made a mistake moving in with him. She tried to understand his restlessness, but she wanted someone who would settle down and be the family man she needed. How could she stay with someone who yearns for adventure, even craves danger, without considering how it affects her and Halona? She decided enough was enough. She tossed her gloves onto a shelf in the garden shed, and then headed into the house.

***

Fala joined Alex and Halona, who were at the breakfast bar, then grabbed a drink from the fridge. "So, how was your trip to Iceland?"

"Pretty exciting, actually. I hope you don't mind, but I have to go back in a few days, and I'm not sure how long I'll be gone. It could be awhile."

Fala opened her bottle of water and took a big swallow, then recapped it. "Halona, go outside and play. I need to talk to Alex in private."

Halona knew that tone in her mother's voice all too well, and she quickly scurried outside to Trixie and Barney. She closed the door and then leaned her ear against the wood to listen.

Alex stood staring at Fala, dreading the tidal wave of anger about to hit him, but rather than slam her bottle down, like she normally did when she got angry, she carefully set the bottle on the counter. As they stood in brief awkward silence, just staring at each other, Alex became anxious. Fala had never acted this way before.

Waiting to make sure Halona couldn't hear them, Fala finally spoke. "What is going on here, Alex?"

"What do you mean?"

"This will be the third trip you make to Iceland. You went from 'Oh, I'll just be gone one night' to being gone the whole week, and now you're heading back and you have absolutely no idea when you'll be back. So I'm asking you, what is going on? Why do you keep leaving? What is so important that it can't wait?"

Alex turned away as he struggled to find the right answer to lessen Fala's anger, but he drew a blank. The question felt like a trap, and the only thing that could get him out was the truth, but he couldn't tell her the truth. Not yet.

He turned back to her. "We just need more time and resources to explore the tunnel."

Fala crossed her arms to keep from swearing. "I bet there's not even a tunnel!"

"What? That's just ridiculous. Of course there's a tunnel, Fala. Why would you say something like that?"

"Well, for one, I haven't seen a single thing about this mysterious tunnel on the news. If all these great geological minds were brought together to discuss it, you'd think it would be worth mentioning on the news. And don't give me that top-secret excuse. How can a tunnel be top secret? Is it covered in gold? Does it lead to the lost city of Atlantis? And second, you just finished exploring it and now you have to go back to explore some more? What is that all about? Why didn't you get it all done on this last trip? Did you even find anything?"

"Well, no."

"Then why go back?"

Alex stood staring at Fala, not knowing what to do. Everything he said was just the wrong thing.

Fala threw her hands up in the air. "Exactly my point. There's no reason for you to go back."

"Yes there is, Fala. You just don't understand what I have to deal with right now."

"Then explain it to me, Alex. Because I sure would love to understand what is going on."

"I wish I could, but I just can't."

Fala looked at Alex, tears glistening in her eyes, then after a few moments, she spoke in a quiet, broken voice. "Alex Cave, are you cheating on me?"

Alex was stunned by such a question, almost hurt she would think he'd be capable of such a thing. "No, Fala. How could you think such a thing?"

"I just don't know what to think anymore. You're constantly running off and you give me such vague details about these trips, and then refuse to answer any of my questions. You make promises you can't keep, and it makes me feel you don't enjoy being home with Halona and me. Either we're so boring you have to run away from us all the time or there's another woman."

He held her close to him, running his fingers through her soft raven black hair, then lifted her face and kissed her passionately on the lips. "There could never be another woman for me. I love you, Fala."

"I love you too, Alex."

As they kissed, Alex thought to himself he had just poured his heart out to this woman, and deep down, knew he had to tell her the truth. "Fala?"

"Yes."

"You're right. I haven't been forthcoming with the details of this trip, and I apologize for that. I want to be honest with you. Even if it means you getting upset with me."

The loving moment passed and a stern look washed across Fala's face as she backed up away from him. Her heart raced as she feared what Alex was about to tell her.

"There is, in fact, a tunnel recently discovered in Iceland, and Okawna and I have to explore it further. But I've also been working with Director Donner on this."

She slowly shook her head, chuckling to herself. "I knew it."

"I'm sorry I lied to you."

"And all the other trips?"

"Yes, most of those were jobs I was doing for Donner."

"You just cannot keep a promise to save your life, can you?"

Fala grabbed her purse and keys on her way out of the kitchen. She stomped toward the door, heading out to her car.

"Fala, wait! Where are you going?"

"I need to get out of here to clear my head and not look at you. I just can't stand the sight of you, so I'm taking my daughter into town for some dinner."

Alex's heart broke hearing those words, and to know she couldn't stand the sight of him tore him apart. "I'm sorry, Fala. I never meant to hurt you."

"Well, it's too late for that now, isn't it? You broke your promise and then you lied about it, multiple times. So forgive me if I don't accept your apology right away. I've got to go."

"Well, what about me? Is there anything to eat here, or should I go into town?"

Fala turned around, slamming the door as she walked back towards Alex, fire and rage burned in her eyes. "I couldn't care less what you eat, Cave! I'm not your damn cook! Do whatever you want, since you're so good at doing that, anyway!"

Alex watched helplessly as Fala stormed out the door. He had never seen her so angry. For one, she had never sworn before. And two, she only called him 'Cave' when she was extremely angry with him. He cautiously walked out onto the porch and saw Fala buckling Halona into her SUV. He knew better than to speak, even if he could think of something to say to ease her pain.

Fala slammed the door to her rig and saw Alex standing on the porch, looking back at her, so she rolled down the window to stare back At him. "Don't even think of sleeping in bed with me tonight! You can sleep on the damn couch."

The image of Okawna saying 'sofa city' flashed through Alex's mind. He was right, and there was nothing he could say to Fala that would change her mind. He watched her speed off in her SUV, throwing gravel across the driveway and yard. When Barney trotted up and sat down beside him, Alex looked down at him. "Women." When Barney looked up at him and whined, Alex reached over and scratched his head. "You get me, so that's one good thing."

Chapter 8

ICELAND THE GLACIER:
Alex stared out through the open side door of the helicopter while guiding the pilot to a flat area of volcanic rock near the tunnel entrance. In his hand was the button to release the cable attached to a square wooden crate dangling below him.

The crate swayed slightly before touching the ground, and then Alex released the cable and leaned back inside. "It's down, Ron."

Ron set the helicopter down on the glacier a short distance away, then shut down the engine while Alex and Okawna climbed out. He was scheduled for another passenger, but when he heard Alex and Okawna were looking for a ride, he knew he had to be in on their adventure. It had cost him twenty dollars to trade fares with a rival pilot, but he didn't care.

Alex noticed the grin on Ron's face as he approached to help them unload the seven-foot tall crate. "I'm glad you're staying to help."

"Are you kidding? I wouldn't miss this for the world."

Ron flinched when he heard a gunshot. "What was that?"

"That was Okawna, shooting some anchors into the rock to hold the machine in place."

Alex opened the six-foot wide front wall of the crate and leaned it against the side, while Okawna and Ron released the straps on a wedge-shaped aluminum frame. Three small tires were mounted to the bottom; one in front and two on either side near the rear. One tire also spun the drive belt for a small automotive generator, which supplied electricity to the front and rear lights, and charged the battery.

Once on the ground, Okawna and Alex raised the three outside railings and inserted the locking pins. After they raised the two seat backs and had them locked in place, their go-cart was ready to roll down into the planet.

Ron admired Alex's invention. "From what you've told me, it should be one scary ride."

Alex reached further back into the crate, grabbed the end of a slender black cable, and held it out for Ron to look at up close. "It's woven carbon fiber."

Ron looked into the crate, where a large, six-foot diameter steel reel held the rest of the cable, and then he turned to Alex. "Is that going to be long enough?"

"I sure hope so. There's three miles of cable on that reel. If we can't find the bottom by then, we never will. Inside the cable are wires to voice-activated speakers. One in the cart and one here at the control panel, so we can communicate."

Alex took the black cable and attached it to the rear of the cart, then inserted the small plug into its mate hanging from a small junction box inside.

Alex indicated for Ron to study the controls for the hydraulic pump just inside the crate, while he explained how they worked. "The governor should maintain a steady drag to hold us back, and if I call for more speed, open this bleed valve a few more turns. When I say to slow us down, close the valve a few turns. When we're ready to return, start the engine and close this valve over here. When that's done, all you do is reverse the turning of the valve, and you'll drag us back to the surface."

"Got it. Don't you have any brakes?"

"No, because if we used them, it would create slack in the cable and it could become tangled on the reel."

"Personally, I think you two are crazy."

Alex smiled and looked down at Okawna, who was waiting behind the steering wheel, then held his hand out to Ron. "I agree. See you when we get back."

Ron stepped out of the way while Alex climbed in and sat in the seat next to Okawna, and with a final wave, he watched them disappear down into the bowels of the earth. A few seconds later, he heard a loud howl of delight from Okawna as the thin cable spun from the reel.

***

It only took a few moments for Okawna to find the sweet spot for steering, and the centrifugal force held them partway up the side of the tunnel as they corkscrewed into the planet. After ten minutes, Alex noticed there were no more spikes in the wall and raised his voice for the two-way microphone.

"What's our speed, Ron?"

"Six miles-an-hour."

Okawna grinned over at Alex. "What do you think? A little faster?"

"We have no idea how far we need to go, and I'd hate to come to an abrupt stop against a rock wall."

"Good point. In fact, we shouldn't be going this fast. The spiral is getting tighter, and it's getting steeper."

Alex spoke into his microphone. "Start slowing us down, Ron."

"All right, just tell me when to stop. Here we go. You're at five and a half miles-an-hour. Now four."

Alex felt the drag from the cable slowing them down, and then the headlights illuminated a sudden shadow on the floor and screamed into the mic. "Stop!"

When their go-cart came to a quick stop, Alex felt the straps of his seat harness dig in. He remained hanging nearly vertically, staring down at the end of the tunnel, only two-feet from the front tire, and put his hand on Okawna's shoulder. "That was close."

"Whew! No shit!"

Ron's voice came through the speaker. "Hey! Are you guys okay?"

Alex looked over at Okawna, who gave him a thumbs up. "Yeah, we're all right. We've found the end, and it's nearly vertical. Start easing us down and I'll tell you when to stop."

Alex waited while the front wheel of the cart rolled forward into the bowel-shaped cavern. Bright light from the cart filled the room, and it was easy to see what was at the bottom. On the far side, the torpedo had hit the floor straight on, smashing the delicate sensor equipment and camera on its nose. He waited as the cart rolled forward until flat on the floor. "That's good, Ron. We're going to check it out, so I'll holler when we're ready to come back."

Okawna looked over the railing on the right side while he undid his harness. "What do you make of that?"

Alex climbed out and knelt down beside the ten-inch square hole in the solid rock. "It's only two-inches deep. Something was removed from here recently, and I'm betting it was some kind of gravity device. If it wasn't too tall, it could've been smuggled out of here in a backpack. I'm betting Sloan and Essex already have it."

Okawna didn't say a word as he climbed out and detached the cable from the rear of the cart, and then he grabbed the frame. "Help me turn this thing around."

Alex saw the fury in Okawna's eyes as he got up and moved around to the front end. "I know how you feel."

"She did this on purpose, Alex. She led us on a wild goose chase down to the end of this tunnel, knowing exactly what it looked like down here. We would have died, but she didn't care. She just wanted to keep her dirty little secret hidden."

Alex wasn't so sure. "It would not have been dangerous if we weren't in the cart."

"Even so, she could have told us it was a dead drop straight down at the end."

"Agreed. You know, Donner said Essex has a research facility in Nevada. When we get back, let's check it out."

Once the cart was pointing uphill and they were strapped back in, Alex told Ron to haul them up. Neither of them spoke on the way, each lost in their own thoughts about what to do when they got back to the States. When they returned to the surface, they re-packed the cart, attached the lift cable, and climbed into the helicopter for the ride back to Reykjavík.

Chapter 9

FALLON, NEVADA:

Sloan followed Essex's directions as they drove across the desert south of his research facility. The one lane dirt road seemed to go on forever, occasionally skirting the side of a small mountain in the middle of nowhere. When they finally arrived at their destination, she parked the SUV a short distance from an elevated concrete block. She shut off the engine as she looked around, noticing several concrete bunkers about a thousand yards away. "This looks like a test site."

"Yes, it was an experimental explosives test site during the Cold War. I bought it from the Department of Defense when I purchased the land for my research and development compound."

Sloan opened the door and stepped out. "Grab the device and let's learn how it works."

Essex turned to look over his shoulder into the back of the SUV. During the long ride, he could not stop looking at the silver block, expecting it to activate at any moment.

He turned back to the front window and then looked over at his driver. "We should spend a good deal of time studying the device before trying to activate it, Janice."

Sloan slammed the door shut, moved to the rear of the car, and opened the hatch. "Essex, you're a wimp." She grabbed the device and carried it over to the three-foot square concrete block, then placed it in the center. She heard a distant rumble, so looked across the desert, and hundreds of miles away, a military jet was soaring over the mountaintops.

When Essex moved up beside her, she smiled and showed him the three colored lights. "I'm assuming these three touch pads control the way it functions, like when it repelled us up the tunnel, instead of dragging us down."

When she reached out to touch one, Essex grabbed her arm. She jerked it away and glared at him. "Never touch me again!"

"I'm sorry, it's just that how do you even know which ones to push? We have no idea what will happen when you touch them."

"I saw the amber and ruby lights glowing when it was still on."

She touched the two lights just to scare Essex. When he flinched, she chuckled. "Double wimp."

Essex relaxed when nothing happened. "It seems you have a broken gravity device. Let's just take it to my facility and backward engineer it."

Sloan reached into her pocket and brought out the one inch long by quarter inch square crystal. "It won't do anything without this. When we floated up out of the tunnel, I realized this device was still on, so when we started getting to high off the surface of the glacier, I removed this key, the device shut down, and we landed on Alex and Okawna."

"Won't it affect us like before?"

"No, I was next to it when it was on and didn't feel anything. I'm sure it only affects things directly above it."

"Damn it, Janice, you could have told me. I've been worried sick it would activate at any moment."

Sloan grinned sadistically. "It was payback for trying to kill me in the tunnel."

"I didn't have a choice. The rope was around my neck and I couldn't breathe."

She stared at him, not sure if it was true, until she noticed the rope burns on his neck. "Are you ready?"

Essex stepped back. "Go ahead."

Sloan inserted the key and turned it until it stopped, then moved to the opposite side. She touched the amber and ruby-colored touch pads one at a time, but nothing happened. When she touched the turquoise one, the concave surface suddenly radiated neon green light, and she turned and smiled at Essex. "It's on, and we're still alive. What did I tell you?"

Essex flinched when a bird suddenly slammed into the ground a few feet away, then more birds started hitting the surrounding ground. "What the hell? Turn it off!"

Sloan pressed the touch pads, but it didn't stop. She carefully reached around to the opposite side and turned the crystal key, but it didn't work, then a variety of birds began slamming into the ground a few feet away. She removed the key, but the machine stayed on, so she slid it into her pocket. "I can't shut it off! Let's go!"

They ran between falling carcasses back to the car, jumped inside, and watched a dozen more birds slam into the ground in a circle around the device. Essex, being in the aviation industry, hoped no aircraft would fly over this part of the desert in the immediate future. He had no idea how high the gravity distortion would be, and something as dramatic as a plane being torn from the sky would draw mass media attention, and that wasn't the type of attention he wanted right now. Even so, if word got out he was involved in activating the device, the price of his stocks would plummet, and he would be bankrupt within a year. He looked over at Sloan. "I'm not taking responsibility for this. If we can't shut that thing down, it's going to be your problem, not mine."

Sloan abruptly turned to face him. "Listen, you sawed off little shit! We're in this together, got it?"

Essex had seen that look in Sloan's eyes once before, and it scared him. "Listen. Let's just get out of here before something bigger falls from the sky."

"All right, but I seriously have no idea how to turn that damn thing off."

She started the engine, backed away from the test area, and headed back toward Essex's facility. She knew he was correct about it bringing down a plane and drawing attention. She grinned, thinking perhaps it could be mounted to the top of a vehicle and driven to an underground location. That way, she would have time to find out how to control it, which would increase its value considerably.

Essex got an idea. "What about the professor? I've called some important friends who have heard rumors about Mister Cave. He seems to have a knack for this type of thing, so we should at least call him so he doesn't waste his time going down to look for it."

"I wouldn't be surprised if he's been down there and back already. Did you know he's good friends with Martin Donner, the Director of National Security?"

"Yeah, well, that means he has a lot of clout for whatever he wants to do. He's probably the best bet for shutting this thing down."

Sloan didn't care if Essex wanted to become best friends with Cave, but she still had a business to run, so she turned to glare at him. "Not a word about this to Alex, is that clear?"

"Eventually, that thing is going to pull something other than birds out of the sky. Hundreds of people could die if an aircraft is yanked out of the air. I'll send a couple of my people out here to guard it, but we have to contact Cave."

Sloan knew for the moment Essex was the only witness who knew she was the one who turned it on, and for the time being, she needed his assistance, so she wouldn't get rid of him just yet. So far, she had not been convicted of any crime, but she would press her luck when Cave got involved. In fact, she couldn't count on Essex's hired thugs to keep their mouths shut, either, and knew she had to scare the shit out of him. "No! Not a damn word to anyone! No guards, and definitely no Cave, or else I'll remove your manhood! Are we clear?"

Essex was tiring of her threats and stared out across the desert through the side window. "Crystal."

"Good."

"You're a fool, Sloan. Exactly what do you suggest we do?"

"Nothing, for the moment."

Essex turned and glared at her for a few moments, then sighed in resignation and leaned back in his seat. He regretted becoming business partners with such a reckless, violent person. He had a feeling dealing with Sloan would end up with him in jail, or worse, bankrupt. Of course, she'd probably kill him before either of those things happened.

Sloan silently cursed herself for acting so hastily with such an advanced piece of technology. But turning it on was the only way to learn about its true capabilities, and it could be worth a fortune to the right people. She knew Cave could get involved, and if the bastard managed to shut down the gravity device, he would still need the key to re-activate it. Her lips transformed into a sneer. If the government wanted it bad enough, it was going to cost them a lot of money.

She glanced over at Essex, leaning back in his seat with a faraway look in his eyes. She knew since Cave was well connected, it wouldn't take him long to find Essex and learn the location. She didn't know how long it would take him to shut down the device, but knew she wanted to be nearby when it happened. Her lips transformed into a sneer at her new plan. "I'm a genius."

Chapter 10

HUMPBACK HARBOR, OREGON:

Eighteen-year-old Aaron Avery wiped his hands with a red shop towel as he walked out of the small repair shop above the marina. "The Sheriff's boat motor is back together, Uncle Jerry. I could drop it off on my way home, if you'd like."

Jerry Avery was fond of his young nephew and knew he was sweet on the sheriff's daughter, Denise. "Don't worry about it, Aaron. I'll take it over tomorrow morning."

When he saw the anguish in Aaron's eyes, Jerry found it difficult to suppress a grin. "I would imagine the sheriff's still at work, so there's no hurry."

"It's not a problem. Really, I'll take care of it."

Jerry looked out over the marina to stretch out the moment. This would be Aaron's third year working for him at the repair shop, and kept his high school grades up, which he admired. When he looked back into the boy's eyes, he could no longer keep him hanging, and chuckled. "Go on then. Get that thing out of my shop."

Aaron grinned. "Good one, Uncle Jerry. You had me worried for a minute. I'll bring my truck over."

Aaron headed around the corner of the building to the large parking area for the marina. He enjoyed working at the shop, and having an uncle like Jerry was great. He took the time to teach him everything he knew about everything, and oh, how he loved his machines.

Aaron climbed into his pickup truck and then drove to the garage door on the parking lot side of the shop. As it opened, he saw Jerry waiting inside, so he backed up to the outboard motor on the hoist. He set the brake and shut off the engine, then climbed out. "Have you figured out what you're going to say at the celebration on Saturday, Mister Mayor?"

Jerry grunted in response and helped Aaron load the large outboard motor into his truck. "You know I didn't want the damn job in the first place."

"Yeah, but you're the one who managed to get the financial backing to rebuild the marina. Nobody likes Mister Curtis as Mayor, and the only reason he got the job is because his great grandparents settled in this harbor, and he's related to most of the residents."

Jerry thought about the look on Curtis's face after the election and smiled. Curtis thought he would automatically be re-elected until someone added Jerry Avery as a write-in. His smile slipped away as he thought about having to give a speech in front of a crowd. He was a simple man of simple words and worried about making a fool of himself. He suddenly had an idea. "You're good with speeches. Why don't you give it?"

"No, that's your job, Mister Mayor. I'll tell you what. I'll write it, and you just have to read it."

Jerry held out his hand. "Deal."

Aaron accepted the handshake. "I'll have a great speech for you by Friday. That way, you can check it before you have to read it Saturday morning."

"Sounds good. Thanks, Aaron."

"You're going to stay with us for the weekend, right?"

Jerry had his bachelor pad overlooking the ocean only twelve miles away. "You know how I hate to impose on you and your brother."

"Jadin is coming for the celebration."

Jerry smiled at the thought of seeing his favorite niece, since she didn't come around much after she started working for NASA. "It would be nice to see her again. Fine. I'll stay for the weekend."

When Aaron drove away, Jerry closed the garage door, and then strolled through the shop past more motors waiting for parts. He headed out to the front of the shop and then sat on an old wooden bench as he stared down at all the boats filling the mooring slips and anchor buoys. It had cost a small fortune for all the updates to the ancient mooring facilities, since most of it had been pieced together over several hundred years.

Originally, the harbor belonged to the Native Americans, who lived off the abundance of seafood until the whaling industry began using it as a staging area for their ships. Now days, the town was supported by tourism. Some of them would pull off the coastal highway looking for historic places of interest, but most of the town's income was derived from fees collected by the marina.

It was also a popular place for people to refuel their boats while heading south along the west coast. When the salmon off shore were getting ready to head up the local river to spawn, Humpback Harbor was the destination for sports anglers from around the world. Other times of the year, the marina was filled with whale watchers, so there was always something going on in the little harbor.

Jerry stared across at the new entrance into the harbor, now safely tucked behind a rock breakwater. He grinned with pride at what he had managed to accomplish for his hometown.

On the other side of the boat ramp, he admired the new concrete pier where the dilapidated wooden dock used to be. An aluminum ramp stretched down to the main floating dock, which branched off to floating mooring slips with all new facilities for the boaters. Just past the marina office, at the head of the pier, a long row of shops and eateries lined one side of the wide boardwalk, with a metal railing secured into the rim of the basalt rock surrounding the harbor.

Jerry sighed in resignation at his destiny. He didn't want to be the Mayor, but next Saturday, the large parking lot would be filled for the official opening of the marina. All the local people would be there, but he was sure there would be a lot of tourists, plus the people on the boats filling the marina. There was even a rumor the North Bend Newspaper was sending a reporter to cover the event. He hated being the center of attention and having all eyes on him, but at least he didn't have to write a speech. He just hoped Aaron would keep it short.

***

Aaron smiled as he turned into the driveway at the sheriff's house, but it slipped away when he saw his older brother's patrol car parked near the front porch. Brad was twenty-five, and had no business flirting with Denise, even if she would be eighteen in three weeks. He especially had no business hitting on her since she was the sheriff's daughter and Brad was the new deputy sheriff.

When he turned the corner past the large garage, Aaron saw Denise sitting in a chair on the front porch, twirling her long blond hair provocatively with her fingers. He rolled his eyes and grinned when he saw his brother standing on the steps in front of her, leaning against the rail with his hands in his back pockets to show off his chest and shoulders, like a strutting buck.

Aaron backed up next to the large rescue boat, shut off the engine, then climbed out. He couldn't stop grinning as he strolled over to join them on the porch and plopped down into a chair.

Brad noticed the smirk on his brother's face. "What's so amusing?"

"Oh, nothing. Since you're so big and strong, how about giving me a hand putting the engine back on the boat?"

Brad realized his brother was teasing him, and then in two quick steps, wrapped his arm around Aaron's neck in a fake chokehold. "Smart ass."

When Denise heard Aaron's laughter, she smiled. With their parents killed in a car accident, Brad had taken care of Aaron for the past year, and they had grown very close. Their older sisters, Christa and Jadin, had jobs in other parts of the country, so Brad did the best he could to raise his brother. Fortunately, their Uncle Jerry was around to help while Brad was away at the Police Academy.

Aaron squirmed out from under Brad's arm, hunched down in a wrestler's stance, then grinned up at his tall brother. "Don't be afraid, big man. I promise not to hurt you." Their fun was interrupted when the sheriff's SUV pulled into the driveway.

Rick Slade climbed out of his patrol car and indicated for his new deputy to come over. Brad had wanted to be a deputy sheriff all his life, and had done well at the Police Academy, so he had hired him the day after graduation. His only concern was with the young man taking an interest in his daughter.

Brad walked down the steps and joined Rick. "Is there something going on, Sheriff?"

"Your uncle just called about a domestic disturbance at his campground. I'd like for you to go find out what's going on."

"I'll take care of it."

Rick noticed his daughter smile as she watched Brad walk away to his vehicle. Even though she was nearly eighteen, she was still his little girl, so he had a hard time adjusting to her becoming a woman.

"Tell your mom I'll be late for dinner. I have to transport a bear poacher from the State Park Headquarters to the county jail."

"I will. Bye, Dad."

Aaron sat in a chair next to Denise. "The poacher must be a real badass if the Park Rangers had to call your father to pick him up."

"I don't think it was because my dad is a Marine."

"You mean ex-Marine."

"There's no such thing as an ex-Marine, Aaron."

"Right. Well, I'd better get this motor onto your dad's boat."

"I'll help you."

They walked down the steps and over to the large rubber rescue boat on a trailer, which was parked on the concrete slab in front of the garage. Mounted on the stern was a matching outboard motor. Aaron slid the front door of the garage open and walked inside to bring out the engine hoist and Denise followed him into the large open bay. "I saw that look you gave your brother earlier, Aaron."

"I don't know what you mean."

"You don't have to be jealous of your brother."

"I'm not jealous, I'm envious. He got all the muscles."

"Yes, he's very muscular. But you got all the brains."

Aaron chuckled. "Are you saying you think Brad is stupid?"

"That's not what I meant. He's street smart, and you're more mechanically inclined. That's all."

"Oh, that makes me feel so much better. All right, I think I've got it now. Thanks for helping."

Denise stopped next to the portable hoist, crossed her arms, and tried to look stern. "My help comes with a price, Aaron Avery."

Aaron stopped to stare at her, knowing she was going to ask him more questions about Brad. "Oh, yeah. And what price is that?"

"First, take me into town and buy me a milkshake. Second, take me to North Bend, so I can pick up my car. Brad was supposed to, but he might be gone for a while."

Aaron began pushing the hoist outside. "No."

She walked beside him. "Excuse me? Why not?"

"First, you didn't say please. Second, if Brad is so muscular and so smart, then have him drive you down there when he gets back. I'm just a lowly grease monkey, remember? And I've got to get back to the repair shop."

"Aaron Avery! You can be so mean sometimes!"

"Maybe if you say you're sorry, I might reconsider."

"Fine. Aaron, I'm sorry you're a grease monkey."

Aaron had known her all his life, and she had been a spoiled brat since she learned how to manipulate boys to do her bidding. He stared back, showing her he wouldn't budge until he got a genuine apology.

"Fine. Aaron, I'm sorry for not saying please. And if I said anything that might have hurt your feelings, then I apologize for that, too."

"Much better. Thank you. Now, I'd be glad to take you into town."

Denise smiled. "Thanks."

Aaron stopped the hoist with the lift arm positioned over the outboard motor in his truck, then jumped up into the back. Once the chain was attached, he jumped down.

Denise watched him pump the handle, lifting the motor. "Did you know Susan Curtis has a crush on you, but her father told her to stay away?"

Aaron stopped and looked at her. "Why did he tell her to stay away from me?"

"Because you work for your uncle. Mister Curtis is still upset about losing the election."

When the motor was in the air, Aaron grabbed the hoist and rolled it up to the back of the boat. "Try to keep it from banging into anything while I move it over the transom and then tell me when it's lined up."

Aaron continued lining up the motor to suppress his anger. He couldn't care less if Susan had a crush on him, but using Jerry as an excuse was going too far. When he thought the motor was in the right position, he stopped moving the hoist. "How does it look?"

Denise noticed Aaron's scowl. "It's lined up. Start letting it down."

Once the motor sat firmly on the transom, Aaron pushed the hoist out of the way and climbed up into the boat to secure the bolts and hook up the controls. Denise twirled her hair and examined her nails. "Are you about done? I need to get to North Bend before the dealership closes."

"If you're in such a hurry, how about rolling the hoist back into the garage for me?"

Denise grabbed the hoist and dragged it back inside, then pulled the garage door closed. When Aaron jumped down, she climbed into his truck while he got in and started the engine.

She reached over and put her hand on his thigh. "I really appreciate you doing this for me. You're such a good friend."

He put the truck in gear and drove down the driveway. *A good friend?*

***

When Jerry saw the patrol car drive up in front of his office, he walked outside and opened the passenger door. "I'll go with you, Brad."

When Jerry climbed in, Brad headed for the campground, a quarter mile away down the ocean front road. "What's the problem, Jerry?"

"Oh, just two drunks arguing about something. I didn't understand the woman who called it in because she was talking so fast, but I figured if the police showed up, they might settle down."

"You couldn't handle it on your own, like my dad used to do?"

"I ain't as young as I used to be, Bradley. Don't forget, I'm six years older than your father was, and these young people nowadays think they can do whatever they want. They have no respect for their elders."

"Not all of them, Jerry. Why don't you sell the campground?"

"This has been our dream for forty-nine years."

"You mean '*your*' dream. Dad only stayed here because of you."

Jerry abruptly stared at Brad. "What did you just say? Your father and I did it together, damn it!"

Brad realized he had crossed an emotional boundary. "I'm sorry, Jerry. It's just that I really miss him and mom. I keep thinking about how it could have been different."

"You're thinking if he and your mom had left the business to me and moved away, they might still be alive?"

"Yeah. Something like that."

"I know your mom and dad loved living near the ocean. Even if they had sold the business, they wouldn't have ever left this place. Their deaths were just a case of bad luck, was all."

"I suppose you're right."

Brad drove across the bridge over the river, which flowed out into the ocean on the other side of the road, then turned off the highway and entered the campground. "Which campsite?"

"Thirteen. It's at the end of the riverfront sites."

"I know where number thirteen is, Jerry. I used to work here, remember?"

"Sorry. Force of habit."

A few moments later, a teenage girl flagged them down, and Brad pulled up beside her. "Are you the one who called?"

"Yes, Sheriff. They said they were going to beat the hell out of each other and walked down into the water. When they realized how cold it was, they started laughing, and now they're drinking beers together. I'm sorry. I should have called you back."

"That's okay, ma'am. I'm glad they worked it out."

***

Brad parked in front of the marina office to let his uncle out. "Oh, hey, good news. Jadin is coming for the celebration."

"I know. Aaron invited me to stay at the house for the weekend."

"And?"

Jerry suppressed his grin, climbed out, and was about to close the door.

Brad leaned over the center console to look out at his uncle. "So, are you staying with us or not?"

Jerry looked inside. "I accept, and I'll bring dinner."

Brad grinned. "You're a cruel old man, Jerry."

Jerry closed the door and stepped back, and as he watched Brad drive away, his chest swelled with pride for the young deputy sheriff. He looked across at the line of shops and then strolled along the waterfront in that direction.

Chapter 11

SENTINEL MONITORING STATION, NORTHERN ALASKA:

Even with hundreds of ground-based telescopes scanning the solar system, it still was not possible to see every asteroid or comet on a collision course with Earth, but the Sentinel satellite telescope was designed and launched into space just to identify and track the millions of asteroids and comets. If it discovered any with a trajectory that would enter the solar system, it would notify the station.

Keven Sterling, a sixty-two-year-old astrophysicist, heard a soft beeping, indicating the computer had received a signal from Sentinel. When he looked at the monitor, his jaw dropped open. When he zoomed in on the object, he suddenly leaned forward to check something. If the dimensions on the screen were accurate, the asteroid was nearly ten miles across. Even more startling was its color. He had been watching the stars for most of his life, but had seen nothing like this asteroid. Even stranger, this one was coming at a thirty-degree angle to our orbital plane from another galaxy.

He entered a command into the computer for an estimated trajectory, and when he saw the numbers on the monitor, he frowned. "Oh, now that's interesting."

He entered a number for his friend at the NASA Jet Propulsion Laboratory in Pasadena, California, and a moment later, a young woman with red hair appeared on another monitor. "You're not going to believe what Sentinel just found, Jadin. I'm sending you the video."

Jadin Avery brought up the recording and stared at the asteroid. "Is this a joke?"

Keven leaned back in his chair and grinned at her. "Nope."

"Is that gold?"

"I was hoping you could find out for me."

"Of course I will. Do you have a trajectory yet?"

"Yes, it's on a thirty-degree angle into our solar system, which suggests it's coming from another one, but I have no idea which one. The data indicates it's going to pass us by eight-hundred-miles, but what's more puzzling is its speed. It's moving eight times faster than the normal speed of an asteroid, so it's going to zip right through our system at 800,000 miles-per-hour."

"Now that I have a location, I'll see if I can task one of our telescopes to determine its composition with spectrum analysis. We might have something by the time I get back."

"Where are you going?"

"Home, to Humpback Harbor, Oregon."

"All right. Call me when you have more information. I'll talk to you later."

Keven stared at the streaming video feed of the asteroid, and after several minutes, he noticed it was slowly rotating, which made it sparkle. He recorded a four-minute segment, uploaded it to his fellow astronomers on the Internet, then smiled as he leaned back in his chair and stared at his discovery.

Chapter 12

NASA'S JET PROPULSION LABORATORY, PASADENA, CALIFORNIA:

Patrick Sherman grabbed a copy of Popular Science and leaned his chair back from the desk, but before he could thumb through the magazine, he heard a steady beeping coming from his computer. When he looked at the tracking data on the monitor, he could not believe it was even possible. The moon had just moved closer to the planet. He checked and double-checked the data, cross-referencing with alternate systems, but the result was the same. The moon was definitely closer.

He entered a number for a secure video call to Captain Sheri Larson, the government liaison stationed at his facility, and then her face appeared on the screen. "Captain? You're not going to believe this."

"Hey, Patrick. What's going on?"

"Our distance from the moon has decreased by twenty-eight-thousand miles. I just sent you the data. And no, I'm not crazy. Look at the cross-reference data backing me up."

Larson brought the information up on her monitor. "Oh, no! When did this happen?"

"Less than a minute ago. I don't mind telling you, this scares the crap out of me."

"You're not alone. Who else knows about this?"

"It just happened, but I'm sure I'm not the only one who noticed, so I'm certain the word will spread quickly."

"Of course. I'll contact some people and let them know what's going on so they can start monitoring the tidal effects."

"All right."

When Larson's faced vanished from the monitor, Patrick leaned back in his chair and stared at the information on the screen. "What could possibly cause this?"

***

WASHINGTON, DC:

Director Donner looked up at his monitor and smiled at the woman on the screen. "Hello, Captain Larson. What can I do for you?"

"Good morning, Director. I wanted to let you know right away the moon's orbit has changed, and we don't know why."

Realizing Larson was serious, Donner's posture stiffened. "When did this happen?"

"Just now."

"What kind of affect is it having?"

"Nothing we know about for the moment, but the tidal effect will appear first."

"How bad?"

"It's hard to say until it happens, Sir."

"How many people know about this?"

"The scientist who made the discovery, and the two of us, but we're not the only ones studying the moon, so it's only a matter of time before others make the same discovery."

"All right. I'll contact a few people I can trust. Keep me posted on any new developments."

"Yes, Sir."

When Larson's image vanished, Donner called his contact at the FEMA office and gave her the information so she could get her people involved. He leaned back in his chair, considering if it was too soon to inform the president. A moment later, he leaned forward and selected the button to connect to with him. "Sir? You're not going to believe this."

***

SOVIET MILITARY DEFENSE COMMAND:

Vladimir's eyes slowly closed and his head tilted forward for an instant before he looked up and stared at the computer monitor again. The image he had been staring at for the past 4 hours had suddenly vanished and the screen showed nothing but static. He typed several commands into the computer and waited for the results, and aA moment later, the information appeared.

CONTACT WITH SATELLITE HAS BEEN TERMINATED.

He grabbed the phone and called his commander, and several moments later, a groggy voice answered. "This had better be important, Vladimir."

"We have just lost contact with one of our satellites. One second I was receiving a signal, and then suddenly it was gone."

Vladimir felt a hand from one of the other technicians on his shoulder, and looked up to see the concern in her eyes. "What happened?"

Vladimir listened to the tech, and then just stared at her for a moment before the realization sunk in and he spoke into the phone. "Commander, I have just been informed that the satellite did not malfunction. It suddenly lost altitude and burned up in the atmosphere."

"That is impossible. Satellites do not suddenly fall out of the sky."

"I do not know what to say, Commander. Perhaps the Americans shot it down."

"Keep me informed. I must call the Kremlin and see if our contacts know anything about this sabotage."

***

WASHINGTON, D.C.:

Donner pressed the speaker button on his telephone. "Yes."

"Sir, we seemed to have lost one of our satellites, and Houston says it just fell out of the sky and burned up in the atmosphere. This is bad news, Sir. It was one of our top secret spy satellites."

Donner stared at the phone for a moment. "That's impossible."

"I agree, sir, but there is no explanation."

"Could it be some type of weapon?"

"Sir, even our most powerful laser systems could not have done it with such precision. We have no idea why it happened."

"All right. Keep me informed of any new incidents."

"Yes, Sir."

Donner hung up, thinking it didn't make any sense. The Soviets were far behind our current laser technology, and at the moment, the Chinese wouldn't risk an incident. He grabbed the phone and called the Chairman of the Joint Chiefs.

"This is General Matheson, Sir."

"General, we have a situation that might need your attention. Someone took out one of our satellites, and we have no suspects."

"What do you mean, took out?"

"It suddenly lost altitude and burned up in the atmosphere."

"All right. I'll see what I can find out from our end."

Donner ended the call and turned his chair to look out across the White House lawn. This was too much of a coincidence with the possibility Sloan had stolen the gravity device. He grabbed the phone and selected a contact.

Chapter 13

MONTANA:

Because of the time changes on his return trips from Iceland, Alex had barely slept, and the drive home from the airport seemed to be taking forever. It also didn't help he had not got a good night's sleep before he headed to Iceland, either. Fala had kept her word and put him out on the sofa the night of their big blowout and just as Okawna had said. No couch can come close to a soft, warm woman lying beside you.

He knew when he got home, Fala would be at work in her clinic, and Halona would be away spending the night with a friend. He was looking forward to getting home to the quiet house and comfortable bed so he could finally get some decent sleep.

When Alex parked in front of his home, Barney's tail wagged furiously as he climbed out and bent down for a slobbery kiss, then ran his hands through his thick fur. "How have you been, big guy?"

He grabbed his suitcase and entered the house, dropping it near the hallway on his way to the refrigerator. With a cold beer in hand, he walked out onto the porch and sat down to admire the view across the valley. It had been awhile since he had got a moment's peace to himself and just admire the view from his porch, breathing in the cool, clean Montana air.

His phone rang, and he recognized Director Donner's image. "Hello, Martin."

"Hi, Alex. Sorry to bother you, but we've just mysteriously lost one of our satellites, and I'm thinking it might be related to your gravity machine."

"What do you mean mysteriously lost it?"

"It fell out of orbit and burnt up upon re-entry into the atmosphere. Fortunately, there have been no reports of anyone being hurt from falling space debris, so we're thinking it was completely vaporized in the atmosphere."

"Crap! I bet Sloan turned it on."

"Do you have any idea how powerful that machine is?"

"Well, if it can take out a satellite, I'd say it's pretty damned powerful. Why?"

"The orbit of the moon has suddenly changed, too."

Being a geophysicist, Alex knew the ramifications of a stronger tidal effect. "This is bad, Martin. Very bad. The only thing that could change the orbit of the moon is that damned gravity device."

"Any idea where it could be?"

"Not entirely, but I have a hunch. Your report said Essex has a research facility in the Nevada desert. Somewhere outside of Reno, I think. It'd be the perfect place to stash it."

"I know you're tired, Alex, and I hate to ask this of you."

"I know, I know. I'll check it out, but I'll need a ride to Reno."

"I'll arrange a flight to pick you up in Bozeman."

"All right. I'll call Okawna and see if he's available to join me before he heads to Alaska."

"If you need some backup, I know the Base Commander at the Fallon Naval Air Station."

"We'll pay Essex a visit and find out what he knows first. If that doesn't work, we'll call in the reinforcements and take the place apart if we have to."

"All right. I'll have my people call you with the details. You let them know if you need to stop and pick up Okawna."

"I will. As soon as we figure out what's going on, I'll let you know."

"Sounds good. And thanks again, Alex. Good luck."

Alex ended the call and entered Okawna's number, and on the second ring, Okawna picked up. "I hope you haven't unpacked yet."

"Hey, Alex. What's going on?"

"I just got a call from Donner." Alex filled him in on the details. "Care to join me?"

"Sure. I'm still in Seward, Alaska, waiting for Mike to pick me up. I'll tell him what happened and book a flight to Reno, then see you there."

"Thanks. I appreciate it."

"That's what friends are for."

Alex grabbed his suitcase, carried it into his bedroom, and then undressed and jumped into the shower while he waited for Donner's people to call. The warm water felt wonderful, but it did nothing to help him relax. He was exhausted and mentally drained from all the fighting with Fala.

Once he dressed and threw a few things in his suitcase, he walked back to the living room. He sat on the couch, dreading what he knew was coming. "Here we go," He grabbed his phone and called Fala. "Hey, beautiful."

"Hi, Alex. Are you home now?"

"Yes, I got back a short while ago."

"Good. Look, Alex, I'm sorry about blowing up at you like that. I'm sure I said some hurtful things, and I just feel horrible about it."

"Oh boy. You may want to hold on to that apology, Fala."

Fala's tone immediately turned from apologetic and loving to angry. "Why?"

"I have to catch a flight to Reno at any moment."

"You want to run that past me again? And I want to remind you to choose your words very carefully. I'm hanging on by a thread right now, Alex, and I'm on the verge of leaving you."

"Fala, please, don't do this right now. I'm begging you. Something very serious happened and I have to go to Reno to make sure it doesn't happen again. If I don't go, a lot of people could get hurt. Honest. Fala? Fala? Are you still there?"

"I'm still here, Alex."

When he heard a familiar sniffle, Alex hated himself for causing so many of her tears. "Fala, please don't cry."

"I'm going to let you go this time, Alex. If you come home and turn around to have to leave again, don't be in a rush to come back home, because Halona and I will not be there."

"Please, don't do that."

"Because people's lives are at stake, I'm willing to let you go. But when you come back home, if I don't see some real commitment from you, Alex, then we're gone. It is as plain as that. I cannot keep doing this."

"I understand."

"Goodbye, Alex."

"I love you."

Alex's heart raced, waiting for a reply. When it didn't come, he set the phone on the coffee table, then lay down and stared at the ceiling. She was right, and he knew he had to be there for them and show Fala how committed he was to her. Before he drifted off to sleep, he had made his mind up that when he returned from Reno, he was going to ask Fala to marry him.

Chapter 14

HUMPBACK HARBOR, OREGON:

Jadin Avery parked her rented sedan in the circular driveway of a large, timber style house overlooking the Pacific Ocean, then got out and took a moment to look around. The last time she was home was for her parent's funeral over a year ago, but nearly everything was just as she remembered.

She grabbed her suitcase from the back seat, then climbed the steps to the thick wooden door and entered the great room. She noticed five people sitting at a table on the back deck, enjoying the sunset over the ocean, so she set her suitcase near the stairs and no one noticed her stroll out to join them. "I made it."

The four men stood, and she exchanged smiles and hugs with Brad and Aaron, then hugged the man who was her father's best friend. "Hello, Sheriff. It's nice to see you again."

Rick smiled. "You, too, Jadin."

Saving Jerry for last, she smiled and hugged him tight. "Hey, Uncle Jerry. I've missed you."

Jerry hugged her close for a moment, then held her at arm's length and grinned. "You're just as pretty as your mother."

Jadin felt her face flush. "Oh, you say that to Christa, too, but thanks anyway. It must be our red hair."

She sat at the end of the table, with Jerry and Aaron sitting on either side of her. Then she smiled at Denise, sitting between Aaron and Brad.

Jerry thought Jadin seemed more confident than the last time he saw her. "So, what's NASA got you working on these days?"

"I have my own team now, at the JPL laboratory in Pasadena. We look for and collect data on any objects in space that might be on a collision course with Earth, like asteroids and comets."

Jerry gave her a questioning expression. "That's a big sky to search. Are there enough of you to actually find one?"

"Our chances just improved tremendously. A private company launched a new satellite called Sentinel, and its only purpose is to find what we can't with our limited capabilities."

"Well, let's hope it finds them in time."

She grinned and reached over to put her hand on Jerry's. "The person I'm working with at Sentinel looks a lot like you, Jerry, but with a beard."

Jerry chuckled. "So he's a good-looking fellow, you say. You know, when your dad and I were young, I was the one with all the girlfriends. Of course, once your dad met your mom in his junior year, he was hooked."

Aaron grinned at his sister. "Does he talk to himself, like Uncle Jerry?"

"Nope. Ours is one of a kind."

Jadin realized it felt good to be home again, and over the next hour, she ate leftover pizza and enjoyed listening to the banter and stories. When the topic changed to things they had done with their parents, a knot formed in her stomach over the regret she felt from not spending more time with them before they were killed.

When the Sheriff and Denise left for the evening, Aaron held out a sheet of paper for his uncle to read. "Here's the speech I promised, Uncle Jerry."

Jerry pulled his glasses from his shirt pocket and put them on before accepting the letter. The first thing he noticed was the speech filled the entire sheet of paper, and then he realized Aaron had used a tiny font size and looked up at the young man. "I appreciate this, Aaron. Really, I do, but first, it is way too long. And second, I can barely read this small print, even with my glasses."

"That's just a rough draft, so you can pick out the parts you like. Here's a yellow highlighter. Just mark the parts you want to keep and I'll retype it before the ceremony."

"All right." He noticed a stifled yawn from Jadin and gently squeezed her hand. "I'm glad you came."

"Are you kidding? My uncle is now the Mayor, and I want to see him speak to over five people at one time."

Jerry grinned. "You're getting as bad as me, young lady."

"I know. It's fun, isn't it?"

Jerry gave Jadin's hand one last squeeze, then stood and looked at his family, so proud of every one of them. "I would like to sit here with Jadin for the rest of the night, but I know she's tired, so why don't we let the little lady get some sleep?"

Everyone stood, then Jadin gave Brad and Aaron hugs before hugging her uncle. "Good night, Jerry."

"Good night, sweetie. I'll see you in the morning."

***

SATURDAY MORNING:

Jadin was enjoying a morning cup of coffee in the kitchen as Jerry strolled in. When she saw how he was dressed, she laughed. "Are you kidding me, Jerry? Is that what you're planning on wearing today?"

Jerry looked down at his jeans and shoes. "What's wrong with the way I dress?"

"The jeans and tennis shoes I can deal with, but the plaid shirt has got to go."

"Well, I don't have anything that requires a tie, so this is about it."

"I think Dad's clothes are still in his closet. I'll see if I can find something that might fit you."

"Oh, I doubt it. He was three-inches taller than me."

Jadin left her coffee on the counter, then stood and filled a coffee mug and held it out to Jerry. "Here. I'll be back in a minute."

She walked through the main floor of the house, then down the hall toward her parents' bedroom, but when she grabbed the handle, she hesitated to open the door. The last time she had entered their room, her parents were still alive. She had scheduled a vacation to go home just two weeks before the accident, but when NASA had offered her a team of her own, she had canceled her trip. Ever since the accident, she has lived with the regret of that decision.

She walked into the room and went to one of the two closets, then sorted through her father's shirts until she found a nice one for her uncle to wear, then took one last look around before closing the door. On her way back to the kitchen, Jadin noticed Jerry out on the back deck, but continued into the kitchen to grab her coffee before going out to join him. She smiled at Aaron, who was looking at a sheet of paper on the counter. "Good morning."

"Hey, Jadin. I hope that shirt is for Uncle Jerry."

"I guess you noticed his ensemble. This will make him look more like the Mayor. Has Brad come down yet?"

"Yeah, he got a call early this morning. The Sheriff wanted him to check out some animal disturbances, so he'll meet us at the ceremony."

Jadin topped off her coffee and stared at the sheet of paper. "Is that Jerry's speech?"

He slid the sheet over to Jadin. "It was, but he only highlighted a few sentences. He said they're the only ones he wants to read. It's going to be a short speech."

Jadin read the yellowed areas. "You're right. I'll go talk to him about it."

Jadin took the sheet of paper and her coffee out to the back deck and set them on the table, then held out the shirt. "Stand up and let's see how this fits you."

Jerry remained seated and stared at the shirt, then looked up at her. "You've got to be kidding. You want me to wear a powder blue shirt?"

"Oh, come on, Jerry. The blue will bring out the color of your eyes. Maybe you'll attract a nice lady and settle down."

Jerry chuckled. "I think I'm pretty settled already."

"Well, whatever. I'm not going to let you out in public dressed like that, so stand up and take it off."

Jerry reluctantly stood, took off his plaid shirt, and then set it on the table. "All right, hand it over."

Jadin gave him an appraising stare. "You know, you're still in pretty good shape for your age. Why aren't the women in this area beating down your door?"

"I keep it bolted, and for a good reason."

"And what might that be?"

"Women always want to change their man, and sometimes it's not for his betterment. I like my life just the way it is, thank you very much."

Jadin held out the shirt and watched him put it on. "Much better. Now you look like a man of authority. I would have loved to see the look on Curtis's face when he lost the election."

Jerry grinned. "Even though I didn't want the job in the first place, it was worth it just to see his smug demeanor disappear."

When Aaron walked out onto the deck, he grinned at Jerry. "Good morning, Mister Mayor. Now you look the part."

Jerry headed for the door. "We might as well get started. I have a feeling it's going to be a long day."

Aaron grabbed his jacket off the wall hook near the door. "I'm taking over operating the marina today, so you're off duty, Uncle Jerry. I need to make a stop on the way, so I'll see both of you there later."

***

CURTIS RANCH:

During the thirty-minute drive, Brad wondered what would happen when he arrived at the ex-Mayor's house. Personally, he did not have any problems with Mister Curtis prior to the election, and had rarely seen him in town since then.

He parked his patrol car in front of the barn and climbed out, then a tall, handsome man with salt and pepper hair greeted him and shook his hand. "So, what's going on with your animals, Mister Curtis?"

"The horses have been acting skittish since yesterday afternoon, and I can't figure out why. My dogs and chickens are acting strange as well."

"Have you had any trouble with bears in this area?"

"Once, about ten years ago, but nothing since then. I heard a poacher was arrested the other day, so I wondered if he had a partner."

Brad looked around the area. "From what I understand, he was alone. I'm not sure what I can do to help you, Mister Curtis. Maybe we have a weather front moving through. I hear animals sometimes act strange right before a big storm."

"Yes, possibly."

Brad turned and saw an attractive middle-aged woman hurrying in his direction. When she stopped, he smiled. "Good morning, Misses Curtis."

"Good morning, Bradley. I brought you a cup of coffee to take with you. I'm sure you're eager to get back to the celebration. I'm so sorry you had to come all the way out here, and I'm afraid that was my fault. Thomas didn't want me to call you, but I was so worried it might be a rustler trying to steal our animals, or maybe another poacher in the area, I called you anyway."

"Yes, ma'am, I understand. No need to apologize. That's what the sheriff and I are here for, to help the folks of this town feel safe. If you notice anything else out of the ordinary, call me."

"Thank you, Bradley. That's just so sweet of you."

"Are you both coming to the celebration today?"

Curtis crossed his arms over his chest. "Hell no!"

Mary placed her hand on the deputy sheriff's arm and smiled. "Don't pay any attention to him, Bradley. Of course we are. You tell your uncle we'll expect to be seated on the stage with him, all right, dear?"

Brad knew his uncle had been in love with Mary since high school, but when Curtis stole her away, Jerry never found another woman who measured up to what he had lost. "Yes, ma'am, I'll tell him. Thanks for the coffee, and I'll see you later."

When Brad climbed into his car and drove away, Curtis waited for Mary to turn back around, then noticed she was smiling and had a faraway look in her eyes. "We're not going to the ceremony!"

Mary stopped smiling. "If you don't want to go, fine, but I'm going to hear Jerry's speech."

Curtis's lips formed into a sadistic grin. "Okay, I'll go. I can't wait to hear him make a fool out of himself. Unless he has nobody to listen to him."

"What do you mean, Thomas?"

"You'll see. I'd better finish feeding the animals so I can get ready. I can't wait to see what that hick will be wearing."

He entered the barn and moved out of Mary's line of sight, then brought out his phone and entered a text message. He smirked when he pressed send.

Mary stared after Curtis for a few moments and had a sinking feeling he was up to something cruel to humiliate Jerry in public. She was still very fond of her old boyfriend, and occasionally reminisced about when she and Jerry were together in high school. On more than one occasion, she regretted her decision to leave him for Curtis all those years ago. She turned and walked back to the house.

Chapter 15

THE CEREMONY:

Jadin drove Jerry into the empty parking lot at the marina and stopped behind the repair shop. Once the engine was off, she turned to look over at him in the passenger seat. "Are you sure it's today?"

"That's what I was told."

Jadin opened her door and climbed out and waited while Jerry did the same. "I see a few people over at the shops. Let's head over and find out what happened."

Jerry walked around the car to join her. "No ceremony is fine with me. I didn't want to give a speech in the first place."

Jadin wrapped her arm around Jerry's. "That's not the point. There should be a lot more people here for the grand opening."

"It's not a grand opening, Jadin. It's been open for three months."

"You know what I mean. This marina supports most of the town, so you'd think they would at least come and thank you for finding the financing to rebuild it." She looked up at him. "How did you manage to find that much money?" She noticed a change in his demeanor and a sad look in his eyes, so abruptly stopped walking. "You didn't, did you?"

"Yes, and not a word about this to anyone, young lady."

"But why? You and Dad built that campground together, and you swore you would never sell it."

"My brother is gone, Jadin, and I'm not getting any younger. None of you kids want to take it over, so it's time to let it go."

Jadin crossed her arms. "You still haven't answered my question. Why did you rebuild the marina with the money instead of actually retiring?"

"Because, Jadin, without the marina, this town would wither up and die. This is still my home, and I won't let that happen."

"All right. You know, you really should tell everyone it was your money and not some financial group's."

Jerry smiled and held his elbow out for Jadin to accept, and with his arm wrapped around hers, walked toward the shops. "What purpose would that serve? The only recognition I need right now is a harbor full of happy boaters, and look how full it is."

"All right. It's your call."

Jadin could not believe the difference in the appearance of the marina, and when they reached the new pier, she stopped and smiled up at Jerry. "You did a great job. What time are you supposed to give your speech?"

"The note said 10:00 AM."

"What note, and from whom?"

"Someone from City Hall left it at my shop." He saw the skepticism in her eyes. "It was on official stationery."

Jadin grinned. "I think you've been punked."

"What? What do you mean, punked?"

"Didn't 10:00 AM strike you as being a little early for a celebration? Someone's playing a practical joke on you."

"I bet it was Curtis. 1:00 PM would seem more reasonable."

"Well, it seems there isn't any hurry, so show me your new docks."

Jerry turned and led her down the new pier. "All right, but they're not my docks, this is a city marina."

"You paid for them, so in my opinion, that makes them yours."

"The town will pay me back with a percentage of the mooring fees."

"What's the percentage?"

Jerry looked down at her. "Do you need to know everything?"

"Of course. You're my favorite uncle, and I'm going to make sure you don't get screwed out of what you deserve."

"I'm your *only* uncle, so that's not really a compliment, but thanks anyway."

When they reached the end of the pier, Jadin went down the aluminum ramp first. Compared to the old wooden ramp, this one felt solid as a rock. Being a curious scientist and astrophysicist, when she reached the bottom, she knelt down to look underneath. The thick aluminum frame was secured to the concrete pier with two large hinges, and the bottom rested on four large rubber rollers. When she stood, she gave Jerry a curious expression. "I bet this ramp wasn't cheap. How much did you pay for it?"

"What can I say? We needed something that would last, otherwise there was no sense in replacing the old one. Same with the mooring docks. The new pilings are Teflon-coated steel tubes, and the same with the attachment rings on the docks. The company guarantees the Teflon will not wear down to the steel for five-hundred years. Of course, by then there will be something lighter and smaller available. Things just keep changing."

Jadin smiled up at her humble uncle. Even his house was a modest rambler style, although it overlooked the ocean. When her phone rang, she retrieved it from her coat pocket, and recognized the number from one of her team member's in Pasadena. "Hey, Patrick. What's going on?"

"I'm sorry for interrupting your vacation, Jadin, but everyone's being called back to work. The moon's tidal affect is causing a higher than normal tide, but no serious damage. You should get a higher than normal tidal surge a few hours from now."

"Do you know how much higher?"

"We knew you would want to know, so we figured it out. For the Pacific Northwest, about two-feet above any previous high tide mark, so nothing too drastic yet."

"What about the one after that?"

"The change sent the moon into a chaotic elliptical orbit, and our calculations indicate the next incoming tide shouldn't be as bad."

"That's good news. Has anyone determined how something this impossible just happened?"

"At the moment, no one in NASA has any idea, not even any wild theories. Oh, and one more thing. The Director of National Security has classified this as top secret until he says otherwise."

"All right. Can you arrange a flight for me this afternoon?"

"I'll take care of it and text you the information."

"Thanks, Patrick. Keep me posted on any new developments."

Jadin slid the phone into her pocket and looked up at Jerry. "I'm sorry, Jerry, but I need to head back to JPL after the ceremony."

Jerry stared at her. "That's okay, but can you tell me why?"

"I can't go into any details for security reasons, but we're going to have some strange tides for a while. Nothing for you to worry about."

Jerry thought about it for a moment. "Since when does an astrologist get called back to work if it's nothing to worry about? Asteroids don't have anything to do with tides, Jadin."

"I'm an astrophysicist, not a fortune teller, and my expertise is not limited to just asteroids and comets. I also have a degree in foreign languages, and another in computer science." She stared out across the harbor for a moment. "You're right, Jerry. Asteroids don't have anything to do with tides. I just wish I knew all the details about why this is happening."

No longer arm in arm, they continued along the docks, receiving nods of approval for the new marina from the people on their boats. Jerry knew she was keeping something important from him, but knew she would tell him if it wasn't top secret.

***

When Thomas Curtis arrived at the marina, he smiled when he saw there were only seven cars in the parking lot. Out of habit, he parked in the spot reserved for VIPs and climbed out of his town car. Once Mary joined him, they strolled along the waterfront. Quaint shops, restaurants, and two taverns had replaced the fish processing factories. Back in his day as Mayor, he had fought hard to get approval from the town council to build a hotel in that area instead, but never got the approval.

Mary stopped and placed her hands on the steel railing as she stared down at the water in the harbor, fifteen-feet straight below the rail. She looked out across the marina and smiled up at Curtis. "Jerry did a wonderful job, didn't he, Thomas?"

Curtis hated to admit it, but she was correct. "I suppose so." He grinned at her. "Come on. I want to see what he's wearing."

"You'd better behave yourself, Thomas. You're not the Mayor anymore."

Curtis ignored her when he noticed someone he hadn't expected to see at the ceremony and left her to go over to join him at a table in the waterfront park. "What are you doing here, Fred? I told you not to come here today."

"You're not the Mayor anymore, Tommy, and I don't approve of your trying to boycott this grand opening ceremony."

Mary had followed Curtis and stared up at him. "You're a real bastard, Thomas!" She turned and stomped over to the shops, entering the first one just to get out of Curtis's sight.

Curtis glared at Fred. "I loaned you the money for starting your kayaking business when nobody else would, so you owe me."

Fred stood and smiled sarcastically at Curtis. "And I really appreciate it, Tommy, especially since your bank is charging me nineteen percent interest. Enjoy the celebration. I know I will."

When Fred walked away, Curtis was surprised by the lack of respect, and stared after him for a moment, wondering if this was the way it was going to be today. His hands clenched into fists at his side for a moment, and then they relaxed as he headed toward the new gazebo to check it out.

***

On their way back up the ramp, Jadin noticed the ex-Mayor standing at the railing near the gazebo and looked up at Jerry. "Have you spoken to Curtis since the election?"

"We exchanged nods at the grocery store once."

"It's time to go check out where you will give your speech."

***

Curtis had paid no attention to the man and a red-haired woman walking around the dock, thinking they were boaters or tourists. As promised, he had allowed Jerry to plan and organize the design of the new marina, and he had to admire Jerry's choices. He turned when he heard a familiar voice behind him, and his attention was immediately drawn to the powder blue shirt.

Jadin saw Curtis' reaction and grinned. "Hi, Tom. I bet you didn't expect to see the new Mayor all dressed up for the occasion."

Curtis grinned. "I know it wasn't his decision, Jadin."

"You're correct. I picked it out for him. I think the color makes a statement, don't you?"

Curtis stared at Jadin. Even when she was young, she always spoke what was on her mind, but what irked him was she was usually right about what she said. "What have you been doing, Jadin?"

"Oh, the usual. Trying to save humanity from destruction, things like that."

Curtis ignored her and frowned when he noticed someone else he wasn't expecting to see at the ceremony. "You'll have to excuse me."

Jerry watched Curtis hurry over to Ernesto Rodriguez, standing in front of one of the shops. They appeared to be arguing until Curtis waved his arms in the air and stomped away, and he wondered what it was about.

Jadin took Jerry's hand to move him out of the way when four musicians carried their equipment up into the gazebo. "Let's see how they plan to set up their microphones. I want to make sure you're facing the boardwalk in front of the shops and the park."

"You just can't help trying to take care of everything for me, can you?"

"It's the least I can do for you, Jerry. You were a big help while Brad was going to the Police Academy. I think Aaron had more fun being with you than any of us." She looked at the setup in the gazebo. "That won't work. Come on. I want to see how you look on stage."

Jerry reluctantly followed Jadin up the steps into the gazebo, and looked down at the marina on the other side, fifteen-feet below the park.

He felt Jadin pull on his arm and turned to smile at her. "It sure is a beautiful sight."

"It sure is. Now move over here, at an angle to the street."

Jerry did as instructed, while Jadin leapt down the steps to look at him. When she gave him a thumbs up, he walked down to join her. "Are we done?"

Jadin looked at her watch. "I suppose. The notice on the bulletin board said the ceremony will start with a speech from the new Mayor at 1:00 PM today, about twenty minutes from now." She grinned. "Since I hijacked you from your breakfast to see the marina, how about I buy you some lunch?"

"To be honest, I'm not that hungry. How about a milkshake instead?"

"Good afternoon, Mister Mayor."

Jerry recognized the voice and smiled as he turned around. "Hello, Mary."

"I like that shirt on you. It brings out the color of your eyes."

Jerry glanced over at Jadin, who was grinning. "Why, thank you, Mary. You look lovely today. I wasn't sure if you and Tommy were going to show up."

"Are you kidding? I wouldn't miss it for the world." Mary waved her hand out toward the marina. "You did a wonderful job, Jerry. You should be proud of your accomplishment. I know I am."

Jerry looked Mary in the eyes and felt his face flush. "It was a labor of love."

"Good afternoon, Mister Mayor."

Jerry turned and smiled at the Andersons. "Good afternoon to you, too."

He turned back to Mary and Jadin. "I need someplace to hide until it's time to get up and embarrass myself."

Jadin took his arm and looked at Mary. "We were just going down to get milkshakes, if you'd care to join us."

Mary looked around until she saw Curtis arguing with two young men, then smiled and took Jerry's other arm in hers. "Yes, thank you. I would love a milkshake."

***

Curtis hurried along the boardwalk to the parking lot and abruptly stopped and put his hands on his hips when he saw it was quickly filling up. The people who walked past him no longer called him Mister Mayor, only Tom or Mister Curtis, and it irked him. He had served this community on the Town Council for ten years before accepting the position as the Mayor for the past fifteen years. But they didn't even make the mistake of accidently calling him Mister Mayor, which bothered him almost as much as being beaten by a country bumpkin like Avery.

He turned back to the stores when he heard music coming from the park and noticed the lawn and boardwalk were becoming crowded with people waiting for the celebration to begin. When he noticed Mary was sitting next to Avery, he felt a slight sense of rage, knowing Mary was still in love with the guy. Tom's frown turned into a smirk of satisfaction, since he was the man who took her away from Avery. He hurried back down the boardwalk to be ready when Avery gave his speech. "This should be good."

***

Jadin smiled at people she didn't know who would stop by their table to say hello to her uncle. Several of his old high school friends would, seeing Mary Curtis sitting close to his side and smile at him conspiratorially. When she looked past the crowded boardwalk, her heartbeat increased with a sense of pride. The park was filled with people and several families had set up blankets and chairs, and the older folks occupied the benches, while tourists lined the railing along the boardwalk, and they were all here to listen to Jerry's official grand opening speech. She took Jerry's hand and smiled. "It's time, Uncle Jerry."

Jerry sighed in resignation. "I guess I might as well get it over with."

Jadin stood and guided Jerry and Mary back to the gazebo, but before they went up the steps, Jerry stopped, and she turned and saw the trepidation in her uncle's eyes. "Why don't you wait down here, and I'll get things started."

Jerry let his shoulders relax for a moment. "Thanks, Jadin."

Jadin squeezed his hand and walked up the steps. When the musicians looked at her, she gave them a nod and they played a short burst of announcement music.

She turned and stepped in front of the microphone, and a soft click erupted from the speaker system when she turned it on. She waited until most of the people were paying attention before she began her introduction. "Hello, everyone. I'm Jadin Avery. My uncle is a little shy around people, so I was very surprised when I heard he had become a town official. Let's give a round of applause to the man who made all this possible. My uncle, Mayor Jerry Avery." She smiled and held her hand out to Jerry.

When the applause erupted from the spectators, Jerry straightened his shoulders and tried to keep his nerves under control as he climbed the steps. When Jadin stepped away, he leaned into the microphone. "Hello." The squeal caused everyone to wince, and he moved farther away. "Hello? That's much better. I, uh. I just wanted to say welcome to the official grand opening of the new marina, and have a good time." When he heard the cheers, he felt his face flush, and turned away from the audience.

Curtis quickly made his way to the front of the crowd. "Tell me how you envision the future of our town, Mister Mayor?"

Jerry looked down at Curtis and smiled. "Why don't you come on up here and let me explain it to you in person?"

Curtis smirked up at Jerry, thinking this ought to be good, and jogged up the steps. "I look forward to hearing all about the destiny you have planned for all of us living in this little community."

Jerry waved him over and waited until Curtis was beside him at the podium, then adjusted the microphone and looked out over the crowd. "I don't know who wrote my name down on the ballot, Tommy. I hadn't planned on taking over your job. The only thing I wanted to do was rebuild our marina, and now I've accomplished the task. My first and last official act is to concede to the runner-up and resign from my position as the Mayor of Humpback Harbor."

Jerry walked away from Curtis, and the only sound heard in response was the slight tap of jerry's shoes on steps on his way down from the gazebo.

Curtis' mouth hung open as he stared after Jerry. He looked at the crowd, and they were all staring in numb shock at Avery.

Jadin waited until her uncle was beside her. "Did you plan this from the beginning?"

"Yep. I was just waiting for the right opportunity."

Jadin smiled, but when she looked down at the harbor, her smile slipped away. "Listen, the tide has been dropping fast, and your docks and the boats will sit in the mud in a few minutes."

When Jerry turned around, he saw Aaron standing on the closest dock with his palms up. He stared in shock as the boats tethered to the mooring buoys slowly listed to the side in the gray mud. "I had the harbor dredged before we set the pilings, and I was assured it would be deep enough for any boat, even at the lowest possible tide."

"This is worse than I had imagined, Jerry. I hate to leave so soon, but I've got to get back to JPL and find out why this is happening."

"I think you already know, Jadin." When she chewed on her lower lip, he understood her predicament. "Don't worry, I won't ask you for the details. Just tell me, is the tide going to be just as drastic when it comes back in?"

"I'm sure it will be higher than normal, so you should let everyone know to be prepared for flooding in the lower areas."

"Damn! The campground might not get flooded, but I'm sure some people are walking out on the beach out of curiosity. If the tide comes in as quickly as it went out, they could drown before they make it back to shore. I'd better let Rick and Curtis know what's going on."

Jadin didn't know if Curtis had a change in personality since losing the election, but if he stayed true to form, he wouldn't take her uncle's word on what was about to happen. "I'm going with you."

Jerry walked through the crowd of people who were trying to get a better view of the waterless harbor and found the Sheriff and Curtis looking down from the gazebo. "I need your help, Sheriff. We need to hurry down to the campground and warn the people not to go out from shore to collect souvenirs." He explained what Jadin had told him. "I'm going with you, Rick."

Jadin moved closer to Jerry. "I'll help too, Sheriff."

Jerry looked down at her. "We can handle it, sweetie. I saw you look at your phone, and I would imagine that's your ride back. You need to do your job, so get going."

Jadin hugged him tightly. "I love you, Uncle Jerry. Be careful, all right?"

"I will, and I'll call you later."

When Jerry and the Sheriff headed to Main Street to get the patrol vehicle, Jadin jogged back to the parking lot to get her rental car. When she stopped, she called her lab in Pasadena. "I'm on my way, and I'll be on the plane in twenty minutes. Thanks, Patrick, and I'll see you soon."

When Jadin turned to get in, she noticed a dozen people headed in her direction. She quickly climbed in behind the steering wheel before the parking lot became jammed by scared drivers and headed up the hill to the Coast Highway. A few minutes later, she was cruising to the airport in North Bend at ten miles over the speed limit.

***

Jerry and Rick climbed into the patrol car and headed south. When they drove across the bridge, Jerry looked down at the river, and the question was how high it would get when the incoming tide blocked the outflow into the ocean.

Rick turned off the highway and entered the campground, and it appeared the campers had left their belongings unattended. "This doesn't look good, Jerry."

"Everyone went down to the beach, so we'd better get down there and warn them before they get trapped."

"Won't they just walk to shore as it comes in?"

"Don't argue, just hurry. It's coming in fast this time."

Rick turned around and left the camping area, driving further down the road to the gravel-covered shoreline. They stopped and climbed out, and stared out across the flooded sandbar where the river emptied into the ocean. Off to one side of the outflow, a narrow gap separated the steep bluff from the rushing river.

Jerry stared at the people running from the tidal surge, many of them already sloshing through the thigh high incoming water. "Damn fools!" He hurried down to the beach to help two young children running alone. "Where are your parents?"

"They got trapped on a big rock," the small boy answered.

Jerry stared past them at the rising tide, now filling the gap between the bluff and the river. If the parents were high enough, they would be safe. If not, he knew the nearest access to dry land was a thousand yards in either direction, and their chances of surviving the rapidly rising water were slim.

Suddenly, Jerry saw two heads bobbing above the water, and watched them swim until they could stand up, then slosh through the chest high water as they struggled to get to shore and their children. He pointed past the children, who spun around when they heard their parents' voices. The children waved frantically for them to hurry, and then Jerry grabbed the children's hands and turned them around. "Let's go. We'll meet them on the road."

At first, they did not want to leave, and he was nearly dragging them up the beach. When they were standing safely on the asphalt, they all turned to watch the parents, still sloshing through the waist high water. The tidal bore was moving faster than they could run, and the man and woman looked exhausted, stumbling and occasionally falling forward into the water. A few of the other campers who had already reached the road suddenly ran out to assist the couple back to shore.

Jerry stared at the steadily rising ocean, now moving up to the base of the road. Just by looking at the floating pieces of dry driftwood and seaweed, he realized it was rising much higher than ever before. He spun around when he heard people yelling, and several campers were pointing to their belongings, now floating out to sea on the water from the swollen river. He felt helpless, and when he turned back toward the beach, the tidewater was less than a foot below the asphalt, and if the tide continued to rise, it too would be under water.

He wasn't sure if he was just imagining it, but the water level appeared to be decreasing, and when the wet gravel was exposed, he knew the tide was slowly receding. When he turned around, Rick was smiling at him.

"Get in, Jerry, and we'll drive around the campground to assess the damage."

"Thanks," he said and climbed into Rick's patrol car.

Much to his surprise, Jerry saw only the waterfront campsites had been washed away, and the rest of the campground remained high and dry. "So far, so good, but I have a bad feeling things are going to get worse."

***

Rick took them back to town, and when they stopped, Jerry hurried to the park to talk to Curtis, and found him sitting in front of a tavern with a cold beer in his hand. "Do you really think this is a good time to have a drink, Tommy?"

"It's only one beer, Avery. Did anyone get hurt?"

Jerry shook his head no. "They were lucky this time. I'm going to close the camping areas and send them away for the time being."

Curtis stared up at Jerry and Rick. "I don't think so. As long as they stay off the beach at low tide, they should be okay."

Jerry knew he was wrong, and even though the campground didn't belong to him anymore, he still felt responsible for the occupants. "Listen, Tommy, I'm sure the tides are going to get worse, and the river will eventually flood the entire campground. You need to send the campers away before that happens."

Rick wasn't sure what was going on. "Isn't that your call, Jerry?"

Curtis stood. "Not anymore. The campground belongs to me now, so whatever I say goes. And I say it stays open." He dropped his beer can into the trash and walked away.

Jerry sat down at the table, frustrated. "I know what you're thinking, Rick."

Rick sat down across from him. "The only thing I'm thinking is that you must have had a damn good reason to sell it." When he noticed Jerry look down at the harbor, Rick understood. "You used the money to rebuild the marina. Does anyone else know what you did?"

"Just Jadin, and that's the way I like it. I'd appreciate it if you would keep it to yourself."

Rick was curious why, but didn't ask. "All right." He stood. "I'll go back to the campground and see if I can convince the people to leave on their own."

Jerry smiled. "Thanks, Rick. That's one less thing for me to worry about."

"What else are you worried about?"

"The reason this is happening. Jadin had to cut her vacation short because she was called back to work. She was the one who mentioned the tides might act weird, but nothing this drastic. Whatever is affecting the tides must be a major problem."

When Rick walked away, Jerry stood and walked back along the boardwalk toward his shop. He looked out across the harbor and saw a long line of boats crowding the exit from the harbor, and in a few more hours, the buoys and mooring spaces would be abandoned. "So much for the grand opening."

Chapter 16

FALLON, NEVADA:

South of the Naval Air Station, Okawna turned the rental sedan off the asphalt onto a well-maintained gravel road across the desert. Alex stared out the passenger window, thinking about how empty his life would be without Fala and Halona, and hoped when he asked the important question she would change her mind about leaving him. He felt the acceleration and looked over at Okawna. "You're in a hurry."

"Why not? This is a private road with no speed limit, and according to the GPS, it's still forty miles to Essex's place."

Alex didn't bother to look at the speedometer. He knew Okawna wasn't suicidal, just enthusiastic, and twenty minutes later, they saw a two-story building blocking the view of several hangars and buildings behind it and slowed down. ESSEX SPACE RESEARCH AND DEVELOPMENT CORPORATION was stated in large, stainless steel letters on the side of the building, with ten foot tall barbed wire fences stretching out across the desert on either side.

Okawna stopped their vehicle at the guard station next to a large gate. When a man strolled out, he rolled down his window for the private security guard, and thought it odd he was dressed in SWAT gear.

Sam Kirby lowered his head to look inside the sedan at the blond-haired driver. "Can I help you?"

"We're here to see Mister Essex."

"Do you have an appointment?"

"No, but tell him his good friends, Alex Cave and Okawna, are here to see him."

Sam straightened from the window. "Can I get your last name, Mister Okawna?"

Okawna gave Alex a smirk before looking up at the guard. "That is my last name."

Sam stared back evenly. "Are you trying to be a smartass?"

When Okawna shrugged his shoulders and smiled, Sam was about to tell them to get the hell out of there when the phone in the guard shack rang, so he stepped inside to answer it.

Alex looked over at Okawna. "His good friends?"

"Just trying to be civilized before I torture Mister Essex."

Sam returned to the vehicle. "Go straight past the hangars and turn right at the main building. He's waiting in his office on the first floor."

When the gate opened, Okawna stepped on the accelerator. "That was easy."

Alex noticed a basketball court against the end of a small barracks building, with several white SUV security vehicles in proximity. "Let's look around before we visit our friend."

When they turned the corner at one hangar, the massive doors were partially open, and what they saw inside would make anyone stop. In the huge room were four fifteen-foot long sections of what appeared to be living accommodations during space travel.

Okawna shut off the engine and Alex was about to climb out for a closer look, but an armed guard in the same SWAT gear walked around the hangar door and stepped up to his side of their car. He could tell the man was serious about his job, as he rolled down his window instead and noticed the man's nametag. "Those habitats got my attention, Mister Coburn. Mind if we look around?"

Jim Coburn gave him a cold stare. "State your business."

"We're actually here to see a friend of ours. Maybe you know him. John Essex." Alex waited for a change in the guard's expression, but the big man stared back evenly. "I believe he owns this place."

"Is that a fact? Well, you won't find him in here, so just keep moving."

"No problem. We'll be on our way."

Okawna started the engine and continued toward the main building. When he looked in the rearview mirror, Coburn was staring after them while speaking into a radio and smirked. "He sure was friendly. I think he's calling his friends."

"He had an Army Ranger tattoo on his arm."

"Do you think he's a mercenary?"

"Essex is more involved than he's leading us to believe. Let's push him a little and see what happens. Drive around and check things out before we're asked to stop."

Okawna turned off the main road toward several more hangars spaced along one side of the runway. Alex noticed the last hangar had a six foot wide elevated platform with railroad tracks paralleling the runway for more than a mile across the open desert. When they turned around, he saw three glass spires grouped together on top of the main building.

Okawna slammed on the brakes when a security vehicle suddenly pulled out in front of him, then he looked over at Alex. "Uh-oh, this should be interesting."

The familiar guard climbed out of the vehicle, and Okawna rolled down his window when he approached. "I got a little lost, Officer Coburn. I'm trying to find Mister Essex's office."

Coburn stared back coldly. "You're a funny man. Ha. Ha. Pull this shit again and I'll arrest you two for trespassing."

Okawna just smiled. "Not a problem. Now be a good boy and show us the way."

Coburn gritted his teeth, stifling the urge to rip the man's head off. "Follow me. And no more funny business."

Okawna smiled at Alex while he waited for the guard to get into his car. "I think he's starting to like me."

"You've always had a way with people."

Okawna followed his new friend to the main research and development building, and then waved to him when they climbed out. Alex noticed another entrance farther along the walkway and saw Coburn was still sitting in his patrol car, waiting for them to enter the building, as they went inside and stepped up to the young woman behind the counter. "I'm Alex Cave, and this is Okawna. Mister Essex is expecting us."

"Yes. Go to the end of the hall."

"Thank you."

Alex turned and headed down the hallway, with Okawna at his side. On the walls were artist's renditions of space and examples of living accommodations similar to the ones in the hangar. One showed a mining operation on the moon with the Earth in the background.

Essex looked up when his office door opened, but was surprised as Okawna quickly moved around the desk. His eyes went wide with fear as Okawna pushed him in his chair against the back wall.

Alex closed the door, then sat on the edge of the desk and stared at Essex. "This is a nice setup. You even have living accommodations. Very nice. I want Sloan to turn off the device and give it to me."

Essex glanced from Alex to Okawna, then back again. "First, I want to tell you it wasn't my idea to take the device. I didn't even see her do it. She must have grabbed it when I was unconscious after we fell down the tunnel. It wasn't until we landed back in the States that I realized she had it, and then the stupid bitch decided to turn it on. I warned her not to do it, but she did it anyway and birds started falling from the sky. I begged her to turn it off, but when she couldn't figure it out, I asked her to call you for help, but she refused, so the thing is still on out in the desert. I'm telling you, this was all Sloan's fault."

Alex sighed in frustration. "How long has it been running?"

"Since yesterday. I've been so worried that the device might cause a plane to crash. I know you have connections, and I was hoping you could figure out how to turn it off."

"Why didn't you call me?"

"Sloan threatened to cut off my balls if I told you. You know how she is, Alex. She's crazy."

"How powerful is the device?"

"I have no idea, but it seems to only affect things directly above it. All we saw were the birds smashing into the ground around us, but only if they flew above the device."

Alex stared coldly at Essex. "Fine. Take us out to the test site so we can see what we're up against."

Essex shook his head no. "I'm not going near that thing. It's easy to find, and I'll tell you how to get there."

Okawna placed his shoe on the chair between Essex's legs. "I thought you said it didn't affect you, as long as you weren't directly above it."

Essex stared up at Okawna. "True, but I'm still not going with you. That thing scares the hell out of me. I can give you directions, but that's the best I can do."

Okawna lowered his foot and stepped back so Essex could roll his chair back to his desk. He didn't blame the little man for his fear of the device. Hell, he was scared of the damn thing, too.

When Essex finished drawing a crude map, Alex took it and stared at him. "If it's not there, I'm coming back here and tearing this place apart. And when I'm done with this place, I'm going to have Okawna tear you apart until I find it."

"I'm telling you the truth, Alex. I want it shut down just as much as you do."

When they left the building, Okawna noticed Coburn was still sitting in his patrol car, so he looked at Alex and grinned. "Do you think I should go over and say hello?"

"No, he's going to follow us to the exit, anyway. Just wave when we leave him at the gate."

***

When his visitors left the office, Essex opened his desk drawer and grabbed the bottle of Black Velvet whiskey he stashed inside for emergencies. He brought out a glass and poured a hefty amount, then stared through the window at Alex and Okawna getting into their car. After a large swallow, he leaned back and stared at the ceiling. "This won't end well."

***

Following Essex's instructions, Okawna drove the rental car out across the desert, along a single lane dirt road for two hours. His training as an operative kicked in, and if they were on a CIA mission, he saw the perfect place for an ambush up ahead. For nearly two miles on his side of the road, there was a steep incline with a matching downgrade on the other. Thirty minutes later, they reached the test area and cautiously climbed out and slowly approached the square mirrored box they assumed was the gravity device, while avoiding the bird carcasses scattered randomly in a wide circle around the large block of concrete.

Okawna noticed the charred remains of a metal object a short distance from the device. "I'll bet that's what's left of the missing satellite."

"It looks like another one over there. It's hard to believe that little box could harness so much power."

Alex picked up a stone, and when he hurled it above the device, it was ripped from the air and slammed into the ground on the other side. "When we get a good phone signal, I'll call Donner and confirm the device is causing the satellites to drop out of orbit. And it looks like this is what's causing the moon to move closer. I'll need to talk to David and Henry about this type of control system. When it comes to this type of technology, they're the most knowledgeable people on the planet." He gave Okawna a conspiratorial grin. "Would you be interested in a trip down to Area 51?"

"Oh, hell yeah. When do we leave?"

Alex grinned at Okawna's enthusiasm. "I'll set it up on the way."

***

It seemed a long drive, and since Alex could not call Donner until they were within cell range, he leaned back in his seat and stared out the window at the sagebrush stretching out across the desert, while his mind drifted to thoughts of Fala and their last discussion. He really did not want to let her down again, and for once, he wanted to keep his promise to her. The last thing he wanted was for her to leave.

"You sure are deep in thought over there."

Alex looked over at his friend. "Yeah."

"So, are you going to share what is on your mind? You look troubled."

"It's Fala."

"All this constant leaving isn't sitting well with her, is it?"

"No."

"Man, I told you. You had better keep her happy or she'll make your life miserable. She's already put your ass on the couch, hasn't she?" Okawna grinned when Alex didn't say a word. "I knew it! She did, didn't she?"

"It's gotten a little more serious than sofa city."

Sensing the seriousness of the situation, Okawna stopped laughing. "Uh-oh, what's going on?"

"She's threatening to leave."

"No, shit?"

"Yeah."

"So? What do you plan on doing?"

"I've decided to ask her to marry me."

"No shit?"

"Too extreme?"

Okawna grinned. "No. I was thinking more like it was about time."

"As soon as we're done with this job and can get that device in a secured location, I'm going to pop the question the moment I get home."

"Good for you. I'm happy for you, Alex."

As they neared NAS Fallon, Alex looked out across the desert. Now more than ever, he felt more confident in his decision to ask Fala to marry him. He just hoped he could stay out of trouble long enough for her to say yes.

Alex finally got phone reception and called Director Donner. "We found the device, but we can't turn it off. It's pulling birds out of the sky, Martin, and we found the burnt up remains of two satellites. I think it would be wise for you to tell the FAA to detour all flights around that area. Also, Okawna and I need a ride to Groom Lake. Someone there might know how this device operates."

"David and Henry are still on the island with the spacecraft, and it sounds like they're getting close to figuring out how to fly it. I'll arrange for a company plane to pick you up at the Fallon Naval Air Station and fly you up to our Adak station. From there, a helicopter will take you to the island. Good luck, Alex."

"Thanks. I'll keep you updated." He looked over at Okawna. "I'm sorry, but we aren't going to Area 51."

"I knew it was too good to be true. Did he say why I couldn't go there?"

"Yes, we're going to Alaska to meet everyone at the spaceship. Who knows? If they can get it working, we might even get a ride back to Nevada."

Okawna grinned. "Now that's what I'm talking about."

Chapter 17

HUMPBACK HARBOR CAMPGROUND:

Jerry and Rick climbed into the patrol car and headed south. When they drove across the bridge, Jerry looked down at the river running alongside the campground, which appeared normal. The problem was he did not know how high it would get when the incoming tide blocked the outflow into the ocean.

Rick turned left off the highway and entered the campground, but it appeared the campers had left their belongings unattended. "This doesn't look good, Jerry."

"That's what I was worried about. Everyone went down to the beach, so we'd better get down there and warn them before they get trapped."

"Won't they just walk to shore as it comes in?"

"Don't argue, just hurry. It's coming in fast this time."

Rick turned his patrol car around and left the camping area, then drove a short distance further south to the gravel-covered shoreline on the right. They stopped and climbed out, and stared across the sandbar, where the river emptied into the ocean. Off to one side of the outflow, a narrow strip of land separated the steep bluff from the rushing river.

Jerry stared at dozens of people running from the tidal surge, many of them already sloshing through the thigh high incoming water. "Damn fools!"

Most of them made it up to the beach, but Jerry hurried down to help two young children running alone, and then spoke to the oldest one. "Where are your parents?"

"They got trapped on a big rock."

Jerry stared past them at the rising tide, now filling the gap between the bluff and the river. He knew the nearest access to dry land was a thousand yards in either direction, and their chances of surviving the rapidly rising water were slim.

Jerry felt a sudden sense of relief when he saw two heads bobbing above the water. He held his breath while they swam until they could stand up, then they sloshed through chest high water as they struggled to get to shore and their children.

Rick pointed past the children. "Hey, kids, look! Here come your parents!"

The children spun around when they heard their parents' voices, waving frantically for them to hurry, and then Jerry grabbed their hands to turn them around. "Let's go. We'll meet them on the road."

At first, they did not want to leave, and he was nearly dragging them up the beach. When they were standing safely on the asphalt, they all turned to watch the parents, still sloshing through the waist high water.

The tidal bore was moving faster than they could run, but the parents looked exhausted, stumbling and occasionally falling forward into the water. Suddenly, a few of the other campers, who had already reached the road, ran back out in to the water to assist the couple back to shore.

Jerry stared at the steadily rising ocean, now moving up to the base of the road. Just by looking at the floating pieces of dry driftwood and seaweed, he realized it was rising much higher than ever before. He spun around when he heard people yelling, and several campers were pointing to their belongings, now floating out to sea on the water from the swollen river.

Jerry felt helpless. When he turned back toward the beach, the tidewater was less than a foot below the asphalt, and if the tide continued to rise, it too would be under water. He wasn't sure if he was just imagining it, but the sea level appeared to be decreasing. As the wet gravel was exposed, he knew the tide was slowly receding. When he turned around, Rick was smiling at him.

"Get in, Jerry, and we'll drive around the campground to assess the damage."

"Thanks."

Jerry got into the patrol car, and then the campers moved out of the way to let them pass. Rick turned into the campground, and only the riverfront sites had been washed away. As far as they could tell, the rest of the campground remained high and dry.

Jerry stared out the window while Rick continued through the rest of the campsites. "So far, so good, but I have a bad feeling things are going to get worse."

***

HUMPBACK HARBOR:

Jerry climbed out of the patrol car to go find Curtis, then Rick drove away to find a parking spot. Jerry searched the park but couldn't find him, so he followed the boardwalk to the shops, and found Curtis sitting in front of a tavern with a cold beer in his hand. "Do you really think this is a good time to have a drink, Tommy?"

"It's only one beer, Avery. Did anyone get hurt?"

"No, but they were lucky this time. I'm closing the camping areas and sending them away for the time being. That's the only way to make sure they stay off the beach."

Curtis stared up at Jerry. "I don't think so. As long as they stay off the beach at low tide, they should be okay."

Jerry knew he was wrong in assuming they'd stay away, and even though the campground didn't belong to him anymore, he still felt responsible for the occupants. "Listen, Tommy, I'm sure the tides are going to get worse, and the river will eventually flood the entire campground. You need to send the campers away before that happens."

Rick strolled up and heard the conversation, but wasn't sure what was going on. "Isn't that your call, Jerry?"

Curtis stood up. "Not anymore. The campground belongs to me now, so whatever I say goes. And I say it stays open."

When Curtis dropped his beer can into the trash and walked away, Jerry sat down at the table, frustrated. "I know what you're thinking, Rick."

Rick sat down across from him. "The only thing I'm thinking is that you must have had a damn good reason to sell it."

Rick noticed Jerry look down at the harbor and understood. "You used the money to rebuild the marina. Does anyone else know what you did?"

"Just Jadin, and that's the way I like it. I'd appreciate it if you would keep it to yourself."

Rick was curious why, but didn't ask. "All right. I'll go back to the campground and see if I can convince the people to leave on their own."

Jerry smiled. "Thanks. That's one less thing for me to worry about."

"What else are you worried about?"

"The reason this is happening. Jadin had to cut her vacation short because she was called back to work. She was the one who mentioned the tides might act weird, but nothing this drastic. Whatever is affecting the tides must be a major problem."

When Rick walked away, Jerry stood and walked back along the boardwalk toward his shop. He looked out across the harbor and saw a long line of boats crowding the exit from the harbor, and in a few more hours, the buoys and mooring spaces would be abandoned.

"So much for the grand opening."

Chapter 18

NASA'S JET PROPULSION LABORATORY, PASADENA, CALIFORNIA:

When Jadin entered the terrestrial tracking building, she immediately went over to the large wall monitor and studied the animated version of the moon's rotation around the earth. "Has it started to re-stabilize?"

Patrick stood from his desk. "No, not yet. We're talking a mass the size of Argentina, so it will take some time. Mark and Terry have been monitoring the moon's movement all night, and I relieved them this morning. I'm glad you're back."

A steady beeping sound suddenly interrupted their conversation, and then the image on the monitor changed, showing the moon was gaining speed. The steady increase lasted for eleven minutes before its acceleration leveled out, but the distance from Earth also decreased by another sixteen-thousand miles during the same period.

Jadin sat down and entered a command into the computer, and a transparent red oval shape appeared over western North America, stretching from San Francisco to Bonneville, Utah. "That's the estimated area on the planet where the moon was passing over during that eleven minute period. It appears something in that vicinity is affecting the moon's gravity."

"What you're saying is not possible."

"Okay. Then explain to me how it coincides perfectly when it's over that area of the planet, just like the first time you noticed the change in altitude. We just watched it happen, Patrick."

"Well, we had better figure out what is causing this or we're in a world of trouble, no pun intended. The tidal effect will get much worse, and we've also learned the Great Lakes are being affected, too. We expected it would happen, and now we have conformation."

"This is just too crazy for a logical explanation. We'll have to think outside the box again, but that's why they hired us. Let's you and I toss out some ideas and see where it leads us."

"Mark and Terry are coming back after they get some sleep. I agree, it would be nice to have a theory or two before they get here."

"Right. Let's start with the basic laws of physics and why this is impossible."

Chapter 19

A TINY ISLAND IN THE BERING SEA:

The two hundred foot crater of the ancient volcano was unlike the other islands dotting the Aleutian chain. Not only was it just thirty feet above the waterline at high tide, inside this one was an alien spaceship, partially buried in the basaltic rock. Alex knew its location without acknowledging he had been there before, claiming it was an above-top-secret mission. He also knew that was a major problem with time travel from the Red Energy operation. He could never tell anyone he did it three times before he corrected the fate of the human race on Earth.

Inside the spacecraft control room, David Conway rubbed his tired eyes. For the past three hours, he's been trying to decipher intelligence from the spacecraft's operating system, which consisted of a string of symbols, making it very difficult. He looked over at his friend and mentor, Doctor Henry Heinz, affectionately called Doc by his friends, who was sitting in front of another console. "Are you having any luck?"

Henry looked up and shook his head no, his gray bangs swishing across his forehead. "No, I am not."

David stood to stretch for a moment and then had an idea. "I'm sure Director Donner knows somebody who could help us. I'll step out and call him. I'll be right back."

David stepped outside the ship and paused to admire the section of mirrored surface protruding from the solid rock, which he knew from Alex, was shaped like a forty-foot diameter by twenty-four foot high chromed hockey puck.

He turned and strolled across the gravel to the portable satellite transmitter and receiver station, which was set up at the entrance to a natural cave inside the crater. One of the other problems with trying to decipher the instruction manual was the lack of outside communication capability from inside the spaceship. Something about the craft even blocked signals through the wire and optical cables they tried stringing across the entrance into the ship.

He sat down in front of the monitor, and once he established a secure connection with the Director of National Security, Donner's face appeared on the monitor.

"Hello, David. Any luck with the translation?"

"No, Sir. We just don't have the right computing software. Without an Internet connection to the ship's systems, we just can't do it."

"What can I do to help?"

"We need someone who can create a special program to translate the ship's logs, or we'll never learn the purpose of the ship's control systems."

"I'll make sure you get the help you need. I'll call you back in thirty minutes."

"Thank you, Director."

***

WASHINGTON, D.C.:

Donner pressed a button on the intercom. "Tell Captain Larson to come in, please."

A moment later, a woman wearing an Air Force Officer's uniform stepped into his office. He smiled and indicated a chair and sat down after she did. "Hi, Sheri. What's going on with the moon? Any new developments?"

"A few moments ago, I was informed it moved closer, and the momentum is increasing as well. I'm afraid to say things are not going to get any better until we figure out why it is moving out of orbit and stop it. The closer it gets, the worse the tides will become."

"That means this recent move will make the tides worse than the first time."

"Yes, Sir. For us, the Pacific Northwest coastal areas will have higher and significantly faster incoming tides. I've just read a report about the erosion created by this first higher tide, and it's already causing some landslides. If this continues to get worse, the devastation to the west coasts around the planet will be horrific."

"What about our eastern shores?"

"Only minor tide changes for the moment on our side, but there is a significant change along the European coastlines. The Great Lakes are experiencing increased tidal effects as well."

"I see."

"I wish I had better news, Sir."

"I know this may sound like a strange request, but do you know anyone who can write a sophisticated computer program for interpreting unusual hieroglyphics? Someone with a top secret security clearance?"

Larson thought for a moment. "What do you mean by unusual?"

"All I can tell you is it's related to Area 51."

"Yes, Sir. I understand. I know of only one, and her name is Jadin Avery. She's working with us on the moon situation."

"Good. See if she's available for a conference call."

"What time?"

"Right now."

Larson reached for her cell phone and pressed contacts, and Jadin's image appeared almost immediately. "Hi, Jadin. I'm in Director Donner's office and we need your help. Do you have time to talk to him?"

"Did you say Director Donner? Uh, sure."

"I'm putting you through."

Donner waited while Larson connected him to the call, but when he saw Jadin's picture on his monitor, he thought she looked familiar. "Hello, Jadin. We could use your expertise on a project in Alaska. Do you think you could break away for a few days?"

"I'm kind of busy with the moon situation right now, but when do you need me?"

"I can have a plane pick you up in a few hours."

"Wow, that's not much notice. Exactly what is it you want me to do?"

"We need your help to decipher a coded language, and it could help with the moon situation. Will you help us?"

Jadin grinned and felt her heart rate increase. "Of course. Just tell me when and where."

"I'll have my people set it up and call you back. Thank you, Ms. Avery."

Larson looked across the desk. "She's fantastic, Sir."

"Thanks for the update, Sheri. Let me know if anything changes."

Larson stood to leave. "Yes, Sir."

***

THE ISLAND:

When the bell chimed, David looked up at the clock. As promised, exactly thirty minutes had passed when Donner appeared on the monitor. "Hello Sir."

"I found someone to help you, David. She has the right security clearance and abilities for what you want to accomplish. She'll be arriving this afternoon with Alex and Okawna. Good luck."

David stood and then ran across the beach and into the spaceship. "Help is on the way, Doc. Alex and Okawna are coming, and a language specialist is coming with them."

"That is great news. How long before they arrive?"

"Not until later today. We might as well get out of here for a while. I'm going up to the rim of the crater and look at the ocean. Would you like to come with me?"

Henry smiled and stood up from the seat in front of the control console. "Thank you for the offer, but I will go down to the living area and take a nap instead. Please wake me when they arrive."

"I will. You don't look so good, Doc. Are you feeling okay?"

"I will be fine after I get some sleep."

David accompanied Henry down to the living quarters inside the ship, and once the Doc was resting, he decided to stay with him to make sure he would be all right. He debated whether to call the Director and have him send a medical doctor out, but when he heard a soft snoring from the sleeping quarters, he decided against the idea. He sat down with his e-book reader while he waited for Alex to arrive. The view could wait, but his friend may not be able to.

Chapter 20

DONNER'S JET:

During the flight from Fallon, Alex kept wondering what would happen if they didn't turn off the gravity machine. He knew something powerful enough to affect the moon was more dangerous than nuclear weapons. If the moon kept coming towards Earth, the tidal effect would cause a shift in the tectonic plates, releasing the power of thousands of volcanic eruptions across the entire planet, and nothing would survive.

When the jet taxied to the terminal in Pasadena, California, Alex leaned back in the leather seat while he stared out the window. The message from Donner said to make a quick stop on the way to Alaska and pick up someone to help David and Henry with the translation. He noticed a woman with red hair run out from the terminal, dragging a small suitcase across the tarmac to his plane, and quickly stood and hurried forward to open the door, and when the young woman climbed the steps, he moved back to allow her into the passenger compartment. Once she was safely inside, he thought she looked familiar as he held out his hand. "Welcome aboard, I'm Alex Cave."

She accepted. "I'm Jadin Avery. It's very nice to meet you, Mister Cave. I can hardly wait to get started."

"You can call me Alex. Avery? Do you know a Christa Avery? Because you look just like her."

"Yes, she's my older sister."

Alex smiled. "We worked together for a while. She's a nice lady."

Okawna's soft snoring abruptly ceased when he heard a woman's voice. He brought his seat up, looked down the aisle, and then quickly ran his fingers through his hair before getting up to find out who she was. He stopped in front of Alex and Jadin as he extended his hand. "Hi. I'm Okawna."

"I'm Jadin Avery, Mister Okawna."

"We're pretty casual around here, so you can just call me Okawna."

"All right."

The pilot, Ruben Coltrane, looked back through the doorway at his passengers. "We're cleared to taxi, Alex."

Alex pressed the button to bring the stairs up, and then latched the door closed. "We're all set, Ruben. How long to Stillwater?"

"Approximately thirty minutes until wheels down."

"Thanks. Okay, Jadin. Let's find a more comfortable place to talk."

Okawna led them to the oval-shaped conference table just past the wing, indicating for Jadin to sit wherever she wanted. He noticed her athletic build and found her quite attractive, and sat across from her.

Alex sat where he could face Jadin and clasped his hands together on the table. "Director Donner was vague about who we were picking up. Tell us about yourself."

"I work for NASA, and my team and I track asteroids and comets for NEOs, near-earth-objects. One of my people was the first to see the change in the moon's orbit, which is how I got involved. I have a few other skills, one of which is interpreting ancient languages. It's the reason Mister Donner sent me to help with your problem."

"Did the Director tell you where we're going or why we need your help?"

"Nothing specific, except it's in Alaska, and he needed me to create a program that could decipher a complex language."

Alex smiled and looked at Okawna, who understood keeping it a surprise, then turned back to Jadin. "Can I get you something to drink? I think there's some packaged snacks if you're hungry."

"Just a soda would be fine. Something with lemon if you have one."

When Alex stood, Okawna leaned back and looked at Jadin. "So, where are you from originally?"

"A small harbor town along the Oregon coast."

"Alex is originally from northwest Washington, but lives in Montana. I work on a research vessel out of a small harbor town nearby, called Anacortes. I love the Pacific Northwest."

"Oh, me too. I love it. I've boated up through the San Juan Islands a few times."

She looked up when Alex set a soda on the table, then opened it and took a sip while he sat down. "Thank you. Would you mind telling me what all this has to do with the change in the moon's orbit?"

Alex grinned at her. "It's kind of difficult to explain because the explanation is really out there. Almost unbelievable."

She listened while Alex explained the discovery of the gravity machine and the problems it was creating. "Who would build such a thing?"

"Someone who lived here one hundred and eighty million years ago."

Jadin wasn't sure if she heard correctly. "Wait, did you just say a hundred and eighty million? How could you possibly know something like that?"

Okawna pointed a finger at Alex. "It was his discovery, so you'll have to ask him."

Jadin stared at Alex. "What discovery is he talking about?"

Alex hesitated, hoping to keep it a surprise, but gave in to the pleading expression in her eyes, and explained what happened during the Dead Energy Operation, and how he met her sister. "I've recently discovered another alien spaceship, and if you can interpret the language for us, we might get it working. If we do, we might discover a way to shut down the gravity device."

Jadin stared at Alex, unable to respond. "Wow, this is a lot to take in. How many people know about this?"

"Very few, and we would like to keep it that way."

"Of course. Will I be working with the two of you when we get there?"

"No, we have two people waiting for us who are far more knowledgeable about the ship than we are. You'll be working with them."

"I look forward to it. By the way, I heard the pilot say you're stopping in Stillwater."

When Alex indicated Okawna, she looked over at him. "You said you worked on a fishing vessel out of Anacortes."

"I do, and it's not a fishing vessel, but Stillwater is my hometown. I just need to pick up some clean clothes and say hi to my mom and dad. They're going to meet me at the airport with my stuff."

Jadin grinned. "You still live at home with your parents? Aren't you a little old for that?"

Okawna chuckled. "Actually, I live on a luxurious yacht and explore the oceans of the world in a submarine."

Jadin figured he was joking about living on a yacht. "I prefer solid ground. When you're stuck out at sea, the only thing to look at is water." She looked over at Alex. "You never told me what you do for a living."

"I'm a geophysics instructor at a small college in Montana."

"And you're both friends with the Director of National Security? How is that even possible?"

"We've known him for years. We have a long history with the Director, and occasionally, he asks for our help."

"I see. Well, it certainly was a surprise when he asked for my help. I was excited when he said it had something to do with finding out what's causing the moon to shift orbit, but now I'm absolutely thrilled about the prospect of working on a space vehicle."

Okawna saw an opportunity to gain favor with the pretty woman. "If you can solve our language problem, I'll take you on a ride in it as a show of gratitude."

"I'll find a way. You can count on it."

***

MONTANA:

Before Donner's private plane touched down at the Bozeman Municipal Airport, Alex had called ahead to the college to see if his student aide, Franklin, was available to run by his house and pick up a few things for him. Since he was just making a quick pit stop in Bozeman, he did not want Fala finding out he passed through. It just wasn't the right time to talk to her.

When he stepped off the plane to meet up with Franklin, he was surprised to see Fala waiting in the air terminal with his suitcase. She had her arms folded across her chest, and a look of annoyance and frustration on her face. "What are you doing here?"

"Why? Were you expecting someone else? Say, maybe, Franklin?"

Alex knew he had been busted, and this was not going to go well. "Fala, wait."

She uncrossed her arms while getting right up in Alex's face. "No, you wait! That was a pretty inconsiderate thing you tried to pull. Imagine my surprise when I'm working in the yard, and Franklin pulls up and tells me you are heading back to Bozeman. The fool was dumb enough to tell me you sent him to the house to pick up some things for you because you didn't want to drive all the way home."

"You weren't supposed to be there when he showed up. I thought you were going to be at work and I didn't want to bother you."

"I took the day off because I wasn't feeling well. Ever since our last conversation, I've had a migraine headache."

"That's why I called Franklin."

"You're so full of shit! You didn't want me to find out because you knew I'd leave if you showed up and left to go out of town again. So here we are. It looks like you have a decision to make. What's it going to be? Me or the job?"

"Fala, please. We are so close to finishing this, and I just need a little more time. Please don't make me choose."

Fala stepped back. "It seems like you've already made your decision."

Alex stepped toward Fala. "Yes, I choose you."

"Then tell the plane to leave and you come home with me."

"I can't. Not this time. The fate of the world hangs on me getting on that plane. Fala, please, give me a chance. I'll make it up to you in a big way, I promise."

"Your promises mean nothing to me anymore, Alex. They're just empty words with no merit."

Alex reached for her, but she pulled away. "Goodbye, Alex."

"Fala, I'm begging you, please." Fala kept on walking, not looking back, and he ran part of the way to her and stopped. "Fala! Marry me!"

Fala stopped in her tracks and turned to stare at Alex. "What did you just say?"

Alex ran up and took her hand. "Fala, make me the happiest man in the world and marry me. And when I finish this job, I will spend the rest of our lives together, making you the happiest woman in the world."

"No."

"What?"

"No, Alex, I will not marry you. If it was just me, I might become your wife, but I have to think about Halona. You're an adventure junkie and always will be, and I can't put Halona through you leaving all the time, not knowing whether you'll come back alive. I just can't do this anymore, Alex. I'm sorry. We'll be gone by the time you get back."

When she walked away, Alex went back and grabbed his bag, and then shuffled out through the doorway and across the tarmac to the plane. He climbed the steps and closed the hatch, then told the pilot to take off when he was ready. He shoved his bag into the luggage compartment, then headed down the aisle.

Okawna noticed Alex's demeanor. "Something wrong?"

"She said no."

"What? Who?"

"Fala. She said no."

"I thought Franklin was meeting you."

"Fala was in the terminal waiting for me. She didn't go to work today, so she was home when Franklin showed up, and he told her everything."

"Oh, man. I'm so sorry, Alex."

"And she's leaving, too."

"You mean the airport?"

"No, for good."

"That sucks." He could tell Alex needed to be alone, and went back to his seat.

When the plane leveled out at twenty-five thousand feet, Alex stared blankly out at the clouds whizzing past in the distance, not only feeling the heartbreak, but the weight of the world on his shoulders. He and looked over at Jadin with her headphones plugged in, and Okawna snoring softly, continuing his nap, then wiped the single tear from his cheek.

Chapter 21

THE ISLAND:

When the side door of the helicopter opened, David smiled at the attractive young woman with red hair. "You must be the language specialist. I'm David Conway."

Jadin's jaw dropped when she looked through the doorway and saw the mirrored surface of the spaceship. "This is incredible! It's so big. How many people can it take into space? What type of power does it use? Can it travel faster than light?"

"I wish we knew. We don't know much about it right now. That's why we need your help. There's just so much code and I can't decipher it."

Jadin finally looked down at David, expecting an elderly man. "I can't believe this is real."

She climbed out and moved past him toward the spacecraft to get a better look at the huge hockey puck with a mirrored surface. It appeared to be listing at a slight angle, and most of it was buried in volcanic rock, so she wondered how it could have survived.

David noticed his friend jump out of the helicopter and held his hand out to Alex. "I'm glad you came to help us. This is your ship, after all."

Okawna quickly followed Alex out of the helicopter to shake David's hand. "It's good to see you again, David."

"Yeah, you too, Okawna."

Alex was about to debate the ownership of the spacecraft when he noticed Henry slowly moving in his direction from the ship while carrying a small suitcase. "Is the Doc leaving?"

"He's not feeling too good, so he's going to meet us later in Nevada."

Alex hurried over and took the suitcase from Henry's grasp. "Let me help you with this, Doc. Are you okay?"

Henry smiled up at his friend. "It is nothing too serious, Alex. I am just feeling run down, and I prefer the comforts of home."

"Yeah, I know what you mean."

"Is everything all right, Alex? Maybe you should go see a doctor rather than me."

"Oh, it's nothing, Doc. Way too long of a story. So, are we all set here?"

"Now that David has a firm grasp of this ship's basic functions, I feel confident that once you interpret the code, it will be all you need to operate this machine."

"Well, I'm sorry to see you go. You get to feeling better and I'll see you again in Nevada."

Alex waited while Henry boarded the helicopter and saw him wave out the window as it climbed into the air. He stared after the craft, hoping Henry would be okay, because even though he had only known him for a year, they had grown close during the Cold Energy mission.

After Henry's departure, everyone headed across the gravel toward the spaceship, and Okawna surreptitiously moved up next to Jadin. "I'd be glad to give you a private tour before you get started."

During the flight, she had tried to ignore his advances, but he was relentless. "I'm sure there will be plenty of time to look around once my translation program is working. The gravity device takes priority over anything else."

Okawna loved a challenge. "The offer stands open whenever you want to take that tour. Just for the record, I don't mind close tight areas if we should happen to find ourselves in one."

Jadin rolled her eyes as she moved closer to David. "So, you need help translating a strange language. From which country?"

David turned and saw the excitement in her eyes. "Well, the strange part is right. It's actually out of this world. That's why I need your help."

"You know, my sister was at Area 51 once, and she refused to tell me what happened while she was there, but Alex told me the story during the flight."

"Oh yeah? What's your sister's name?"

"Christa Avery."

"You know, I thought you looked familiar. I knew Christa, too. We worked together at a college in Montana and down in Nevada. We went through a lot of dangerous situations together, but she never told me she had a younger sister."

"It's not like her to talk about family, so it's no surprise she never mentioned me. She's so wrapped up with work and all I rarely see her. You'll have to tell me some stories about her sometime."

Jadin could not stop grinning as she followed David into the ship, but when she stepped into the control room, her eyes went wide. "I can see through the walls and the ceiling!"

"I know. Amazing, isn't it?"

"How does it work? Does it do the same thing in outer space?"

"Like I said, we don't know much until we can decipher the language."

"And to think I've been spending my life staring at computer monitors waiting for space rocks. I need to be working with you people. This is amazing. I've got to learn how all this incredible technology works."

"First things first. Let's get you hooked up to the ship."

David flipped open Jadin's laptop computer and booted the operating system. "I wish I could say I completely understood this technology, but I don't. You need to be inside the ship while the two computers are communicating. Something about its mirrored surface seems to block any type of transmitted signal. We tried stringing cables from here to the communications station, but the information was blocked outside the doorway." He gave the laptop back to Jadin. "Okay, try logging in and let's see if your computer is talking to mine."

"All right."

Jadin entered her password and brought up her translation software. When she pressed open, some computer language started scrolling up across the ship's holographic monitor in front of the control consol.

She looked up at David, still standing in front of the monitor. "Wow. It looks like they're talking. This may take a while."

When Okawna sat down beside her, Jadin looked over at him and saw him grinning flirtatiously at her. "I believe that's David's seat, Mister Okawna."

Okawna softly touched her arm. "I told you on the plane, it's just Okawna."

She turned in her chair to get his hand off her arm. "You don't need to stick around. I'm sure there's something else you'd rather be doing right now."

"Not really. I'd much rather be here with you."

Jadin suddenly jumped up. "We've got it! David! Come over here and see this!"

She sat back down, punching keys on the keyboard. "This is unbelievable. The ship seemed to know what I was trying to do and finished the program for me."

David hurried over and unknowingly got between Okawna and Jadin. When Okawna moved out of the way, David sat down next to Jadin to look at the data. The two computers had categorized thousands of files with subtitles and hyperlinks to all the information in the ship's operating systems.

"You did it, Jadin! Way to go."

Jadin smiled, wrapped her arms around David, and hugged him tightly. "You're going to let me stay and continue to help, right?"

David felt his face flush when her aroma wafted through his nose, causing him to become slightly aroused. "Uh, of course. I'd love to have you stay for a while longer. I think between the two of us, we can get this ship off the ground."

Alex moved around behind the group to see what information was available. "Perhaps we should start with any information about the gravity machine. Specifically, how to turn it off."

David turned and looked up at Alex. "You're right." When he turned back, Jadin was already bringing up the files. Some words appeared as the alien language, which was quickly replaced with the English-language version.

Jadin glanced up at Alex, then back at her monitor. "Here it is. It appears they were going to conduct an experiment with the gravity device after completing their mission on this planet."

David read more of the log entries. "I don't see any specific information for controlling the device. I might learn more by studying this ship's artificial gravity control system to use as a reference, but it's going to take some time. There is a lot of technical information to sift through."

Alex moved around to face David and placed his hand on his shoulder. "You're the perfect man for the job. I'll be outside watching the sunset, so let me know if anything changes."

As Alex left the ship, Okawna stared after him for a moment. He knew there wasn't much he could say to help his best friend, but hoped it might help to talk about it, and went out to join him.

David noticed and turned back to Jadin. "What's up with Alex? He doesn't seem like himself."

She looked at the exit to make sure Okawna and Alex didn't walk in on them. "Well, from what I overheard on the flight out here, his girlfriend dumped him."

"No. Fala left him?"

"Apparently, she was waiting at the airport for him when we landed."

"Man, poor Alex."

**

Alex stared out over the ocean, thinking about his encounter with Fala at the airport. Remembering her last words to him, he realized she was right. He was an adventure junkie, and the more dangerous the adventure, the better he liked it. On some level, he knew he could never live a normal life because he'd always be out there, looking for his next fix. He knew Fala and Halona really needed a wholesome family living environment, and at this juncture in his life, he could not provide that for them.

He could not bear to bring another tear to her eye, so he decided when he returned to Montana, he would not chase after her. In a way, he was relieved, not having to worry about her getting upset with him for leaving all the time. It seemed lately he was gone more than he was at home, anyway.

Okawna heard Alex release a long sigh as he sat down beside him. "Are you doing okay?"

"Yeah, I'll be fine. Over time."

"You want to hear something funny? I think I'm losing my touch."

"What do you mean?"

"With Jadin. I can't seem to make any headway with her. I'm being shot down at every turn, so I think I'm losing my touch."

Alex chuckled. Okawna always had a way to make him feel better.

"I'm serious, Alex."

Alex heard someone yell his name and turned to look down inside the crater at David. When David waved anxiously at him, he and Okawna hurried back down the rim, and then ran across the gravel to the ship. When Alex entered the control room, David and Jadin were smiling at him. "What have you learned?"

David stopped smiling. "First, let me just say I'm sorry, Alex."

"For what?"

"After looking through all this material, I realized I was the one who almost got you killed in Iceland. I activated the gravity device by accident the first time you saw the melted rock floating into the air. Let me show you." Once everyone gathered around him, David pointed at a touchpad. "The amber button engaged the anti-gravity system on this ship. That is how this craft can move through the atmosphere."

Alex leaned over the console to look at the dull amber color of the touchpad. "It's off now, right?"

"Yes. I wasn't sure what it controlled, and I had pressed it several times while we were still learning how to operate the control systems. We didn't notice the difference here, but evidently, I activated your device."

Alex looked up from the console. "So, the other gravity device should be off."

"Perhaps not. The woman you spoke of turned it on this time, so I don't think I am in control anymore."

"There's one way to find out. I'll ask Donner to launch a drone to toss something over the beam. Have you deciphered any of the logs about how they can control gravity?"

"The technical achievements of this previous race of humans are remarkable, Alex. They used anti-gravity when they were near the gravitational pull from a planet. Their original concept was to use the gravitational pull from massive space objects, like Jupiter, for space travel. They would use the attraction to propel the ship through space, but they discarded that idea when it was also changing the trajectories of heavy asteroids, sort of like a gravitational magnet."

"I'd better make my call. Thanks, David."

***

It was after sunset while Alex and his friends waited at the communication station inside the cave, now bathed in white light, to watch the video feed from the drone. The lights from the city of Reno flew across the screen as the aircraft headed deep into the desert, then the picture changed to night vision, and several minutes later, the drone slowed down and approached the test area.

The outline of the concrete slab appeared directly ahead, and within moments, they saw a small winged aircraft leave the drone and move toward the gravity beam. In an instant, the little test craft smacked into the ground next to the device, while the drone veered away from the test area.

Alex turned to face his friends. "Damn! Any ideas on how we could shut that thing down?"

David stood. "I'll go back to the ship and continue going through the technical logs."

As everyone walked out of the cave, Alex heard his satellite phone and recognized Donner's number. "Hello, Martin."

"I have a lot of nervous people to deal with, so the sooner we get this thing turned off, the better."

"I take it you watched the feed from the drone? We'll keep working on solving the problem."

"I know you will. Good luck."

David waited for Alex to join them inside the spaceship and then indicated the amber touchpad. "I believe I can turn the device off from here, but it will need to be directly over the gravity beam."

"Won't the ship be caught like everything else?"

"No. The anti-gravity device in this ship will neutralize the increased gravity, but first, we'll see if this ship can fly. Also, since the other ships had a cloaking system, let's hope this one does too, and it still works."

"I was just on the phone with Donner, and it's imperative we shut down the device as soon as possible. If the cloaking system doesn't work, we'll just have to fly down in the daylight and stay low to the ground. How long before you know if this ship can fly?"

David grinned. "Now that I know what each of the colored pads control, the systems appear to be functioning."

Okawna grinned. "That's what I'm talking about. Start the engine and let's see what happens."

David reached forward and tapped a series of pads, and one by one, the colored lights changed from red to blue. "The engine is on, and all indications are normal."

Okawna frowned when everything remained silent and looked around the interior. "Are you sure? I don't hear any engine noise."

"This piece of technology is completely different from our own, Okawna. I assure you, the engine is operating correctly."

Okawna grinned with excitement and sat in one of the other three chairs. "All right! See if it can break loose from the rock on its own. If not, we'll have to bring in the demolition specialists."

Alex thought about their mission. "Hold on a second, David. Do you know which button controls the cloaking system?"

David studied the illuminated pads. "Yes, this white one indicates we should be cloaked now."

Alex turned and headed toward the exit. "I'll be right back. I want to see if it's working."

Alex hurried out through the opening and turned to look at the ship, then went back inside. His disappointment must have been apparent, because his friend's hopeful expressions slipped away. "We'll have to take the chance of being seen. Find out if it can still fly."

When David tapped another series of pads, the ship shuddered as the rock holding it in place fractured, but it remained trapped in the volcano. He entered the sequence again, but the ship remained locked in the rock.

When the ship didn't move, Alex stared down at David. "What's wrong?"

"I don't know. Everything appears to be operating properly."

Jadin grinned at David. "Did you press the amber button?"

David felt his face flush as he held his finger over the button. "Sorry. Let's try this again."

When David pressed the amber pad, the rock surrounding the ship shattered and the spacecraft suddenly lurched up, as if sensing freedom from its one-hundred and eighty-million year volcanic prison, and he smiled and looked up at Alex. "We're at two-hundred-feet above the rim of the crater. Should I set us back down?"

"No, we should head for Groom Lake while it's still dark. Perhaps you'll fix the cloaking system on the way. If not, from there we'll be able to stay away from populated areas during the day on our way to get to the device."

"All right. Buckle up, cause here we go."

When Jadin sat down next to David, she realized something wasn't right. "I guess you know this thing doesn't have seatbelts."

"Don't worry, we'll be fine. This thing has an inertial dampening system."

Chapter 22

OREGON:

Jerry was standing outside his shop watching the tide coming in nice and steady, but the water was already above the highest tidemarks on the new pilings. He suddenly realized if the tide rose ten-feet higher, the main pier would be under water, and the floating docks would rise higher than the pilings. When that happened, the ramp would be torn from its hinges. The new ramp had cost a fortune, and he would be damned before he let it be destroyed.

He hurried into his shop, grabbed a pair of pliers and a sledgehammer, and then walked to the end of the pier. He knelt down next to the left hinge and used the pliers to remove the safety clip, then swung the hammer to drive the kingpin out. When the hammer bounced off the three-inch diameter steel rod, he swung it again, but the kingpin would not budge. He turned and moved over to the right hinge, removed the safety clip, and swung the sledgehammer with all his might, but it just bounced off like the other one. "Damn!"

When he noticed Aaron's truck drive up next to his shop, he set the hammer down and went back to greet him and Denise. "I was just about to call your big brother. I need his help."

"I'll give you a hand. What do you need done?"

Jerry appreciated the boy's offer, but Aaron was small in stature compared to his brother, and right now, he would need someone bigger to drive out those kingpins. "I'm trying to get the ramp loose, so the hinges don't break. The tide's coming in fast, and I'm afraid the docks will rise higher than the pier. When that happens, the ramp is going to be sticking into the air until it snaps in half, and I'm not going to let that happen."

"Let me try it."

"I don't think you'll be able to, but all right."

Jerry led them down to the end of the pier and stopped to pick up the sledgehammer, then held it out to Aaron. "We need to drive these large pins out."

Aaron took the hammer, but set it on the ground. "It will be a lot easier if we wait until the ramp is even with the pier. That way, there won't be as much weight on the pins."

"That makes sense. Why didn't I think of that? Okay, we'll just wait then."

Denise put her hand on Aaron's arm. "That won't be long. Look how fast the water is rising."

Aaron turned and ran back to the shop, grabbed a short-handled sledgehammer, then ran back to the ramp. "We need to do both pins at the same time, or it won't work. One side will bind up and break."

"Got it."

When Jerry grabbed his hammer and moved to the right side kingpin, Aaron did the same on the left and stared down at the rising docks until they were level with the pier. "Now!" He swung his hammer, hit the pin, and then heard a deep kirplunk when the pin popped out into the water.

Jerry swung with all his strength and felt a thud through the handle. When he looked at the pin, it was only halfway out of the holes. "Aaron! Bring your hammer!"

Aaron hurried over beside Jerry and saw what had happened. "What do you want me to do?"

"Put your hammer head into the hole, and I'll hit it with mine."

Aaron trusted his uncle and didn't hesitate. He knelt down on the pier and held his hammer in place. "Now!"

Jerry swung and hit it perfectly, and the end of the ramp suddenly popped up and was now resting on the floating dock. He dropped to his knees beside Aaron and wrapped his arms around him. "You did it!"

When Jerry let go, Aaron got up. "No, *we* did it, Uncle Jerry."

Jerry grabbed his nephew's hand to help him up. "Thank you."

Denise got their attention. "We'd better get moving. The water will start flooding this pier in a few moments."

The three of them ran up the pier to the front of his shop and then turned back to see what would happen next. Jerry stood watching helplessly while the water quickly washed over the concrete surface as the docks were sliding up along their pilings, and if the tide did not stop rising, the rings would slip over the tops, and then the docks would float away, taking his ramp with them.

Jerry held his breath and stared down at the floating docks, still steadily moving up toward the silver-pointed caps on the end of the pilings. Two-feet higher and the docks would be free. When they slowly moved down, he released a long sigh of relief. When the water level continued to drop, he grinned at Aaron and Denise. "I damn near wet my pants. We had better put a couple of pieces of pipe under the ramp as it comes down, so it won't get caught on the edge of the pier."

Aaron dashed into the shop, grabbed two short lengths of two-inch pipe, and set them on the ground. For the moment, all they could do was watch the water recede.

Debris carried from shore by the high tide was piling up on the pier, and Jerry realized it would hinder their rush to get back to the ramp. When he thought the time was right, he reached down, grabbed the two lengths of pipe, and held one out to Aaron.

Aaron was always worried Jerry might get hurt, but the look of determination in his uncle's eyes meant nothing was going to stop him from saving his ramp, so he accepted the pipe. "Let's get started."

Aaron looked on in admiration when Jerry nimbly dashed between small logs and across the seaweed. He should have known better than to doubt his uncle's abilities, especially since Jerry and his dad had grown up along the Oregon Coast and mainly did manual labor most of their lives.

Jerry showed Aaron how to hold his pipe between the ramp and the pier. "Just remember this. The moment the ramp hits your pipe, let go, because it could flip up and break your arm."

"Okay."

It didn't take long for the docks to drop even with the pier, and Jerry held the pipe in place. Inch by inch, the front edge of the aluminum ramp got close, and then it touched the steel and he let go. He stumbled backward on the debris before landing on his butt, and then looked over at Aaron, also sitting on his rear, with Denise kneeling beside him. He looked back at the ramp, silently sliding along the makeshift steel rollers until it dropped out of sight. He heard the splash of the pipes hitting the water, knowing he could retrieve them and the pins at low tide.

Aaron hurried over to Jerry. "It worked. Are you okay?"

Jerry smiled up at Aaron and held out his hand. "Great. Help me up, would you?"

Aaron grabbed his hand and pulled, noticing the slight grimace on his uncle's face. "Are you hurt?"

Jerry stood and shook his head no. "I just bruised my butt when I landed on that small log." He looked down over the edge, where the ramp was now safely resting on the concrete dock, then turned when Aaron moved up beside him. "It worked."

"Well, Uncle Jerry. It looks like things are back to normal. At least for now. I wonder if this will happen again with the next tide."

Jerry didn't reply. According to Jadin, the tides would continue to act this way and maybe even get worse.

A distant wail of a siren quickly grew louder, followed by the appearance of the sheriff's truck with his rescue boat in tow. Jerry could see Rick in the driver's seat as he turned the trailer around and backed the large gray rubber boat down the launch ramp. He ran up the pier and around the front of Rick's truck to the driver's window, and then walked beside his friend, helping to guide him down the boat launch. "A little to the left. What's going on, Rick? What's the rush?"

"It's just like you suspected. The river backed up over the bank and tore up your campground. I managed to convince most of them to leave on their own yesterday, but the holdouts were swept away to the ocean. I sent Brad and a few volunteers to the campground to search for survivors on shore, and I'm headed out to rescue any survivors in the water. I just hope I don't end up collecting bodies instead."

"I'll get my boat as soon as we get yours in the water."

"Thanks, Jerry. We can use as many people as we can to help rescue folks."

"Hold on a second while I move some of that crap out of your way."

After unloading the sheriff's boat, Jerry ran back to his shop and grabbed a remote control hanging just inside the doorway. When he pressed the button, a large garage door opened, and then the trailer under his nineteen-foot motorboat rolled down the boat launch on a set of railroad tracks, and he turned when Aaron and Denise ran up beside him. "Could you help me clear the rails?"

Aaron and Denise hurried down past the end of the trailer, while Jerry stopped the winch next to a level slab of concrete, making it easier for him to climb into the boat. He waited while the kids tossed driftwood and seaweed onto the far side of the boat launch, and when nothing remained on the rails, Aaron ran back up to the boat to climb in.

Jerry got in the boy's way to stop him. "No, Aaron. Stay here."

"Why? I heard what the sheriff said, and I want to help."

Because of his experience with water rescues, Jerry knew it might be a gruesome sight when they arrived at the search area. He thought perhaps Aaron was too young to see what they might find, but as he thought about it, he also realized he might not be able to help anyone into the boat by himself. He moved out of the way and grabbed the remote control for the winch. "Fine, you can help, but do exactly as I say. Let's go."

When Aaron stepped into the boat, Jerry pressed the remote control, then the winch whined as the trailer continued its journey down to the water. Jerry started the engine and backed away from the trailer, then headed for the breakwater leading out to the ocean.

***

Jerry slowed his boat down to idle as he slowly approached a tangled mass of debris floating off shore. Some brightly colored material appeared out of place among the leaves, branches, and brush, then Aaron looked over at his uncle from the passenger seat. "I think I see a flesh color in the water, just to the right side of that light blue spot."

"I see it. I really appreciate you coming with me, Aaron."

"Well, when I heard what happened, I just had to help."

When Jerry was within eight-feet of the blue object, he saw blond hair bobbing on the surface, and turned to Aaron. "Just a word of warning. Seeing a real dead person is not the same as seeing a body in a movie. It's not something you can prepare for, it just happens. Try to avoid staring at the face, if possible. I know from personal experience, it helped to keep me from throwing up."

"I will. Thanks, Uncle Jerry."

Jerry put the engine in neutral, grabbed a boat gaff to ease the debris out of the way around the woman, then held her alongside the boat before looking at Aaron standing beside him. "There's no easy way to get her on board, except to grab a leg and an arm and hoist her over the side into the boat. I'm sure she won't mind."

Aaron stared down at the back of the body and felt a little queasy, but overcame his reluctance and reached over the side to grab her arm. He almost let go when he felt the ice-cold flesh, but Jerry was already holding her leg, so he held on and waited for his signal.

Jerry noticed the trepidation in Aaron's eyes when he reached down to grab the woman's wrist, but the boy bravely took hold of the woman and looked at him for further instructions. "Okay, on three, we pull her over the gunnel. One, two, three!"

Jerry pulled up on the leg as Aaron pulled on the wrist, and the body slid over the side. When he looked at Aaron, the boy's complexion was nearly white.

Aaron jumped back when the body flopped onto the deck with a dull thud. The girl was face up, her eyes still frozen open in terror, and Aaron felt his stomach heave. He fought hard to keep it down, but lost the battle and threw up before making it to the edge of the boat. When nothing more came out, he stood and wiped the tears from his eyes and the drool from his chin. When he turned back toward the body, the face was covered with a small colored blanket, and Jerry was sitting on the rail, watching him. "Sorry about that, Uncle Jerry."

"Don't worry about it. The first one is always the toughest. Are you ready to look for another one?"

Aaron looked down at the corpse. "I guess."

"All right. Take the gaff and keep the crap from getting tangled in the propeller while I back away."

Once clear of the mess, Jerry slowly drove his boat through the scattered debris, then heard the sheriff's voice on the radio and grabbed the microphone. "Hey, Rick. So far, we have one DOA female on board."

"We just brought six survivors and two bodies into the harbor, so that's the last one. You can come back in."

"All right, we're on our way."

***

When he arrived at the marina, Jerry saw Curtis waiting at the top of the pier. He and Aaron rode in the boat as it was winched out of the water up to his shop, then they left the body inside until the county coroner could take possession. They climbed out, and Aaron had trouble keeping up with Jerry's quick pace. His uncle suddenly stopped and drove his fist into Curtis's jaw, knocking him to the ground. At first, Aaron was shocked, but then he regained his composure and grabbed Jerry's fist before he could clobber Curtis again.

Jerry stood over Curtis, staring down at him on the ground moaning, and wiping blood from his mouth. "You just killed three innocent people, you son of a bitch!"

Curtis stared up at the rage in Jerry's eyes. "I didn't kill anyone, you crazy bastard."

"Three people are dead because you refused to close the campground. As far as I'm concerned, that's the same as murder."

Curtis pushed himself off the ground and stood, wiping the blood from his jaw with the back of his hand while staring at Jerry. "I made a mistake, all right? How was I to know the river would flood so much?"

"Because I told you it would, damn it! I built that campground, so I ought to know what would happen when high tides roll in." A siren wailed and Jerry turned to look, only then noticing two more ambulances arriving in the parking lot, so he turned back to Curtis. "You're a real bastard, Tommy. I hope you have insurance for the campground, and it had better include liability coverage, because you're going to need it."

When Curtis walked away, Aaron turned to his uncle. "I don't get it. Why does old man Curtis need insurance for the campground?"

Jerry heaved a deep sigh and placed his hand on Aaron's shoulder. "Because I sold it to him ten months ago."

"I guess it's a good thing you got rid of it before all this happened." When he looked at his uncle, he didn't seem too happy about it. "Isn't that a good thing?"

"If I hadn't sold it to Curtis, no one would have died. I would've still been in charge and I would've shut the place down before the tides came back in. The place would've been empty, and those three people would've been driving home instead of being stuffed in a body bag and taken to the morgue."

"You can't think of it that way, Uncle Jerry. Just like when mom and dad were killed. We can think about all the what-ifs, but it doesn't change the fact that they are gone. We just have to move on with our lives."

Jerry stared at the people being treated for minor wounds and abrasions. "I suppose you're right. It could have been worse if the sheriff hadn't persuaded so many campers to leave yesterday. When did you get so smart?"

Aaron shrugged. "I guess just from being around you."

"Well, thank you for your help today. That took a lot of courage, and I'm very proud of you. You know, I think it's about time you dropped the uncle part. Just Jerry would be fine with me."

Aaron smiled. "Thanks, Jerry."

Chapter 23

GROOM LAKE, NEVADA:

Henry was in a golf cart driving along the streets between the hangars, grateful the moon had set, making it the perfect time for Alex and his friends to arrive in the spacecraft. Since the mirrored surface of the ship would reflect the smallest amount of artificial light, the entire base was in a shroud of darkness. He stopped next to four scientists standing outside Hangar 5, and the only sound was the thrumming of desert insects. To the casual observer, the approaching alien craft was invisible.

Two parallel rows of red lights on the concrete tarmac slowly increased in intensity, marking the approach to the entrance of the hangar. The reflection of the red dots slowly moved along the mirrored bottom of the spaceship as it silently entered through the opening between the hangar doors, and once inside, the red lights blinked off.

Henry and the scientist moved through the narrowing gap in between the doors into the hangar just before a quiet thud indicated they were closed. The LED lights mounted to the ceiling burst into brilliant white light, illuminating the forty-foot diameter mirrored hockey puck on the concrete floor.

Although no one outside the ship could see him inside, Alex saw them applauding through the transparent wall, then grinned at David. "That was an amazing ride."

"I've got the best job in the world. Thanks for arranging this for me, Alex."

Jadin got up from her chair and hurried over to David, then wrapped her arms around his neck and kissed him on the cheek. "That was awesome."

Alex saw Henry standing outside the ship and moved over to the control panel, then tapped a pad that opened the airlock doors down in the cargo hold. He moved back to the side and saw Henry enter the ship.

Henry entered the cargo hold and continued up the stairs along the outside wall. He stopped on the second level and looked into the small living area, then continued up and stepped into the control room. When he reached the top of the stairs, his friends were smiling at him, so Henry did the same. "You did it, David."

"No, it was all of us working together that made this possible."

Henry turned to Alex. "Director Donner would like for you to call him as soon as possible."

"All right. Have your people remove the cylinder from the ship's cargo hold right away and lock it up with the other two."

"We only have one so far, Alex. We are still waiting for the one from the cave on the island to arrive."

Alex stared at Henry. "That's odd. It was supposed to be here eight months ago. I'll ask Donner about it and be back in a minute."

***

Once Alex stepped outside the ship, he brought out his phone and called the Director. "We made it, Martin."

"That's good to hear. I'm afraid we have another immediate problem. There's a chance the gravity machine could cause problems with the International Space Station when it passes over that part of the desert."

"Just when I thought things couldn't get any worse, this happens. How long until it's in alignment?"

"Seven hours. I know it's a lot of pressure."

"I know, Martin. I think we finally have a plan. We're having a problem with the cloaking system on this ship, so we'll need to stay away from any populated areas on the way out to the device. We figure Sloan has her people watching the test area, so David will need to stay above ten thousand feet to avoid being seen. Okawna and I will fly back to Fallon, so we can be at the location when the ship arrives. Once he turns off the device, we'll be on the ground, ready to take it back to Fallon and have it shipped back here."

"I'll have some Marines waiting for you at NAS Fallon as backup."

Alex wished he had the help, but that meant more eyes on the spacecraft. "I would prefer to keep this as covert as possible. The fewer who know about the spaceship, the better. It's your call, but if we want to keep it a secret, we really don't have any other choice."

"I see what you mean. I trust you, Alex, so I know this operation is in good hands. The base commander is a friend of mine, so he'll have a car waiting for you at the air terminal. Good luck, Alex, for all our sakes."

"Thanks."

Alex dreaded having to tell everyone what was going on. With a sigh of resignation, he stepped back into the cargo hold. When he stepped into the control room, his four friends were staring at him. "All right, we have an actual deadline to get this device shut off. Seven hours."

Jadin and David spoke at the same time. "What?"

David got up from his chair. "What if we can't get it turned off in that timeframe?"

"We have to. Otherwise, in seven hours, it'll drag the International Space Station back into the atmosphere."

Jadin leapt out of her chair. "No, no, no! Alex, we have astronauts on board and they're not equipped for sudden re-entry. They'll all die if it is pulled back down to Earth. I need to call this in so NASA can organize an evacuation mission."

Alex stared at her. "Can they do it in seven hours?"

Jadin's shoulders slumped. "No, that's not near enough time. I don't think they even have a procedure for such a thing."

"Then there's no point in calling them."

David gave his friends a determined look. "Don't worry, Alex. We'll get that thing shut off in seven hours." He plopped down in the chair behind the control console and entered the coordinates into the computer, and then a map appeared on the holographic screen. "Fortunately, because of our location in a vast expanse of barren desert, we can be there in ten minutes without passing close to any populated areas. Who's with me?"

Jadin didn't hesitate. "I'm in."

Henry shook his head no. "I shall remain behind."

Alex turned to him. "We'll call you from the test site when we're ready, Doc."

When Alex and Okawna left the room, Henry looked across at a separate small control console. It had been leaning at a slight angle when they first entered the ship, but when they pushed it back into its storage bracket, nothing seemed to work.

He strolled over and stared at the touchpads, which appeared to be different from the main console. "David? Is there any information about what this controls?"

David brought the information up on the viewscreen. "There is a lot of data about controlling the weather and cleaning the atmosphere, but there is too much to sift through without overloading our own computers while they are connected to the ship." He noticed a flash drive in Jadin's briefcase and indicated it to her. "Would you mind if I borrowed that?"

Jadin grabbed the white plastic device and looked at the number on the side, then gave it to him. "That one is empty."

When David finished downloading the information, he held it out to Henry. "Here you go, Doc. Let me know what you find out."

Henry slid the device into his pocket. "I shall wait in my office and come back once I hear from Alex."

When Henry left the room, David smiled at Jadin. "He seems to be feeling much better."

Jadin thought about Jerry. "I think he just needed a break. The same thing happens to my uncle. Are we ready to do this?"

David nodded. "I just hope it works."

Chapter 24

MONTANA:

Fala pulled into Alex's driveway, shut off the engine, then turned to look at Halona strapped into the back seat. "I'll be back in a minute. I forgot to unlock the door for the movers, so they can load our things in the truck."

"But Mom, I don't want to leave. I like it here."

"I'm sorry, sweetie, but Alex and I just couldn't work things out."

"I love Alex, and I don't want to leave him. What about Barney? He'd be lonely without me and Trixie."

"That's enough! We are moving and that's final. I don't want to hear another word about it."

"Fine." Suddenly, the quietness of the yard caught Halona's attention. "Mom, where's Barney?"

"I don't know. I'll look around for him." Fala opened her door, climbed out, then glanced back inside at Halona. "You stay in the car, all right?"

"Yes, ma'am."

Fala closed the door and looked around for the dog as she walked toward the house. "Barney? Come here, boy."

She was positive she had not left him in the house, but when he didn't come to her, she hurried up onto the porch, unlocked the door and stepped inside. "Barney! Come here, boy!"

She looked through the rooms, passing by stacks of moving boxes neatly positioned by the back door. As she looked around Halona's room, tears blurred her vision for a moment, seeing how empty it was. Where the walls were once covered in her colorful drawings of castles and princesses, they were now bare, and her puppy paw-print bedspread was no longer there. Instead, all that remained was a bare mattress.

"Barney! Are you in here, boy?"

When she looked through her and Alex's bedroom, she saw one of Alex's old shirts hanging on the back of the closet door, and even though she wasn't near it, she could still remember his scent. It gave her butterflies every time she smelled his aroma. He just had that effect on her.

Then her eyes drifted to the bed, and a few tears rolled down her cheeks. The thought of never holding him in her arms as he slept, never feeling his soft lips on hers, never feeling his warm muscular body against hers, it all became too much to bear.

She turned and walked away, wiping the tears off her cheeks as she left the room, then remembered Barney never strays too far from the house. She suddenly had the feeling something was terribly wrong, so ran down the hallway and out the door.

When she stepped outside, Fala's eyes went wide when she saw someone sitting in the back seat with Halona. She ran to the car, only then realizing someone was also sitting behind the steering wheel. The driver's door suddenly opened, and then a tall woman stepped out. When Fala saw the gun pointed in her direction, she slid to a stop on the gravel, her mouth open in shock as she held her hands up beside her shoulders.

Sloan grinned when she saw the fear in the woman's eyes. "Hello, Fala. Get in. We're going on a trip."

"I don't understand. Who are you?"

"Get in the car or my friend will put a bullet in your daughter's leg."

When Fala didn't move, Sloan looked into the back seat. "John?"

"No! All right, I'll go with you."

Sloan waited while Fala hurried over to the passenger door and climbed inside, then displayed a crooked smile as she climbed in behind the steering wheel and turned to Fala. "Are we going to have a problem?"

Fala shook her head no and looked in the back seat at Halona. Her stomach tightened into a knot when she saw the small man holding a pistol pointed at her daughter, and to her surprise, Halona didn't look frightened. "Are you all right, baby?"

"Yes, ma'am."

Fala released a soft sigh of relief and then turned back to Sloan. "Who are you, and why are you doing this?"

"Your boyfriend is going to get something I want, and when he does, I need a bargaining chip. That's where you and the girl come in. I plan on trading you for it."

"This has something to do with Alex?"

Sloan smirked at her. "Not unless you have another boyfriend."

Fala shook her head no and then looked out the passenger window. "That son of a bitch!"

"Uh-oh, sounds like trouble in paradise."

Ignoring Sloan's comment, Fala decided to dig for more information and turned to look at her. "So, what is this about exactly? You say you plan on trading us for this thing, and I would like to know what is so important it's worth my life and that of my daughter's. Because right now, none of this makes any sense. Alex is a geophysicist, and I can tell by your desperation this is about more than just a rock."

Sloan laughed. "A rock? Honey, you have no idea what is going on. He really kept you in the dark, didn't he?"

"Yes. I've noticed that a lot lately myself. Alex isn't one who likes to share information. It's like pulling teeth with him sometimes."

"Let's just say all the news about the tides is caused by an unusual device, and I want it."

"A machine is causing the tides to act up?"

"Yes. Now you see why I need you and your daughter for leverage. You also know Alex isn't the kind of person to hand something like that over. Hence, he has something I want, and now I have something he will want even more."

All Fala wanted was to get her and Halona as far away from here as possible, and finally close the chapter in her life with Alex Cave, but now, because of him, she was trapped with this nasty woman. "Please don't do this."

"Just do what you're told, and you and your daughter will be fine."

"I'll do what you say."

Sloan started the engine, drove down the driveway, and then headed toward the airport. "Are you okay back there, John?"

Essex had told Sloan he wanted no part of the kidnapping until she threatened to crush his balls with vice grip pliers. "I will be."

***

When the pilot leveled the plane at thirty-thousand-feet, Essex stood and poured himself a drink. "I wasn't surprised when Alex and his friend showed up at my office, but they acted like it was my fault."

"You were supposed to stay with them so you could keep me informed of their progress. Now I have to pay for someone to watch for them."

"That wasn't my fault. Cave doesn't trust me. You know that, Janice."

"You're such a coward, John. You're so afraid of that device."

"You've seen what that machine can do, so I have every reason to fear that thing. I can always find another way to launch my space travel legacy." Essex looked down the aisle at the little girl resting her head on her mother's lap. Even though he knew it was necessary, he still felt a twinge of guilt, scaring her with his pistol. Although thinking back on it, she appeared to be scared at first, but a moment later, she seemed okay, as if it wasn't a big deal. She was either very naïve or very brave.

Chapter 25

JPL:

Patrick felt a hand on his shoulder, opened his eyes, and looked up at Terry, his team member. "What's going on?"

"You had better look at this. The moon just changed orbit again."

Patrick rolled off the cot in the laboratory and got up. "How much did it change this time?"

"Another sixteen-thousand miles closer."

Patrick stared at the animated image of the moon orbiting the planet. "How is this even possible?"

"I don't know, but you had better call Jadin right away, because the tidal effect is going to get much worse. Los Angeles, London, France, Spain, all the major coastal cities will be underwater, killing millions of people."

Patrick grabbed the phone and selected Jadin's number. "I'm on it."

***

EUREKA, CALIFORNIA:

Sam Uric slipped the tongs around a bratwurst in the hot water, placed it into a bun, and then handed it to a young girl standing beside his cart. When she offered him money, he shook his head no. "This one's on me, Penny, just don't tell your friends about it. Are you still sleeping in the old factory?"

"Yeah, but now that it's summer, it's getting too crowded. Panhandling doesn't work too well with so many of us begging for money. People get annoyed, and they tell you to get lost or worse."

"Why don't you go home, Penny? That old building isn't safe anymore."

"You sound just like my grandpa. You kind of look like him, too."

"Okay, so two grandpas think it's the right thing for you to do. You should take our advice and go home."

Penny turned her back to him, "You don't know what it was like, Sam." She took a bite of her bratwurst and stared out over the ocean. "Hey, check it out."

Sam turned to look and his lips parted. Since he began working the boardwalk fifteen years ago, he had never seen anything like it. Normally, the seaweed didn't grow any closer than eight-hundred yards from the low tide mark, but suddenly the slender brown tentacles and glistening leaves lay flat on the muddy beach, exposed to the sun by an extremely low tide.

Penny turned to look at Sam. "Have you ever seen the tide that low?"

"No, and I do know it's the first sign of a tsunami, but I don't think that's what we're looking at. It's the tidal effect from the moon, and it's going to be much worse than yesterday. We had better get to higher ground."

"Do you really think that's what's happening?"

"Not for sure, but let's not take the chance."

"Okay, but where do we go?"

"Up the hill to the Presley Estates. That's the only place high enough."

"Those rich people aren't going to let us through the gate."

Sam reached down and shut the propane tank off and closed up his portable hot dog stand. "You let me worry about that. Let's get going before it's too late."

"How are we going to push this thing a quarter mile up that steep road to the highway?"

"When I was younger, I used muscle power, but those days are over. I modified this one with an electric motor and those are solar panels on the roof. Just hang on going up the hill and it will do the work for us."

Penny stared up at the small cover above the cookers and accessories. Since she began visiting with Sam three months ago, she had never noticed much difference with Sam's cart compared to all the other vendors along the boardwalk. Now that she knew it was electric, it appeared to be more modern.

Sam grabbed the steering arm, swung it out straight with the cart, and looked at Penny. "Let's go."

The speed of the three-wheeled vehicle caught her off guard, and Penny hurried to catch up with Sam. "You weren't kidding. How fast can this thing go?"

"As fast as I can walk. I used to run with it until the arthritis in my knees told me it was payback time for all the abuse I put them through."

It didn't take long to reach the parking lot, now jammed with cars so their passengers could walk down to the exposed beach. High on the steep mountain, cars on the highway honked their horns as the traffic stopped and everyone wanted to stare across the massive stretch of mud and seaweed.

Sam had difficulty steering his cart between all the cars and silently cursed the ones who left their doors open while they gawked at the view. He looked over at Penny, who was staying out of the way behind him. "I'll have to add a horn to this cart before I come back."

When Sam reached the two-lane road leading up to the highway, he sighed with relief. All the cars had parked off to the sides, leaving a wide space up the road. When they reached the highway, they didn't have to wait for the traffic light to change, since not a single vehicle was moving. Once on the other side, they began the long uphill journey between the slender vertical rods of the ten-foot-tall steel fences on either side of the road to the mansions, high on the ridge.

Penny waited until she couldn't stand the pain in her leg muscles before grabbing the handrail on the back of the cart. "I just wanted to let you know I'm more capable than I appear."

"I imagine you need to be pretty tough to live on the streets, but you don't have to prove anything to me, Penny."

She turned away, not wanting Sam to see the sense of regret showing in her eyes. This was her life now, but she didn't have a choice. She had to get away or end up living in a rundown trailer park in Hicksville, USA.

She looked up when the cart suddenly stopped in front of a large steel gate with ornate stone obelisks supporting the hinges, and a thick lock to keep visitors out. "Now what do we do?" When Sam turned around, she did the same and stared down at the beach, now stretching out toward a sparkling line across the horizon.

Sam felt a sinking sensation in his stomach, knowing why dozens of people were walking far out from shore, but their curiosity could get them killed. What goes out must come back in, and the question was how fast.

When Penny noticed a sparkling line across the horizon, she turned to tell Sam, but suddenly his posture stiffened, and his eyes focused on the scene below.

"Run, damn it!" Sam growled softly.

Penny jerked her head around to look at the ocean, and below the sparkling line, a twenty-foot wall of water was racing toward the parking lot. "Oh, my! You were right, Sam. Why didn't we hear any tsunami warnings?"

Sam couldn't take his eyes off the scene developing below, as the power of the wave slammed into the running figures, driving them face down into the gray mud before smothering them in a deluge of churning ocean. When the wave hit the concrete barriers built to keep it at bay, the water tore them apart like straw. It kept coming in, filling the parking lot with screaming bodies, their flailing arms desperately trying to find something to grab. He dropped to his knees as tears slowly ran down his cheeks.

Penny caught a movement out of the corner of her eye. When she looked down at Sam, he appeared frail and vulnerable. She felt bad for the people below, but she couldn't imagine why Sam was taking this so hard. She realized she really didn't know much about him. He was just a nice old man who sold hotdogs and was interesting to talk to on the boardwalk.

When the wave hit the base of the hillside, massive chunks of mud and rock slid into the ocean, but the water kept rising. The two-lane highway below broke into large chunks of asphalt, tossing the crowded vehicles into the water, before it vanished beneath another landslide.

Penny realized they were trapped and tried desperately to crawl over the tall fences, but there was nothing to stand on for traction. Tears rolled down her cheeks as she knelt beside Sam and squeezed his hand, then the hillside disappeared in front of her feet, and she screamed when the ornate entrance collapsed onto her and Sam as they slid into the ocean.

Chapter 26

OREGON:

When Jerry finally returned home, he sat in his well-worn recliner and turned on the television, then selected a news channel, hoping someone knew what was causing the strange tides. A woman announcer appeared on the screen, and behind her was a picture of the moon orbiting the planet.

"Scientists from around the world have gathered for an emergency meeting in Stockholm, but so far no one has an explanation for why the moon suddenly changed its orbit. Even more disconcerting is the fact it has changed twice in the past few days, and the increased tidal effect is tearing up shorelines around the planet. The ensuing panic on every continent is out of control, as thousands of people desperately flee from the low-lying coastal areas. The experts say the high tides will continue to get worse, and will eventually redefine the shape of the continents."

Jerry closed his mouth. "So that's what Jadin couldn't tell me."

He changed television stations, and one after another, had a red banner heading from the Emergency Broadcast System. He looked through the front window at the Pacific Ocean, wondering if one hundred feet from the bluff would be enough to keep his home from washing into the sea. He thought his heart would break as he slowly stood so he could see the empty marina far below. "All that work for nothing."

He turned and headed into his kitchen, knowing he needed to eat something. He searched through the refrigerator, but nothing looked appealing. He was about to close the door when he saw something that *did* look appealing in the rack, so he grabbed a bottle of beer and strolled out onto the deck to watch the sunset. He took several swallows, and then set the bottle on the end table. He had already lost the campground, and soon his shop, but without the income from the marina, the town would suffer, and possibly die.

When he reached over and grabbed the beer, he noticed the ring of water on the table, then had an idea and grinned. "I'm not going down without a fight."

***

Jerry was already up at first light when he heard his phone ring and saw it was Jadin. "Good morning. Listen, before you get started, I know about the moon, and I understand why you couldn't tell me about it. Now it's my turn to be nosey about your business. Tell me what's going on, Jadin. Will the tides ever get back to normal?"

"Honestly, Jerry, I don't know. We're working on something that might help get things back to the way they were, but that's not the reason I'm calling. The moon underwent another change of its orbit, and things are going to get bad. Real bad. You should evacuate the marina and get the word out to your friends and neighbors to get as far inland as you can and away from the river."

"It's already taken care of. This last tidal surge caused the river to flood, and it washed out most of the campground."

Jadin could sense there was more to it than just the campground. "What happened?"

"I wanted to send all the campers out of the area after the first tidal event, but Curtis overruled me. Three people were killed, Jadin, and Aaron helped me recover one of them from the water. He did well, and I'm very proud of him, but the situation was, and is, very bad here."

"I'm so sorry, Jerry."

"It's okay, sweetie. You just work on getting the tides back to normal. I appreciate the heads up about the tide. Good luck, Jadin."

Jerry filled his large coffee mug and headed out the door. With a little luck, he might use his idea to save the shops and his docks.

Chapter 27

NAS FALLON, NEVADA:

Alex stared out the window of a small private jet, listening to the steady whine from the engines while he thought about Fala and Halona. He knew it was the right thing to decide not to chase after her when this operation was over. Perhaps there would come a time in his life where he would have to stop chasing the adventure and finally settle down.

Okawna looked over at Alex, noticing his dejected expression. "Man, it feels just like working for the CIA again. Only better, right?"

Alex turned to look at his friend, who was grinning. "Better?"

"Sure, we're not undercover, and we get to choose our own missions. You've got to admit, saving the world while having fun is a great line of work."

Alex did not smile. "I suppose so."

"Here's an interesting question. Now that you have your own spaceship, where are you planning to go when this is over? South America? Outer space?"

"I really wish people would stop calling it *my* ship."

"Sure it is. You're the one who found it."

Rubin's voice came through the intercom. "We're on final approach to NAS Fallon."

Okawna grinned. "All right, let's get to work."

***

A young man dressed in a white Navy uniform was waiting for them at the air terminal. "I'm Seaman Clarkson, Sirs. Commander Ramey asked me to set you up with a desert vehicle, and it was a blast driving it over here."

When they walked outside, Okawna grinned when he saw the large, camouflage-painted Humvee. "Now that's what I'm talking about."

Clarkson held out the key. "It's fueled and ready to go, and the crate you asked for is inside."

Okawna climbed inside and turned the key, and when he heard the roar from the large engine, looked out the window at Clarkson. "Nice. Thanks."

Once Alex was inside, Okawna drove off the base and headed south on a two-lane highway. According to the map Clarkson had left on the passenger seat, it was a back way to the road on Essex's property, leading to the test area.

When they reached the gate indicating the end of the NAS Fallon property, Alex climbed out and used the key left in the center console to open it. Once Okawna drove through, he locked it and got back into the vehicle, and then they headed along the dirt road. Half an hour later, they turned onto the familiar road along the mountainside.

Ten minutes more brought them to the cement block, and Okawna parked one hundred feet away. Alex climbed out and strolled over to the donut-shaped mound of feathered carcasses around the device. "I'll tell the Doc we're ready."

***

AREA 51. GROOM LAKE, NEVADA:

When Henry stepped into the control room of the spaceship, David and Jadin stared at him with expectant expressions. "Alex and Okawna are ready. Good luck to you both."

David plopped down into one of the chairs. "See you in half an hour, Doc."

David stared after Henry as he disappeared down the stairs. When one of the touch pads changed color, he knew the airlock doors were closed and the ship was ready. He entered a command, and the ship slowly rose above the concrete floor and moved out of the hangar. Once clear, he smiled at Jadin, and then headed out across the desert.

***

Okawna leaned back against the front of the truck next to Alex and then crossed his arms as he stared up at the clouds. "It's hard to believe something so small could move something as big as the moon."

"I'd love to know what it uses as an energy supply."

Okawna's hands dropped to his sides as he straightened up and pointed at the sky above them. "Now that's something you don't see every day."

Alex looked up in the direction Okawna indicated and saw a strange mirage floating across the sky. "It's moving pretty fast. I hope David knows how to slow down."

Within moments, the spaceship stopped moving when it was above the gravity device, and a small section of the atmosphere high above their heads appeared to be shimmering. Alex realized the two gravity systems were counteracting each other, which meant the ship could stay in the air above the gravity beam without a problem. He sighed with relief when the desert mirage surrounding the spaceship raced away across the heavens, meaning David had turned the device off and was getting out of sight.

Just to be sure, Alex threw a rock over the gravity machine and it sailed through without dropping. He went forward to retrieve the device, and once he located the area with the touch pads, he carefully picked it up and carried it back to the truck. When Okawna opened the back door, he smirked at him. "I was right. It's light enough and small enough to be hidden in a backpack. Here, feel for yourself."

Okawna held his hands up and backed away from the device. "No way. Keep that thing away from me. Just put it in the truck and let's get out of here."

Alex grinned at his friend's reluctance, fully understanding his position. This device was more dangerous than a nuclear bomb, so he couldn't blame him for not wanting to hold it. He carefully set the device in the wooden crate strapped to the floor in the back. After inserting blocks of foam rubber around it, making sure none of the foam touched any buttons, he closed the lid. He grabbed a hammer and some nails on the floor, sealed the lid, then closed the door and went around to the passenger side to sit in front with Okawna.

Okawna climbed in behind the steering wheel and started the engine, then stomped on the accelerator, leaving a cloud of dust in his wake as he headed back to Fallon. An hour later, he heard Alex's phone ring and looked over at his friend's concerned expression when he answered and knew something was wrong, so he stopped in the road.

Alex turned on the speaker so Okawna could listen. "What do you want, Sloan?"

"How did you manage to shut down the device?"

"Do you really think I would tell you?"

"I want it, Alex."

"Not a chance. There's no way I'm letting you get your hands on this thing again."

"Oh, I think you'll change your mind. I'm sending you a live video feed. I suggest you watch it."

Alex turned the phone so Okawna could see the video, and what was on the screen took his breath away as they stared at the image of Fala and

Halona, bound and gagged. He didn't recognize where they were being kept, but he suspected it was somewhere at Essex's facility. As the video zoomed in on Fala, they heard Sloan's voice in the background. "Nod to your boyfriend, so he knows this is real."

Alex's heart broke when he saw the scared, pleading expression in her tear-filled eyes as she nodded her head. His gut tightened into a knot, and he felt sick to his stomach, and then looked over at Okawna, whose jaw muscles flexed in anger while his eyes blazed with hate.

"Let's play a game, Alex. It's called, let's make a deal."

Alex decided to try to appeal to her sense of reason. "Don't do this, Janice. This thing is more dangerous than you could possibly understand."

"Oh, I understand plenty. I understand 12 million dollars. That's the highest bid I've gotten on that little gem. You have something I want, and I obviously have something you want. Let's trade."

Alex realized there was no reasoning with Sloan, so he looked over at Okawna while he spoke. "You know I can't do that."

"Is that your final answer, Alex? Let me remind you of what will happen if you pass on this deal."

On the screen, Alex watched Sloan put the barrel of a silenced pistol against Fala's head. "No! Don't!"

"Then do we have a deal?"

Alex knew if he gave Sloan the device, she would sell it and there's no telling how that person would use it. It could be in a heavily populated city like New York or Chicago and the devastation would be horrific. He loved Fala more than life itself, and to lose her would be to lose Sevi all over again. Tears blurred his vision, but he knew what he had to do. He looked over at Okawna, whose eyes were glistening with his own tears, then back at the screen. "I love you, Fala. I hope you know that, but I can't. I'm so sorry. No deal, Sloan."

A gunshot suddenly rang out over the phone, and the image of Fala vanished. "Fala! Damn you, Sloan!"

"The little girl is next, Alex. So what's it going to be?"

Alex tilted his head back and stared up at the roof, feeling like a chunk of his heart had been ripped out. He had to make a choice, and tears slowly ran down from the corners of his eyes as he looked down at Halona's image on the phone. He looked over at Okawna. "Please forgive me."

The look in his friend's eyes was a dagger through his heart, but the slight nod he received let him know his friend understood he had no choice, and he looked at the screen. "The answer is still no, Sloan."

Alex flinched when he heard another gunshot and turned to Okawna, whose face was flush with rage. His own anger reached into his soul, and then he realized he was nearly crushing the phone in his hand, and set it on the dash.

Okawna's hands clenched into fists around the steering wheel, nearly ripping it from the dashboard, and he fought hard to hold back his tears as he stared at the screen. "You're a dead woman, Sloan!"

Sloan's face appeared on the screen. "I want that device and you will give it to me. See you boys later."

Okawna stared over at Alex. "I really hate that woman. I can't believe Fala and Halona are gone. How am I going to explain this to my parents? They were my family!"

"I know. They were my family, too, and it was the two hardest decisions I've ever had to make. Even though Fala ended our relationship, I still loved her, and I loved Halona as though she were my own daughter." He wiped the tears from his cheeks with the back of his hand. "I can't believe Sloan would stoop so low as to drag them into this, but I couldn't risk this thing being turned on again. Could you imagine the death and destruction it would cause?"

Okawna stared over the dashboard at the desert. "Yeah, I know. You made the right choice, Alex. I don't blame you, because I would have done the same thing." He noticed a cloud of dust moving in their direction from further up the road and twisted in his seat to grab his pistol. "We have company, Alex. How much you want to bet they are Sloan's cronies?"

Alex turned to face Okawna, his face flush with rage as he held up his pistol and pulled back on the slide, chambering a round. "I don't care who they are. I just want Sloan. If anyone gets in my way, I'm putting a bullet in their head."

Okawna shifted into four-wheel-drive. "It looks like two vehicles, one behind the other. Time to play a game of chicken."

***

Jim Coburn noticed the cloud of dust moving in his direction and studied his location. The single lane road had a steep incline on one side and a steep drop off on the other, so it was the perfect spot for an ambush so he looked over at the driver, Sam Kirby. "Pull over just up ahead so we can block their escape. Sloan must have a thorn in her butt about these two guys. She said stop them by any means necessary, and take the box-shaped mirror, whatever the hell that means."

When Kirby pulled over and stopped, Coburn climbed out and walked to the other black SUV behind his truck. "If they don't stop, shoot out their tires. If that doesn't work, take them out. We'll dump the bodies where no one will ever find them."

***

Okawna realized the other drivers had stopped at the area he would have used for an ambush, and then looked over the embankment on his side of the road. He stared over at Alex, who had his elbow hanging out through the side window and a pistol in his hand. "When I say go, fire a few rounds, then hang on."

Alex felt a rush of adrenalin as he swung his gun out the window. When Okawna stepped on the gas, they quickly closed the distance to the cars, and as they drew near, they saw four heads appear silhouetted in the open door frames. Several puffs of dust exploded from the dirt road in front of the Humvee as warning shots, and Alex realized they knew what they were doing. More bursts of dirt erupted in front of their tires, but Alex continued to wait for Okawna's signal. Two more bullets ricocheted off the front hood, and they were nearly on top of their enemies, then five bullets burst against the windshield, leaving small scars, much to Alex's surprise and relief.

Okawna glanced at Alex. "Go!"

Alex fired six quick rounds, ducked back inside, then grabbed the inside hand holds. Okawna fired two rounds from outside his window and then threw the steering wheel hard over to the left. The rear tires threw dirt and gravel into the air, peppering the two vehicles to keep the shooters under cover as he headed straight down the bank, and then the front bumper slammed into the level dirt at the bottom, bouncing them into the air. He made a wide circle around the attackers before roaring up the embankment behind them and back onto the road.

The rear window exploded, sending shards of glass flying throughout the vehicle, and then Alex felt a heavy thud in his headrest. He turned to aim through the missing window and fired three quick rounds, and watched the men duck behind their doors when their own rear windows shattered, and then the two vehicles quickly shrank in size behind them and he turned forward to look at Okawna, who had a grim look on his face. "Nice move."

Okawna glanced in the rearview mirror. "Yeah, that was fun, but I still want to kill someone."

Alex leaned back in his seat and felt a small lump against the back of his head. When he leaned forward and turned to look, he recognized the blunt end of a jacketed bullet protruding through the leather.

He slid the headrest out and showed it to Okawna. "One of them is a good shot. I'm just glad this Humvee was combat ready."

"I'd say that was a close call, all right. One of them must have been using some heavy-duty ammunition to pierce the bulletproof glass. Did you notice the SWAT gear they were wearing looked familiar?"

"Yeah, I'll bet they're the same ex-military security guards from Essex's compound. They'll have to go to the test site to turn around, unless they try the Okawna maneuver."

"I almost didn't make it up the hill, and I've got wider tires. They'll never make it."

"I don't think we've heard the last from Sloan. I'm sure she'll come up with another crazy stunt to get this device. She's already proved she'll stop at nothing to get it."

Okawna slammed his fist against the dashboard. "I really hate that woman, Alex!"

They were still thirty minutes from the base when Alex heard his phone ring. Between the chaotic driving and the firefight, his phone had been knocked onto the floor, and he gently sifted through the shards of glass on the carpet between their seats and brought it up to see who was calling.

When he recognized the number, he looked over at Okawna. "You're not going to believe this." The phone rang again, so Alex answered. "What do you want, Sloan?"

"Very impressive, gentlemen. I underestimated you and your abilities."

"Thanks. Why don't you tell me where you are and you can thank us in person?"

"You're a funny man, Alex."

"Every time I hear your voice, I want to reach through the phone and rip your throat out. I know you didn't call just to complement our ability to escape your men, so get on with it and quit wasting my time."

"That's what I like about you, Alex. You get right to the point. I just thought you'd like to know there is no way you could turn that device on again. In case you didn't know, you're missing a piece. A very important piece. A key, if you will."

"Why would I want to turn it on again? I could give a shit about some key."

"Well, don't you think your friends at the Department of Defense would be interested in having all the pieces of that device? It could make a powerful weapon against an adversary if we should ever find ourselves in another world war."

"No way, Sloan. They plan on locking this thing up and throwing away the key as soon as we get back. No one in their right mind would create a weapon out of this."

"Don't be so sure, Alex. Who do you think my highest bidder is?"

"There's no way the DOD would pay 12 million dollars for something as dangerous as this."

"Not the DOD, but a contractor who works for the federal government would."

"You're lying, Sloan."

"Say what you will, but think about it. What a perfect way to eliminate one's enemy with a single device. Or it could create a shield around us. No aircraft could fly in, no satellites orbiting over the U.S. spying on our every move, no possible way of invasion, and all without a single casualty. So, now that you know the truth, let's talk about how much this is worth to you and Mister Donner."

Alex knew nothing Sloan said was the truth, and she was only telling him what he wanted to hear so she could get her hands on the device again. He couldn't care less about a key. What he really wanted was the chance to kill Sloan and decided to play along. "All right. Tell me how much, and where we can meet to make the exchange."

"I'll call you in the next day or so. I have a couple bodies I need to dispose of, then we'll talk price."

"Go to hell, Sloan. I swear I'll find you, and when I do, you're going to wish you had never met me."

"Oh, I already wish that, Alex. You have been nothing but a thorn in my side this whole time."

Okawna leaned over to the phone to see her face. "You'd better sleep with one eye open, because I promise I'm coming for you."

Alex ended the call. "As soon as we drop this machine off, we're going to Essex's facility and tear the place apart until we find Sloan."

"Hey, do you think she was right about the government wanting to get their hands on this device and turn it into a weapon?"

"I doubt what she said was true, but I'll let Donner know he may want to check into it and see if anyone on the inside is trying to acquire it."

***

NAS FALLON:

Four Marines were waiting when Okawna drove into a remote hangar. They climbed out to load the wooden crate with its dangerous cargo on to a plane Donner had sent for them. When they boarded the jet, Alex pressed the button to retract the stairs, and then locked the door and looked into the cockpit at Ruben. "Let's get this bird in the air."

Alex and Okawna sagged into the comfortable passenger seats in the cabin as Rubin taxied out of the hangar and down the runway. A few moments later, they were soaring above the Nevada desert.

Chapter 28

HUMPBACK HARBOR:

When he arrived at the marina, the light fog made it feel like a ghost town. The windows in the shops were still closed, and not a single boat remained in the harbor. He parked behind his shop, then climbed out and entered the office. When he reached for the remote control for the boat winch, he discovered it was gone. "Crap!"

He checked the counter drawers and the ones in his desk, but couldn't find it. His heart rate increased as he searched the floors on both sides of the counter, but the remote control appeared to have vanished. He continued through the office into the shop and froze in mid-stride when he didn't see his boat. "What the hell?" When he realized the control was in his boat, he chuckled. "You're losing it, old man."

He opened the garage door, and there it was, resting on its trailer where he had left it for the coroner. He went over and looked inside, and when he saw the small blanket he had placed over the girl's face, he thought about Curtis, and his stomach tightened into a knot. He slipped the blanket under his arm and returned to the office, tossing the cloth into the trash on his way into the shop.

Since the small tool chest on the boat only carried the bare minimum needed to work on the engine, Jerry took a moment to decide which tools he would need once he was on the docks. He grabbed the three-quarter-inch drive socket set off the counter, a pry bar, and the small sledgehammer, then took one last look around for anything he might need. He carried the tools out and climbed into the boat, and with the push of a button, the winch whined, and the trailer slid down the tracks.

Jerry waited until the boat floated off the padded supports into the water, then set the electric trolling motor to full speed and drove to the end of the first dock, with the ramp still stretched out across its concrete surface. Now that the fuel lines were shut off at the head of the pier, his priority was disconnecting them, the power cable, and fresh water hose from the docks. He tied off and climbed out, then used a wrench to unscrew the water tight fittings.

When that task was complete, he took a moment to look through the fog, only then realizing how many attachment rings he would need to remove for his plan to work. When the charge on the invoice was for three hundred of them, he thought the engineer was mad, but as it turned out, he used them all. In order for his plan to work, each one of the three hundred rings would need to be unbolted from the docks. He sighed, knowing it was going to be a long day, then grabbed the socket set and carried it over to the first ring, then knelt down to remove the first of twelve large bolts.

After three minutes, he realized he had forgotten the most important piece of equipment. Kneepads. He got up and then looked down at the single eight-inch long bolt he had managed to remove. "This is going to take forever."

When Jerry heard someone call his name, he recognized Aaron's voice coming from up on the pier, and looked up at the boy and Denise standing at the end, looking down at him. "Good morning."

Aaron noticed the ratchet in his uncle's hand. "What are you doing?"

"Jadin called and said the tides are going to get worse. The next high tide will lift the docks over the pilings, and they'll float across the harbor and smash into the shops. I was planning on towing them out into deeper water and anchoring them to the buoys."

"Do you want some help?"

"I appreciate your offer, but I just learned from experience it will take too long to get them unbolted."

Aaron saw the frustration in his uncle's eyes. "So, what are you going to do now?"

"I'm not sure. Did you hear about the moon?"

Aaron shook his head no, but Denise answered. "Yes, it's all over the news. My dad thinks that's why the animals are acting up."

Jerry stared across the water at the shops. "If I can't get the docks towed out to the buoys, everything in the harbor will be destroyed."

"What if you had a lot of help?"

Jerry grunted. "It would take an army of people to get it done in time."

"What size wrenches are you using?"

"A three-quarter-inch socket. Six-sided works the best."

Aaron grabbed his phone and entered a text message, then his phone chimed, and he smiled at Jerry. "Help is on the way."

Five minutes later, ten young men and six young girls strolled down the pier, and then the captain of the football team held up a ratchet and socket. "Hey, Mister Avery. I heard you need some help."

Jerry recognized the high school students. "Thanks for coming, Peter. I need to unbolt all the docks before the tide comes in."

Peter smiled as he looked around at the other students, then back at Jerry. "Aaron said if we help, you would buy us all the pizza we can eat. Is that true?"

Jerry's eyes went wide when he looked at Aaron, who grinned at him, and then he turned back to Peter. "Sure thing."

Peter turned to the other students, who held their wrenches in the air, and then he looked at Jerry. "Just show us what to do."

Jerry ferried the first group of six students out to the docks in his boat and showed them what to do before he returned to pick up the next group of six. On the last trip, he took Denise, Aaron, and the last two students over and they got to work, except for Denise. When he stepped out of the boat, she held out her hand for his ratchet.

"I'll need that, Mister Avery."

"Thanks, Denise, but I can do it."

Denise grabbed the wrench from his hand. "I know, but I figured since you're so old, your joints would start to hurt, like my grandma. Besides. You don't have any kneepads"

Jerry realized he had forgotten them again and smiled at her. "I sure appreciate it." He looked at Aaron. "How old do they think I am?"

Aaron shrugged. "Anyone over forty is old compared to them. We'd better get started, Jerry. The tide is already going out."

Jerry stared down the length of the floating docks at the young people furiously turning their wrenches, but even with all the help, removing the bolts would take too long. With only one boat in the harbor, towing them out to the buoys would be another time-consuming task. He heard a siren and looked up in time to see Rick and Brad arrive in the parking lot with the rescue boat.

Aaron placed his hand on his uncle's shoulder. "This is your project, Jerry, so why don't you go back to shore and keep everything organized?"

"All right. I'll try to get you some more help."

When he reached the shoreline, Jerry nudged his boat onto the gravel next to the boat launch, and then climbed out to walk up to his shop. Rick and Brad were waiting for him, so he explained what he was trying to do.

Brad held his phone out for him to see. "Aaron sent a request for help to just about everyone in Humpback Harbor, and the pizza offer worked. You'll be broke after you feed all these people."

"That's the least of my problems. If the tide is going to rise as high as Jadin predicts, the shops will only get some minor flooding, but if the docks rise over the pilings, they'll be driven into all the structures, and there won't be anything left in the harbor worth saving." He looked over at the rapidly filling parking lot and then turned to Rick and Brad. "Let's get your boat in the water so you can start ferrying people to the docks. I just hope they brought their own tools."

While Rick and Brad backed the boat trailer down to the water, Jerry approached the gathering of shop owners and helpers, and then explained what might happen to the marina. Everyone began shouting questions at him, but he didn't know the answers to most of them, and nodded to one of the shop owners as the rest quieted down. "Do you have a question, Dan?"

"Are you sure the tide will be that bad? I mean, the shops are fifteen-feet above the high tide mark."

"Haven't you heard? The orbit of the moon has changed, and it's raising hell with the tides."

"Yeah, I heard about it."

"Well, my niece works for NASA, and she's the one who told me it's going to get bad this time. Now, you can either grab a wrench and help with the docks or get your buildings ready for the flood. Either way, we had better hurry."

Jerry watched Dan and three more shop owners run down the boardwalk toward the shops, but the other people held up socket wrenches, and he smiled. "Thank you. Head down to the sheriff's boat, and he'll give you a ride over."

One woman pointed to the water. "It won't be long until we can walk across to the docks."

Jerry spun around to look, and the water was receding rapidly. "We need to hurry, so let's get down to the boats."

Jerry was about to lead the way when Curtis arrived with a blustery look on his face and hollering his name. "Great, that's all I need right now."

Curtis stomped across the parking lot and glared at Jerry. "Where is your nephew?"

Jerry stared back evenly. "Which one?"

"Aaron, damn it. He sent me a text message at 6:15 this morning, and I want to know how he knew my private number."

Jerry ignored Curtis and turned to the group of volunteers. "Let's get going."

Curtis's hands clinched into fists at his side. "Don't you dare walk away from me, Avery!" When Jerry didn't respond, Curtis hurried to catch up with him. "What the hell is going on here?"

Jerry didn't stop or look at Curtis. "We're trying to save the docks and the stores, so either help or stay the hell out of the way." When Curtis grabbed his arm, Jerry jerked it away and glared at him. "I'm serious, Tom."

Curtis held his arms up. "All right, I'm sorry. Just explain to me why this is necessary."

"I received a call from Jadin this morning, and this next tide is going to be disastrous if we don't finish in time."

"I see. Well, if Jadin is worried, I guess we should prepare for the worst. What can I do to help?"

"Did you bring any tools, like Aaron asked?"

"Uh, no, I was too pissed off to pay any attention to what he wrote."

"Fine. See what you can do to help the shop owners get ready for a flood."

Curtis looked down the row of shops and then turned back to Jerry. "I'll do what I can."

Jerry stared after Curtis for a moment before he turned around, and all but two of the volunteers were in the sheriff's boat as it backed away from shore. The sound of a honking horn drew his attention, and he saw another truck and boat waiting for the sheriff's rig to get out of the way.

Brad climbed into the sheriff's patrol car and towed the trailer back to the parking lot, then stopped next to his uncle. "I'll stay here and direct traffic, but the sheriff needs to know how you plan on towing the docks with no ropes."

"It slipped my mind, I guess. After you park, grab the rolls of polyethylene rope from the sales rack and load it into Jack's boat before he backs down."

"I'll take care of it. The tides going out fast, Jerry. You had better get going before your boat gets grounded on shore."

"Thanks."

Jerry hurried the rest of the way down the boat launch, where the two volunteers helped him shove his boat back into the water. They all jumped in, then Jerry headed out to the far end of the docks to check on the progress of removing the rings. He tied off and waited for everyone to climb out, and then he walked back along the fifty-foot long sections of mooring slips. He noticed each of the dock rings still had one bolt holding it in place, and turned when he heard someone running in his direction.

Aaron staggered to a stop in front of his uncle. "This first row is ready to be towed, and the second row will be ready by the time you get back."

He noticed Jerry looking down at one of the rings. "We had to leave one bolt in place to keep them from drifting out with the tide. Once the tow rope is attached, I'll remove the last bolt and jump off."

Jerry grinned at his nephew. "I should have thought of that. That's the third thing I've forgotten to do so far today. I guess I'm not as sharp as I used to be."

"You've got too much on your mind, but don't worry. Between the two of us, we'll have everything covered."

"Thanks, Aaron."

Jerry nodded to the driver of a boat coming alongside the dock. "I appreciate the help, Jack."

Jack held up the end of a yellow rope. "What do you need me to do?"

Aaron smiled and held up his ratchet and socket. "I've got this, Jerry. I know your volunteers could use a little pat on the back, if you know what I mean."

"Right. Okay, I'll go see how they're holding up."

Aaron waved Jack to the end of the docks. "This section goes first, Mister Murphy. I'll meet you there."

Jerry hurried along the first row of mooring slips to the main dock and noticed another boat and trailer rolling down the launch ramp. He cringed when the wheels slid off the end of the concrete into the mud, bottoming out the trailer.

Brad and the owner, Eric walked along the tongue and shoved the boat the rest of the way into the water. When Eric jumped into his boat, Brad climbed into the truck to drive it back up to the parking lot, but the two-wheeled-drive vehicle couldn't get enough traction to drag the trailer wheels back up onto the concrete, and smoke bellowed from under the tire for a few moments, and stopped when Brad shut off the engine. He climbed out and slammed the door closed, then noticed his uncle standing on the main dock. "That's the last boat we can get in the water, Jerry. The tide is just too low."

"All right, four boats it is. Could you check on the shop owners for me?"

When Brad waved and hurried up the boat launch, Jerry headed down the next long row of mooring slips, stopping and touching each volunteer on the shoulder, while thanking them for their help. He approached Denise, who was kneeling down in front of the ring plate. "How are you holding up?"

She flipped the hair out of her eyes when she looked up, then wiped the sweat from her brow with the back of her hand. "My arms are getting tired and I'm wearing holes in my new jeans, but other than that, I'm okay, Mister Avery."

"You're doing a great job, and I really appreciate it."

"Have you seen Aaron?"

"Yes, he is coordinating with your dad for towing everything out to the buoys. I'd better get back to my boat and help."

Jerry hurried back to the end of the first row of docks and saw Rick and Jack returning from towing the first two sections out to the buoys. He climbed into his boat and brought it around to the next dock, where Aaron was waiting for him.

Aaron tossed the end of the rope to his uncle. "So far, no problems, but the rest of the sections will be sitting in the mud in a few more minutes."

Jerry tied the rope to a cleat near the transom, eased the throttle forward until the slack in the rope was gone, then dragged the unit across the water. He was nearly to an empty buoy when he lost speed, and when he looked over the side, he could see the bottom of the harbor, and realized the dock was dragging along the mud. He shut the motor off and raised it out of the muck, and waited while his boat quickly listed to one side.

When he turned back toward the rest of the docks, Rick's boat lay at an angle on the mud, as were the other two boats, and the volunteers on the remaining docks had stopped working and were staring across the water at him. He crawled over the side of his boat onto the gray mud and brown seaweed, and sloshed through the puddles back to the end of the next row of mooring slips, the tops of which were two feet above the mud.

Rick reached down and helped Jerry up onto the dock. "What's our next move?"

Jerry heard a multitude of footsteps and looked past Aaron at the volunteers gathering behind him. He turned and looked at the waterless entrance into the harbor, and knew they had little time before it rushed back in and turned back to Aaron. "How are we doing with the rings?"

"We've managed to get about three-quarters of them ready to go."

"All right. Let's rope them together in longer sections. They might be harder to tow, but it's the only way to get all of them out to the buoys before they rise over the pilings." He looked at the people standing behind his nephew. "I really appreciate your help, and I hate to say this, because I know how tired you all are, but it's all or nothing, and we don't have a lot of time to make this work."

Denise held up her wrench. "I've had enough of a break. I'm in."

When the rest of the people followed Aaron back to the other docks, Jerry's chest swelled with pride as he turned to Jack. "How many rolls of rope did Brad give you?"

"Only two. He said the other ropes were too small for towing."

"All right. Let's get the rope from your boat and cut it into pieces long enough to lash each of these units together."

Rick saw Jerry was ready to jump down onto the mud, so he grabbed his arm and eased him away from the edge. "Jack and I can handle it."

Jerry stepped back as Rick jumped down and followed Jack to his boat, and when they returned, he reached down and helped them up. "We'll start at the far end and work our way back, so hold the spool for me."

When they were ready, Jerry grabbed the end of the rope and dragged it down the row of docks. When he stopped, he knelt down and started tying the first two docks together. When Rick arrived, he cut the rope and handed the end to him, then continued with his knots.

**

Curtis stopped loading boxes from the shop into the back of a van and stared out across the empty harbor. When he saw Jerry kneeling down on the docks, he rubbed his sore jaw. He had ignored Jerry's warning yesterday, and three people had died, so he wasn't about to ignore him again and hurried back into the shop. "We're out of time, Mrs. Berry. Leave the baked goods and get to higher ground."

"But that's all on consignment."

"At least you'll still be here when it's over, so lock your door and get out of here right now. I mean it."

"Oh, all right, Tommy. It's hard to leave, because this is my only income. I just hope my shop is still here when this is over."

So do I, Curtis thought, while he waited for her to lock the door. When she drove away, he went into the next shop to see if he could lend a hand.

Chapter 29

OREGON COAST:

Brad parked his patrol car on the bluff overlooking the marina so he could watch the tide and warn Jerry when it started coming in. More importantly. How fast. He climbed out and stared at the receding tide, exposing the underwater terrain of his small section of the Oregon coast. He stared out at the caramel colored kelp draped over jagged mounds of brown basalt rock and gray mud, before dropping over an edge far from shore. He heard his name and grabbed the portable radio from his belt. "I'm here, Sheriff."

"How does it look?"

"The water is about a mile from shore, and it's still going out. I could never have imagined this is what the coastline looks like beneath the water. I just wish it were under better circumstances, so I could enjoy the view. Hold on a second and I'll send you a picture."

"Not now, Brad. Save it for later. How low is the water from normal slack tide?"

Brad tried to determine a distance down to the water, but from his vantage point, it was hard to tell where the regular tide line would have been. "I can't be sure from here, but I'd guess at least eighty-feet."

"All right. Call as soon as the tide starts coming in."

"I will, Sheriff."

Brad pulled his phone from his pocket, aimed the camera out over the Pacific Ocean, and recorded a panoramic view. When he finished, he leaned back against the front of his car, hoping Jerry's idea works.

***

HUMPBACK HARBOR:

When all the docks were ready to go, Jerry gave grateful handshakes to everyone who had helped. "Again, I can't thank you enough, but all of you should head back to higher ground before the tide comes in. I guess I'm paying for a lot of pizzas when this is over, so I'll see you then."

Jerry turned and headed down the second set of docks to join up with Rick, Jack, and Eric, then looked at the sheriff. "Any word from Brad?"

"He's in position and says the water level is down by about eighty feet from slack tide."

"All right. That means it will come in fast. I'd better get to my boat before it's too late."

Jerry sat down on the edge of the dock, dropped over the edge onto the muck, then headed out across the small puddles and seaweed to his boat. He climbed in over the side, and then stared back over the stern at his towrope, which was ready to go. He knew his section of docks would float off the bottom first, and he had to finish his task before the other boats could get past him.

He looked toward the rest of the mooring slips, and his friends were all waiting in their boats as well. Each of them had a towline attached to drag the second and third rows of docks out to a buoy. He noticed Rick talking on the radio, and when he waved at him, Jerry turned around and stood behind the steering wheel, ready to lower the outdrive and start his engine.

A moment later, a three-foot high wall of churning brown water raced up the channel into the harbor, then he felt the boat surge up off the mud. He lowered the outdrive and started the engine, then looked back at his section of docks. They were floating, so he shoved the throttle forward and slowly gained speed against the incoming water.

With two massive outboard motors on the back of his boat, Rick had no problem towing his sections of docks from between the rows of pilings. He was able to keep them in place against the surging tide until Jerry could get out of the way, but when he looked back, it was apparent Jack's boat was struggling to keep his section from being dragged toward the steep sides of the harbor, and Eric's boat was also having difficulty dragging his section from between the pilings. "Eric! Just leave yours there for now and help Jack!"

Jerry pulled up beside an empty buoy and set the throttle to maintain a strain on the rope, and then he snagged the orange rubber ball with his boathook. He tied the loose end of the towrope to the steel ring and released the slipknot on the boat cleat, then nearly lost his balance when his boat surged forward. He managed to grab the steering wheel and then swung the boat around toward the remaining docks.

Rick waved Jerry over and waited while he pulled up alongside him. "You'll never be able to tow the last section by yourself, so be ready, and I'll help you as soon as I can."

Jerry waved he understood. Now the final set of docks would be his responsibility, and with a little luck, he would make it before they rose over the pilings. He drove back toward the end of the last row, passing Jack and Eric towing the third section out into the harbor. Even with two boats, he could see they were struggling to drag the docks against the powerful surge.

When he reached the end of the last section, he noticed Aaron and Denise were still at the far end, working on the last ring. He tied his boat off, then jumped out onto the dock and ran along the sections of mooring slips until he was standing beside them. "You shouldn't be here. What's the problem?"

Aaron jumped up. "It's this last ring, but the bolt head has been stripped and we can't get it out."

"Both of you head back to my boat. Denise, you stay there while Aaron brings me back a set of vice grips." When they just stared at him, Jerry lost his temper. "Just do what I say, damn it! Hurry!"

When Aaron and Denise took off running, Jerry saw the sheriff's boat on its way back, then turned when Aaron came back and stopped. "Give me the pliers and get back to the boat. You and Rick will need to work together to get this section out to a buoy."

"No way! I'll take care of this, Jerry."

"Stop being foolish and get going."

"I'm a lot younger and faster than you, so let me do it."

Jerry grabbed Aaron by the shoulders and stared him in the eyes. "That's right, you are much younger, and you have your whole life ahead of you. Now stop arguing and get the hell out of here." Aaron didn't move. "Now!"

Aaron flinched. Jerry had never yelled at him this way before. When he saw the rage and panic in his uncle's eyes, he turned and ran back down the docks to Jerry's boat.

Jerry knelt down next to the stripped bolt head and adjusted the pliers. Once it was tight, he pulled on the handle, but the jaws of the pliers tore away more of the metal as they slipped off the bolt head. "Damn!"

Jerry looked up when he heard a boat horn and saw Aaron and Rick were ready to drag the section out into the harbor. He stood and waved for them to pull, and then he grabbed his pocketknife, knelt back down, and sliced through the ropes connecting his float to the others.

Aaron felt the boat moving and looked back over his shoulder, where Jerry was on his single float, and then his grip tightened on the steering wheel. "Damn you, Jerry!"

Jerry heard Aaron holler his name, but ignored him and continued working on the last bolt. When the wrench slipped off the bolt head again, he reset the tension and had to use both hands to squeeze it closed. When he pulled, the wrench snapped off the head and his hand slid over the ragged steel rod, tearing the skin off his knuckles. "Damn!"

He stood and cradled his injured fingers against his chest with his other hand and saw the top of the piling was only three feet above the ring. He spun around and saw all four boats were having difficulty towing against the rushing water, but at least they were away from the shops. He felt the dock moving up the piling, and when he realized his battle was lost, he sat down. In a few moments, his dock would float over the piling and be shoved toward the shops by the surging tide, and he couldn't stop it.

He suddenly had an idea and reached over to grab the short section of rope he had cut loose a few minutes ago. He tied one end to the ring, made a slip-loop on the other end, and waited in tense anticipation, while inch-by-inch, the ring slid toward the top of the piling.

When it slid over the cap, he tossed the loop in the rope over the piling and cinched it tight before the dock drifted too far away, and felt a shudder through his knees when the rope snapped taut. The strain was too much, and the line frayed until it snapped and slapped against his face, knocking him back onto the concrete surface. He lay in numbed shock, trying to breathe while looking up at the spinning sky, not realizing the rope was tight across his chest.

***

Aaron heard a loud snap and looked back over his shoulder, then saw Jerry topple backward onto the dock. He appeared unconscious as the float raced toward the row of shops, and then he stared in stunned disbelief as the dock slammed into the gazebo, shattering the wooden structure into a hundred pieces.

When he lost sight of his uncle, Aaron slammed his fist against the steering wheel and concentrated on keeping his emotions in check, but he couldn't stop the tears from rolling down from the corners of his eyes. A few moments later, his boat made significant headway as the tide became slack, and he and Rick quickly attached their set of docks to the mooring buoys.

Rick turned and smiled at Aaron, but the young man gave him a grim expression and turned his boat back toward the shoreline. It was only then Rick realized there was no sign of Jerry or his floating dock. When he stared at the row of shops, they were all still standing, but the gazebo appeared to be a tangled pile of broken boards, with the dock protruding beneath them.

Chapter 30

GROOM LAKE, NEVADA:

When the special jet entered the hangar, David waited while the engines shut down and the side door opened. When he saw Okawna coming down the steps, he went over to greet him. "Hey, Okawna. I heard about your family, and I'm really sorry."

Okawna thought of David as a little brother. "I know."

David held his hand out to Alex. "I'm sorry for your loss."

"Thanks, David."

Jadin gave Alex a hug and stepped back. "I'm so sorry." She turned to Okawna. "I know it must have been hard, and you made the right decision, but I am truly sorry for your loss, Okawna."

"Thanks. I'm glad you finally dropped the mister part."

She indicated the exit. "Doctor Heinz is going to meet us at the elevator down to the vault." She noticed the wooden crate Alex had removed from the lower luggage compartment of the plane. "Is that the gravity machine?"

Okawna answered for him. "Yes, the bane of my existence. I'll be glad when it's locked up."

"Can I see it?"

Okawna's eyes went wide. "No way. Don't you dare open it, Alex! We are not letting that thing out of its cage. I'll draw you a picture later."

David indicated across the hangar bay. "I have a golf cart waiting outside. Follow me."

Alex grabbed the handle on the crate and headed across the hangar. He grinned when Okawna moved to where Jadin and David were between himself and the device.

Rubin came down the stairs from the jet. "Take your time, everyone. I'm going to get some dinner for Mack and me. We'll be waiting in the plane when you're ready to head home."

Jadin turned to Rubin. "I don't need a ride. I want to stay here so I can continue to study this incredible ship. Do you realize we now have a viable means of exploring the galaxy?"

Alex snapped his head around and saw Rubin give Jadin a questioning stare, so interrupted. "Yes, that's what the engineers are saying about the new Z-29 rocket ship, but I wouldn't get too excited just yet. You and Mack take your time and enjoy your dinner. It will be awhile before we're ready to go."

Alex turned and gently grabbed Jadin's elbow, guiding her to the golf cart. "Come along, Jadin, we'd better not keep the Doc waiting."

Jadin quickened her pace to keep up with Alex. "What's going on?"

"I'll tell you once we're outside."

They left the building, and after setting the crate in the back of the golf cart, Alex allowed Jadin into the back seat and sat beside her behind Okawna, but didn't speak until the hangar was shrinking in the distance behind him. "Jadin, there are a few things you need to understand while you're here. Rubin and Mack don't have a high enough security clearance for that kind of information. Knowledge about the spaceship is classified as higher than top secret, so you can't tell anyone about it or the gravity machine until you clear it with Director Donner."

"I'm sorry, I didn't know. I'll be more careful from now on. I promise. But I wasn't lying when I said I wanted to stay on and study the ship. It would help if you could put in a good word for me with Director Donner. I know if anyone could help me get a transfer, it would be you, Alex. In fact, how is this base listed as a government facility? Area 51?"

Alex smiled. "Groom Lake, Nevada works better. I'll see what I can do."

"Thanks, Alex. I can hardly believe the way my life has changed since I met you and my new friends."

When David stopped the golf cart in front of the main building, everyone climbed out. Alex went around to the back and grabbed the crate, then followed his friends into the building.

They went to the end of the hallway, where Henry was waiting by the elevator, and indicated for Alex to set the small crate on the cart. "What an incredible piece of technology. Perhaps one day we will know enough about how it operates to study it more closely."

Okawna stared at the crate. "No way. You had better put it under lock and key, and then throw the key as far away as possible. I say good riddance."

Henry reached out and clasped Okawna's hand in both of his own. "I am so sorry for the death of your loved ones, my friend, and my heart shares your sorrow."

"Thanks, Doc. That means a lot to me."

Henry did the same with Alex's hand. "You were so happy, and I am truly sorry for your loss."

"I appreciate it, Doc."

Alex did not have the heart to tell Henry or the others it was his decision that got Fala and Halona killed. Okawna had no choice but to watch it happen.

Henry noticed the weary expression on Alex and Okawna and spoke to the group. "All of you deserve some time on your own to relax and be with your families. I will take it from here."

When Henry pushed the cart into the elevator, Alex stopped him. "Sorry, Doc, but if it's all right with you, I'd feel much better if I could make certain this thing was locked up and secure where Sloan could never get to it."

Okawna nodded vigorously. "Me too. I know I've said it a hundred times, but I really hate that thing. I, for one, would sleep better knowing Sloan or anyone else couldn't get to it."

Henry saw the anxiety in Okawna's eyes. "But of course."

When the elevator doors opened, Henry, Alex, and Okawna stepped inside with the wooden crate, and Henry noticed Jadin and David hung back. "You are not coming with us?"

David shook his head no. "I'm going to start on the log entries again."

"And I haven't checked my phone in a while. I need to find out how my team at JPL is doing, and the same for my family in Oregon."

The elevator doors closed, and the men began their descent, so Jadin and David strolled back along the hallway and out through the front doors. Jadin looked down at her phone and saw a missed call, a voicemail from Patrick, and a message from Aaron, which she opened immediately as she stopped. It read; Marina ok, but Jerry is in bad shape in the hospital in North Bend. Hurry home.

She tried calling him back, but he didn't answer. As she turned to run back inside, she bumped into David.

"Whoa! What's wrong?"

"It's my Uncle Jerry. There's been a terrible accident."

When Jadin rushed past him into the building, David hurried behind her. They stopped at the elevator, and he noticed she was chewing on her lower lip while they waited for the cab to return.

The elevator doors opened, and Alex noticed Jadin's tears. "What happened?"

"It's my uncle Jerry. He's been in an accident."

"Come on. We'll get you home as quick as we can."

Alex found Rubin, who got him, Okawna, and Jadin up in the air, but David stayed behind. He wanted to be with Henry, to continue examining the log entries.

***

AIRPORT. NORTH BEND, OREGON:

They landed in Oregon first, so Jadin could be with her family. They knew she was anxious to get to the hospital, so the boys followed her off the plane to say goodbye.

Jadin hugged Alex. "Thanks for everything."

Okawna stood by, wondering whether Jadin would hug him as well. He knew he had not acted very mature in most of his encounters with her, and he would not blame her for being reluctant.

Jadin reached out to shake Okawna's hand. "Goodbye, Okawna."

"I apologize for flirting with you so heavily. It was only in fun."

"Don't worry about it. Actually, I kind of enjoyed it a little."

Okawna's mouth opened. "You mean I actually had a chance?"

"Oh no. You never had a chance, but the attention was nice."

She leaned in and gave him a quick hug. "There. Do you feel better now?"

"Yes, thank you."

After leaving Jadin in Oregon, Rubin dropped Alex off in Montana before taking Okawna to Alaska. Before they went their separate ways, Alex and Okawna agreed to spend the next couple of days devising a plan to take out Sloan.

Chapter 31

NORTH BEND, OREGON:

At the car-rental desk in the airport terminal, Jadin lightly tapped her fingers on the counter while waiting for the man to print out the contract for her to sign. She made an unrecognizable signature on the paper, snatched the key off the counter, and then headed for the door. The drive from the airport seemed to take forever, even though it was ten-minutes from the city, and she felt a sense of relief when she saw the large 'H' on the blue sign pointing down another road. When she pulled into the parking lot at the hospital, the front tires bounced against the bull rail before she shut off the engine and leapt out.

***

When a woman burst through the front door, the young man behind the reception counter flinched. "Can I help you?"

Jadin glanced at his name tag. "Yes, Simon. I'm looking for Jerry Avery."

"Yes, the older gentleman from Humpback Harbor. Go left at the end of the hallway, and it's the third door on the right, room eighteen."

"Thanks."

She ran down the hallway to a room to a large window with open shades and saw Aaron and Denise sitting inside. She had never seen her uncle seriously injured, and thought how helpless he appeared in a hospital bed. When she realized there were no clear plastic hoses attached to his body, she sighed with relief and eased the door open, and then quietly entered the room. "How's he doing?"

Aaron stood to hug his sister. "I'm glad you made it. He has a bunch of bruises and two fractured ribs, but the doctor said he'll be okay. Jerry is one tough old man."

"How did this happen?"

Aaron indicated for Jadin to sit down next to Denise, and then he leaned back against the bed and explained everything. "Jerry saved the entire marina, except for the gazebo. A foot of water managed to flood some shops, but there was no major damage, thanks to Jerry."

Jadin's chest swelled with pride when she looked over at her uncle, who was snoring softly. "Did they say when he could be released?"

"They want to keep him under observation overnight, and they'll call me tomorrow when he's ready to be picked up."

"That's great. There is something you need to know. The moon will not get any closer, but it's going to take some time before the tides stabilize. From what you've told me, there will be too much drag on a string of docks attached to just one buoy, and it won't hold. Before the next tide, you need to separate them into shorter sections and spread them out among all the buoys."

"I'll get Brad and the sheriff to help me take care of it."

Denise smiled at Jadin. "You should have seen Aaron while all that was going on. He was amazing. He did a great job of keeping us organized when Mister Avery wasn't around. He deserves as much of the credit as his uncle for saving the shops."

Jadin smiled up at her brother. "I'll stay with him for the rest of the night. Why don't you two go home?"

Aaron grabbed his jacket off the door hook. "That works for me. I still have enough daylight to get started on the docks."

Denise turned to Aaron. "I'll help." She weaved her fingers through his, holding his hand. , and smiled when she saw a huge grin spread across his face.

Jadin knew Aaron had always had a crush on Denise, and the corners of her lips formed a small smile. "Be careful."

When the door closed, Jadin stood and moved to the edge of the bed to look down at her uncle. "You did great, Jerry." She took his hand in hers, and then gently rubbed the back of it with her thumbs. When his eyes slowly opened, she smiled and stopped. "It's good to see you in one piece."

Jerry recognized the face smiling down at him. "I thought you left for Pasadena."

"Yeah, well, I heard you tried to be a hero and save the docks, so here I am. Aaron told me what happened. I can't believe you tried something so crazy."

Jerry struggled to sit up, but grimaced and lay back down. "What do you mean, tried? From what Aaron told me, it worked out just as I hoped it would."

"Oh, right, except for the part about you riding a dock into the gazebo."

Jerry grinned. "All right, so maybe that wasn't what I had in mind, but the rest of the marina was saved, and that's all that matters. Hey, I hope you haven't eaten yet, because I wound up sleeping through dinner and I'm starving. Denise told me they were serving roast beef for supper in the cafeteria, and my mouth is already watering just talking about it. How about being a good niece and get me a wheelchair?"

"I don't think so. You stay in bed and I'll bring you a tray with enough food for both of us, okay? I'll be back in a few minutes."

Jadin hurried along the hallway and entered the cafeteria, and was about to grab a tray when her phone rang. When she brought it out to answer, she noticed everyone giving her a look of annoyance, and the woman at the cash register indicating the sign above the entrance into the dining room, which stated phones must be turned off while inside the hospital. She quickly left the room and headed out of the building through a side exit, and when she brought her phone out, recognized Patrick's picture and answered. "I'm here. What's going on?"

"I have the information you wanted about the asteroid. The composition of that thing is incredible."

"Great. I could use some good news. Send me an email with the data."

"It's on the way. When are you coming back to the lab?"

"I'm not sure. I may not be coming back to stay."

"Are you kidding me? The moon is still a major problem, especially if it changes again. We need you back here, Jadin."

"Well, maybe it won't happen again. Listen, I may be transferred to another project, but don't worry. If I don't make it back, I'm going to recommend you to become the team leader. I think you would be the right person to take over." The line was silent. "Patrick?"

"Are you sure I should take over? I mean, with everything that's going on right now, I'm not sure I'm the right man for the job. I mean, we're in completely uncharted territory here, Jadin."

Jadin saw the email had arrived to her in-box. "You'll do fine, Patrick. I have confidence in you. This is a new learning experience for all of us, so think of it as an adventure."

"I suppose you're right."

"I may be out of cell phone reception for a while, so I'll check in with you when I can."

"Thanks."

Jadin sat down on a bench to study the information from Patrick. When she read the analysis of the asteroid's composition, her jaw sagged.

Chapter 32

ALASKA. SENTINEL ASTEROID TRACKING STATION:

Since his discovery, Keven had spent most of his time at his desk in the monitoring station. The footage he had sent to friends on the Internet began getting hits and comments from people all over the world he didn't even know. Many of them asked him to name it the Sterling Asteroid after himself, but he refused. Instead, he named it Gold 101, because of its color. He looked up when a woman wearing an Air Force Officer uniform walked in. She appeared to be in her late forties and smiled as she strolled over to greet him.

Larson reached out to shake hands. "Hello, Mister Sterling. I'm Captain Sheri Larson."

Keven accepted. "Is this an official visit?"

"Yes, and no. You're creating quite a stir on social media."

"So I've noticed. It's the most fun I've had in years. I've got more followers now than ever before."

"Please tell me more about this Sentinel satellite, and how it managed to discover this unusual asteroid."

Keven brought up the streaming video feed from Sentinel on the monitor. "Sentinel is orbiting around our sun, always keeping its telescope pointed out across the universe. That way, it can sense the temperature difference between warm asteroids heated by the sun against a cold background of space. Sentinel determines the speed and trajectory of any large object and, as luck would have it, its telescope was pointed at our sector of space when it detected an unusual object. When Sentinel determined it was shooting across our small piece of the universe, it let me know about it."

"Will it keep watching the asteroid or is it programmed to move on to another sector?"

"Last night, I gave the command to stay on this quadrant, which will take a few months to search. That way, we can continue following this asteroid's trajectory." His phone rang, and he recognized the number of his friend at JPL and then looked at Larson. "Excuse me a minute. Hey, Jadin. What's going on?"

"I'm sorry I took so long to get back to you with the information on your jewel. I just received a call from my team in Pasadena and sent you the digital composition of the asteroid. It's solid gold, so it has tremendous mass."

A knot formed in Keven's stomach as he entered the information into the computer, and when the updated trajectory appeared on the monitor, his jaw dropped. "Good grief! We're in deep trouble, Jadin. I have an Air Force representative with me right now, and I think both of you should hear what I have to say."

"Is it Captain Larson?"

"That's right, do you know her?"

"Yes, put me on video conference."

Larson sat down and looked at the image on the screen. "Hello, Jadin. From Mister Sterling's expression, something has changed."

"That's correct. How bad is it, Keven?"

"Sentinel's early estimated trajectory was wrong, because we didn't know the asteroid's exact composition. I hate to say this, but the damned gold rock is going to change direction when it passes by Jupiter."

"Do you know if it will come close to us?"

Keven gave Jadin and Larson a grim expression. "I'm afraid so. The gravitational attraction of both objects will alter its course enough to sling it on a new trajectory. Even though it won't hit us straight on, it's traveling at 800,000 miles-per-hour and it will clip the edge of the Earth with enough force to send shock waves through the planet. Entire continents will be ripped apart, and thousands of volcanic eruptions will cover the surface in lava and ash."

No one spoke until Larson broke the silence. "How much time do we have?"

"Six days."

"Do you know where it will hit?"

"Central Europe, but it doesn't matter. When it ricochets off the side of the planet like a pool ball, nothing will survive."

Sheri stood and grabbed her purse off the desk. "I need you to stop posting video clips on the Internet. As of right now, this has become classified at the absolute highest level. Excuse me while I call this in. I'll be right back."

When Larson turned and hurried out through the door, Keven stared at Jadin's image on the monitor. "Who does she work for?"

"It changes, but at the moment, she's working for the Director of National Security."

"I guess that means she has some clout, for whatever good it will do us."

"Well, I have a little clout myself, so let's see what develops."

"It doesn't matter how much clout you have, it just isn't possible to stop an asteroid with that much mass."

Sheri walked in and sat down. "I know Sentinel is privately funded, but I hope you understand if word of this gets out, there would be mass hysteria."

"Oh, I understand completely. So what's the plan?"

"I'm heading back to Washington D.C. If you wouldn't mind, I'll establish a secure link to your information from Sentinel. That way, I can keep an eye on things from there."

Keven gave her an affirmative nod. "Under the circumstances, do whatever you need to do."

Sheri looked at Jadin. "That means both of you are now under a government gag order, so you're prohibited from discussing this with anyone but me."

Keven crossed his arms and leaned back in his chair. "Now, just hold on a minute. I don't own this facility, I only work here. My bosses are going to want to know about this new development."

"I need your full cooperation, Mister Sterling." She could tell Sterling didn't like being told what to do, so changed tactics. "I'm sorry. It's just that history has taught us a valuable lesson about what happens when civilizations are threatened. People can become ugly when it comes to self-preservation. Do you remember a few years back when people went insane at the mere thought of our planet losing all its oil?"

"Yes, that was not pleasant at all. All right. Don't worry, I'll keep it a secret as long as I can, Captain."

Larson stood and shook Sterling's hand. "Thank you." She turned to the monitor. "Also, I have just been informed your transfer has been approved, Jadin. So, good luck to you."

When Larson left the building, Keven stared at Jadin. "What transfer?"

"I'm sorry, but I can't tell you just yet."

"All right. Good luck, my friend."

"Thanks, Keven."

He ended the call and stared at the picture of the strange asteroid. When he saw a flash of gold, he entered a command to have Sentinel determine the speed of the rotation. "Were did you come from, beautiful?"

Chapter 33

GROOM LAKE:

When Henry stepped into the spacecraft control room, David looked away from the ship's holographic monitor and stood. "Hey, Doc. Now that the information from the ship's computer is in English, I just can't stop reading these reports about the crew's missions."

"Does it say anything about how to stop an asteroid?"

"Not yet. Why do you ask?"

"I just finished talking to Director Donner and our moon situation is the least of our worries now. An unusually heavy asteroid made of gold is about to collide with our planet."

David waited for the Doc to show some sign he was joking, but it never came, so he slowly sat back down. "Oh, shit."

Henry indicated the control console. "Perhaps there is some information in the computer."

David entered the search criteria. "Right. Here is the information I was studying about this ship's artificial gravity system. I'll cross reference it with the crew's logs."

"Very well. Let me know if you discover anything important."

When Henry started to leave, David held up his finger. "Hold on a second, Doc. I just found something. They experimented with using the gravitational attraction of a sun or planet to gain speed in space when traveling at sub-light speeds, but discarded the project when they discovered the artificial gravity field around this ship was omnidirectional"

"The accomplishments of that ancient civilization are amazing. I wish I could have met them."

"Hey, listen to this, Doc. According to the log, even with all their unique technology, they could not stop an asteroid from hitting one of the Earth-like planets they had colonized millions of years ago. It says here the gold asteroid hit with enough force to shatter tectonic plates before it bounced back into space. It destroyed the entire planet."

Henry's shoulders sagged. "Well, I guess that seals our fate. If it could not work for them, and they knew how to use the technology, then how are we expected to do it? I shall go inform the Director that there is nothing we can do to stop our eventual demise."

"Maybe not. I just found an entry about the crew's next mission. They built the gravity device to change the trajectory of an asteroid."

Henry smiled and clasped his hands under his chin. "David, do you think this ship is still capable of space travel?"

"I can't say for sure, and there's only one way to find out."

"In that case, I propose we test the space capability of this craft."

"Don't get too excited just yet, Doc. According to the rest of the entry, it was only a theory. They never tested it."

"Then let us test the theory ourselves."

"But what if it doesn't work?"

Henry shrugged his shoulders. "At this point, I do not think we have a choice."

David stared at Henry for a moment. "All right. Tell Mister Donner I'll need my crew back if we're going to pull this off."

"I will call him right away."

***

MONTANA:

During the drive home from the airport, Alex dreaded having to return home, knowing everywhere he looked, he would see Fala and Halona. He just couldn't believe they were both dead. When he pulled into his driveway, he realized something wasn't right when Barney wasn't there to greet him as he normally does. Sloan must've kidnapped Fala and Halona here at the house, which would explain Barney's odd disappearance. Barney would not have allowed a stranger up into the yard, especially if they had intentions of harming his family. *Damnit! Sloan must've killed Barney as well.*

He looked in every direction, expecting to see his dog lying in a pool of blood with his tongue hanging limply from his mouth, but he found nothing. For a moment, he thought perhaps they had dragged Barney's body into the barn, but there was no sign he had been taken anywhere. His head snapped around when he heard a familiar bark from far off in the woods. "Barney!"

Another deep bark was much closer, and then his next best friend loped up the hill to greet him. He could not stop smiling as he knelt down and held his arms out wide. "Come here, boy." A moment later, Barney ran up and enthusiastically licked his face. Alex hugged him and ran his hand through his thick fur. When he felt something tangled in the hair, he worked it loose and stared at a small tranquilizer dart. "So Sloan didn't plan to kill you after all."

He suddenly stopped smiling when he thought about Fala and Halona and then stood. It felt good to be home again, except for the deep ache he experienced as he looked at his empty house. He grabbed his suitcase from the back seat and climbed the few steps to the porch, with Barney at his side. His phone rang before he made it to the door, and he recognized Donner's number. "I just got home, Martin. What's going on?"

"You're not going to believe this, but an asteroid is headed straight for us. The impact will be a global killer. Nothing will survive."

Alex closed his eyes and sighed. "I see. I can't seem to get a break. How long before it hits us?"

"We have six days."

"Talk about cutting it close. What can I do to help?"

"David has requested all of you return to Groom Lake. He and Doc might have a plan. After all you've been through already, I hate throwing this new development in your lap, but I'm sure you will think of something. You always do."

"Thanks, Martin. I hope David and Doc's plan will work. I'll call Okawna and fill him in. Hopefully, he hasn't boarded the *Mystic* yet."

"Can you also call Jadin? David has requested her presence as well."

"Sure thing, Martin."

"Great. I'll have Rubin and Mack return and pick all of you up. Good luck, Alex."

Alex selected the contact, but it rang nine times before Okawna finally picked up. "Hey. Where are you?"

"Please tell me I am not about to regret having answered the phone, Alex, because it seems like every time you call, something bad is about to happen,"

"I just got a call from Donner about an asteroid heading our way."

"No shit?"

"We have six days to move it off course before we are all killed."

"So what do we do?"

"David has requested we all return to the ship. Apparently, he and Doc have a plan. Let's hope it's a good one."

"Okay. I'm still in Seattle. Maybe there's a reason my flight to Alaska was already delayed."

"Do you mean like an Oman?"

"You know I don't believe in that voodoo crap. I take it Ruben is on his way to get everyone, so I'll be here waiting."

"Thanks. See you soon."

***

OREGON:

Jadin balanced the tray of food on one hand as she opened the door and entered Jerry's room. "I didn't know what vegetables you prefer, so I brought you a little of everything."

Jerry sniffed the air and smiled. "Everything goes well with roast beef, except Brussels sprouts. In my opinion, they don't go well with anything."

Jadin set the tray on the adjustable table and rolled it to the side of the bed. "The beef cuts with a butter knife and it's fantastic."

Jadin turned when she heard a knock on the door and saw a Highway Patrol Officer looking into the room. "Can I help you?"

"Are you Jadin Avery?"

"Yes. What's this about, Officer?"

"Sheriff Slade asked us to deliver a message to you. You need to call someone named Alex Cave. He said it's urgent and he cannot get a hold of you."

She pulled the phone from her pocket. "I forgot I had put it on mute. Thank you, officer. I'll take care of it." When the officer gave her a nod and walked away, she turned to face Jerry. "I'll be back in a moment."

When Jadin left the room, Jerry stopped eating and stared after her. With everything happening with the moon, he knew she still needed to be doing her job, and he didn't want to make her feel guilty about having to leave so soon. He continued eating while he waited for her to return, and when she walked in, he saw the anguish in her eyes and eased the table out of the way. "Shouldn't you be working on the moon problem right now? I'm glad you came, Jadin, but I'll be fine. Nothing a good night's rest and some aspirin can't fix. Now give me a hug and get back to work."

Jadin had no idea if she and her friends could stop the asteroid, and if they failed, it would mean the death of everyone on the planet. How could she tell her uncle everything he had accomplished and fought to save was all for nothing? She held his hand. "It's not the moon. It has finally stopped moving closer to the Earth, but something else has come up, and I may not see you for a while."

He noticed Jadin appeared to be unusually anxious about this new problem. "Are you all right?"

Jadin nodded she was, but her lips trembled with sadness as she bent down and kissed him on the cheek. "I hope to see you soon, Jerry."

"Do what you got to do and I'll be waiting for you. Now get going."

Jadin stood and turned away before Jerry could see the tears welling up in her eyes, then waved as she left the room. She wiped them from her cheeks as she hurried along the hallway to the exit. When she reached the front desk, Simon was still sitting behind the counter. "Do you have any tissues back there?"

Simon stood and reached under the counter. "Are you okay, Ma'am?"

Jadin grabbed the box and shook her head no before hurrying out to her car. She took a moment to rein in her emotions, then climbed in and started the engine. Donner's jet would land in fifteen minutes, and she still needed to return the rental car before boarding the plane, so she tossed the box of tissue onto the passenger seat and headed for the airport.

Chapter 34

GROOM LAKE:

When Alex, Okawna, and Jadin arrived at the base, Henry was waiting for them in a golf cart outside the air terminal. "I am so glad you have returned, my friends."

Okawna climbed into the back seat with Alex and recognized the wooden crate in the rear compartment. "What the hell is that thing doing here, Doc?"

"We think it may help with our dire circumstances."

Henry parked outside Hangar 5 and the trio climbed out. Alex grabbed the crate and grinned at Okawna's reaction when moved past him into the hangar. The airlock doors at the bottom spacecraft were open, and he led them inside and up to the control room. When they reached the top of the stairs, David was waiting.

David got up from his chair. "Welcome back. I just wish it was under better circumstances. Now, let's talk about why we brought this device back out into the open."

Okawna folded his arms across his chest and stared at the young man. "That thing scares the hell out of me, so it better be a damn good reason it's here."

"Oh, it is, I assure you. I know why they built the gravity machine." David explained everything he had learned about the device from the log entries. "That machine might solve our problem."

Alex held the crate up. "That's good news. Now that we have it, we can do what they had planned on doing. It was their invention, so it ought to work, right?"

David shook his head no. "Even *if* we manage to get it into space, there is no guarantee."

"What do you mean, if we get it into space?"

"This ship is an engineering marvel, but it crashed for a reason, and I think I know why. The gravity machine is a prototype, and just like when I accidentally turned it on while it was in the ground, somehow the device reacted with this ship's antigravity system. The original crew could no longer keep this craft in the air above the planet, and, well, we might have the same problem. Plus, we have no idea if this ship is still capable of space travel."

Jadin turned to Alex. "We should open the crate and inspect the device."

Alex set the crate on the floor, and then realized all the nails had already been removed from the lid, so he pulled up on the cover, and with a little effort, the lid popped open. He set it aside, and looked at Henry. "Who opened it?"

"I do not know. It has not left the vault since we locked it."

Okawna exchanged troubled expression with Alex, and then stepped back and stared at David. "This thing is still off, right?"

David gave him a nod it was, but he too was anxious about how powerful this small object was. "As far as I can tell, it is."

Jadin knelt beside the crate, and then looked up at Alex. "Wow, can I pick it up?"

Okawna took another step back. "I don't think that's such a good idea. What if it comes on again? Remember the tunnel, Alex, and the weird shit that happened there because of this?"

Alex still could not get over how someone who scoffed at danger could be so scared of a little box. "I think it'll be okay, Okawna. Go ahead, Jadin."

Jadin picked it up and studied the different sides, then saw the colored lights under the surface. "That's amazing."

Okawna stepped closer to see it up close. "Yeah, and whatever you do, do not to press the pretty lights."

She looked over at David and smiled. "It's incredible something this small can change the laws of physics. I have got to learn how this works."

Alex looked at the computer monitor in front of David. "Did you find any mention of a key to turn it on?"

"I did. It's a small square-shaped crystal. Jadin, do you see a place where it can be inserted into the device?"

Jadin carefully studied the four sides of the mirrored surface. "Yes, right here. On the opposite side of the control buttons. So all we have to do is find the key and we can use it to change the trajectory of the asteroid, correct?"

"Not exactly. The theory is sound, but it may not even work."

Alex turned to look at David. "What theory?"

"Gravity depends on mass, with the larger mass always winning the tug-of-war. Their theory was to change the mass of the asteroid enough so that this ship could change its trajectory. Once it's on the path they choose, they turn it off and let the asteroid continue on its new course."

Okawna had an idea. "So, all we have to do is dump that thing on the asteroid and turn it on?"

"That's going to be tricky, Okawna. According to the diagram, the gravity device needs to be anchored to the asteroid, and that means if we manage to reach it in time, someone will need to leave the ship to attach the device."

Without hesitation, Okawna raised his hand. "I'll do it. Anything to get that thing out of here and out of our lives. Besides, it sounds like fun. It's not every day I get to do a spacewalk."

Alex wasn't so enthusiastic. "I'll go with you."

Henry realized they still had a problem with the plan. "Getting custom-made spacesuits is difficult. It is going to take time and money, which we have little of either right now."

Alex turned to Jadin. "You're with NASA. Don't they have any suits close to our sizes?"

"Close doesn't work in outer space, Alex. Not when you're trying to work with tools."

Alex thought about it for a moment and then grinned. "We won't be working with tools."

Jadin stared at Alex while he explained what he had in mind. "In that case, I'm sure we have suits that are close enough. Let's find a tape measure, and I'll tell them what we need."

Alex looked out through the side of the ship. "I'm sure we can find a tape measure in the hangar. We only have six days before it hits, so let's get started."

David stood up from behind the control console. "I'm afraid not, Alex. First, we need to test the ship. Second, we don't have the key to activate it. I could turn it off with this ship, but there's no way to turn it on without the key being inserted into the device."

Okawna looked over at the gravity device. "So, we've got to find Sloan, or the whole thing is a bust."

Alex felt his enthusiasm slip away and looked at the others, who appeared to be feeling the same thing. He sat down and stared at the device, knowing the odds of success were getting smaller.

David saw the anguish in Alex's eyes. "I'm sure you hate that Sloan woman."

Alex's hands clenched into fists. "More than you could possibly imagine. When I find her, she'll wish she'd never crossed me."

"She's probably hiding in plain sight. That's what I would do if I were her."

Alex thought about it. "It's a possibility. Okawna and I only made it into Essex's office, but his complex is immense, and Sloan could easily be somewhere in the facility."

Alex sat up to look at Okawna and saw the cold look in his friend's eyes. "Do you feel like breaking into Essex's compound?"

"Anytime."

"I'd better call Donner."

Alex hurried down the stairs and stepped out of the ship, then pulled the phone from his pocket and asked for a secure line directly into Donner's office. A few seconds later, the director answered, and Alex told him about David's discovery in the crew's log entries and their plan of action. He also explained their need to visit Essex at his compound to find Sloan and the key. "That's the only way the plan will work."

"I don't know, Alex. What makes you think Sloan is at his facility?"

"David gave me the idea she might hide in plain sight. Okawna and I recognized two of the men who showed up to take the device from us and they work for Essex, not Sloan."

"I'll get a federal warrant, and the FBI can take the place apart."

"On what grounds? For the moment, we can't charge him with a crime, and I'm not positive Sloan is there with him. I'm only playing a hunch, Martin, and if I'm wrong, it's only Okawna and I who will be charged with breaking and entering. Not you. If this becomes a federal issue, the public will find out their world is about to be destroyed in a matter of days, and we both know what kind of panic will ensue if that happens?"

"I see your point. I'll have the Marines at the air station back you up."

"I appreciate the offer, but the fewer people involved on this, the better. It's your call, but I think stealth is the best option. Okana and I can handle it."

Donner thought about it, and knew Alex always accomplished his missions, and with Okawna to help him, it would probably work. "All right. We'll do it your way. My friend in Fallon and I used to work together. I'm sure he would love to accompany you on a nighttime mission. Strictly as an advisor, of course."

"Of course. Advisor it is."

"All right, Alex. I'll call Ramey and let him know you need his help."

"Thanks. Okawna and I are on our way. I'm just glad your jet didn't leave."

"Since I'm always sending it to you anyway, I've made arrangements to leave it at your disposal for the duration of this mission. And Alex, keep this in mind; don't get caught, especially if Ramey is involved."

"Sure thing, Martin."

Chapter 35

FALLON, NEVADA:

When they landed at the Naval Air Station, Alex and Okawna were met at the air terminal by a young sailor and driven to the Base Command Center, where they entered and approached the front desk and the young woman dressed in a white uniform. "I'm Alex Cave."

"Yes, Sir. Straight down the hall to the left. The commander is expecting you."

Ramey looked up when two men walked into his office and stood from behind his desk as he extended his hand. "I've been expecting you, Mister Cave. Mister Okawna. Welcome to NAS Fallon. I'm Commander Charles Ramey." He indicated the chairs before returning to his own. "Martin and I served together as part of the Navy Seals support team. You sure made a mess of my Hummer, Mister Okawna. What the hell happened to it?"

Alex exchanged looks with Okawna for a second. "I'm sorry about your vehicle, Commander. We were caught in an ambush."

Ramey stared back at his guests. "I don't suppose you can tell me why?"

"I'm sorry, it's classified. What do you know about the research facility south of here?"

"It's owned by John Essex, and they design experimental space equipment for commercial use. Rumor has it he wants to mine the moon. Martin said you're both good man, and to help you if I could. What have you got in mind?"

"We're looking for Essex and his partner and suspect they're holed up at his facility. I can't go into any details, except to say it's imperative we find them."

Ramey grinned. "Well, so be it. This sounds like fun."

"We didn't have time to see the entire complex, so if you can find out what type of added security measures he has in place, it would be a big help."

Ramey grabbed his phone. "All right."

Alex listened to him explain what he needed, and when he was through, noticed the Commander's grin. "It sounds like you've found something."

"You're in luck, gentlemen. One of my people has an aerial photograph of Essex's facility, and it will be here in a moment. Do either of you have any military experience?"

Alex looked over at Okawna and grinned before he answered. "Yes. In fact, we were CIA operatives for a while."

"That makes sense, knowing you're friends with Martin." He looked up when a sailor walked in and handed him a twenty-four-inch square picture of Essex's compound. He set it on the desk and stood to look at it with his visitors, and Alex pointed to the long piece of equipment hidden under the tarp and looked up at Ramey. "I saw this when we drove to the main building. I wasn't sure until now, but seeing this elevated view, I know it's an electro-magnetic launch platform. I guess Essex is serious about space travel."

"That's correct. The damn thing works too." He looked up at the man who appeared in his doorway. "Come in, Sean." He turned to Alex. "Gentlemen, this is Captain Sean Thurman, one of our squadron commanders."

Alex shook the man's hand and then explained what he needed to know. "Can you help me?"

Thurman nodded. "When Essex started construction, he had ground sensors installed throughout the compound, but he didn't count on our jets setting them off if they flew too low over his property. He even filed a complaint with the Department of Defense to raise the minimum altitude for all our aircraft over that sector." Thurman grinned. "We haven't received a formal order yet, so once in a while one of our jets will accidentally stray off course and set off his alarms."

"That's good to know. It would be a nice diversion if we have a problem." He studied the three-hundred-yards of open ground all around the structures. "That means no covert ground assault to the living quarters, and the spires on the roof make it too dangerous as a landing site. We can't take the chance of landing on the ground, so we'll have to land on one of the hangars. Could you help me with that?"

"I have a few aircraft at my disposal. I'll schedule a flight for twenty-two-hundred hours. How many people are going with you?"

Alex glanced at Okawna. "Just the two of us, Captain."

"I see. How are you planning to get out?"

Okawna gave him a smirk. "We have a friend on the inside."

"All right. Meet me inside hangar three at twenty-one-hundred hours. Tell me what kind of gear you need, and I'll have it ready for you." He turned to Ramey. "Will you be joining us, Charlie?"

Ramey smiled. "I wouldn't miss it." He looked at Alex. "I'll see you tonight, gentlemen."

***

The steady rumble from the propellers filled the bay of the C-140 Hercules while Alex sat quietly, thinking about Fala and Halona. His hands clenched into fists when he thought about Sloan and decided this ends here and now. He will not leave until she is dead. He felt a nudge and turned to look at Okawna.

"We're coming up on the drop site, Alex."

Alex stood and reached across to shake Ramey's hand. "I appreciate the support, Commander."

"I just wish you'd let me and a few men go with you."

"We know the layout and we know what we're looking for. We can take care of ourselves."

"So I've heard. Good luck, gentlemen."

When a gust of wind spread through the open bay, the trio turned around to look out the back of the aircraft as the rear hatch dropped open, exposing the light from a crescent moon on the desert far below. Alex looked over at Okawna, who had a dark, determined look on his face, and then the green light flicked on. "Let's go."

When the two men leapt out of the aircraft, Ramey grabbed the handrail and leaned out through the opening, staring at the two black silhouettes plummeting toward the sagebrush and sand. He stepped back inside and gave a command to the crewmember to close the hatch, then walked forward to the cockpit. "Take us home, Captain."

***

Alex and Okawna soared through the air toward the lights of Essex's compound until they were nearly on top of the hangars, and Alex turned his helmet to look over at Okawna and spoke into his headset. "Are you ready to get down to business?"

"Whenever you are. It looks like a security vehicle in front of the hangar where we saw the launch railing. I bet they're there to protect Sloan and the key."

"Lead the way."

Okawna grabbed the drag chute from his pocket, tossed it over his shoulder, then waited for the tug on his harness, but nothing happened. "Hey, Alex, I've got a problem. My chute won't deploy."

Alex knew they were running out of time as they continued to drop, but he was nearly sixty-feet away from Okawna. He quickly turned to join up with his friend to see what went wrong. When he reached his partner, he saw the problem. "The strings on the drag chute are tangled, so it won't open."

"Well, hurry and fix it. That hangar is getting awfully close for comfort."

Alex looked down for an instant, and then moved in closer to Okawna's parachute. "I'll try to drag it the rest of the way out."

Okawna looked back over his shoulder as Alex drifted above his chute, but he lost sight of him. When he looked down, the white roof of the hangar was getting bigger by the second. He trusted Alex with his life, but was getting a little nervous. "How are you doing up there, buddy?"

Alex drifted behind Okawna, gained some altitude, and then sighted in on the drag chute spiraling above Okawna's parachute pack. "Don't worry. I've got this."

Alex folded his arms back and moved to his target, and was within two yards of the drag chute when a sudden side draft pushed him slightly off course. When he tried to compensate, he drifted too far to the side, and then twisted his body around in the air, barely managing to reach out and grab the fluttering piece of cloth, then ripped it the rest of the way out of the pack.

Okawna felt a strong jerk from his harness as Alex shot past him, then an instant later, he watched Alex's chute unfold below him. "Thanks."

Alex dropped onto the roof with a soft landing, and as he was balling up his parachute, Okawna dropped beside him. They glanced at each other, hoping they didn't alert whoever was inside, and then crept over to the edge of the roof. A security patrol car was parked in front of the doors, but they couldn't tell if anyone was inside.

They moved back and continued around to the roof access ladder, bolted to the rear corner of the building. When they didn't see anyone, Alex climbed down and pulled his pistol from its holster, then peered around the corner at the vehicle. It was empty, and he nodded up to Okawna, who slid down the outside rails of the ladder.

The moment he hit the ground, Okawna pulled his pistol out and stayed close to the building as he hurried to join Alex. "What are we up against?"

"The vehicle is empty, so they must be inside. I'll check it out."

Alex hugged the front of the building while he crept over to the front window, carefully stood and looked inside, then hurried back. "I could only see one guard."

Okawna spun around to the security vehicle. "Did you hear that?"

"Yes, from the car radio. Someone is coming to relieve whoever is inside."

Alex remained near the corner while Okawna hurried around to the rear of the building as headlights approached and stopped next to the other vehicle. He recognized the man climbing out and kept his pistol low as he crept out of his hiding spot, and was upon the man before he reacted, aiming the gun at his head. "Easy, Coburn. Nice and slow, I want you to raise your hands."

Coburn turned and gave Alex a menacing stare. He didn't care he was looking straight into the barrel of a gun. He had his fair share of shootings and knew most of the time the person holding the gun was too chickenshit to pull the trigger. However, he knew by looking into Alex's eyes he was one of the few who had no qualms about killing someone. Even though he didn't want this dirt bag telling him what to do, Coburn slowly did as instructed.

Okawna slid up beside Coburn, jabbing his pistol into his side, then reached out and took the man's gun. "I knew we'd meet again."

Coburn glared at Okawna. "And I knew you two were trouble. It's usually the smartasses that cause the most the most problems for me. So, now what are you going to do? Kill me? You realize the moment your guns go off, every guard in this facility will be on you before you have time to piss your pants."

Okawna moved around in front of his new friend and smiled. "We don't give a shit about that. All we want is Essex's partner, Sloan. And you're going to help us find her."

Coburn slowly lowered his hands and crossed his arms over his chest. "Maybe I don't want to help you."

Okawna shrugged. "I guess I could just shoot you then." He pointed his gun at the man's crotch. "Tell me, Coburn, do you like your balls?"

"You wouldn't."

Okawna cocked the hammer on his gun and took aim. "Say goodbye to the boys."

Coburn held his hands up. "Wait, wait, wait! I'll help you, all right? Just don't shoot me."

"Good boy."

"What do you want with her, anyway?"

Okawna glared at him. "I have some unfinished business with her."

Alex eased Okawna back. "Listen, Coburn, have you heard about the recent tidal effects and the moon moving out of its orbit?"

"Yeah. So what?"

"It was Sloan's fault. She had access to something powerful, and it created this whole mess. We were able to stop it, but now we have a problem of another nature, and Sloan has a key we need to stop this new problem. If we can't get it, every living thing on the planet will be dead within a week. Will you help us?"

Coburn thought about it for a moment. "Jim."

Alex's eyebrows rose. "What?"

"Call me Jim. My sister lives in San Diego. She was able to escape further inland when the tides started ripping up the coastline, but she lost her husband and two kids to the landslides. You said Sloan was responsible for all this?"

"Yes."

Coburn uncrossed his arms. "That puts a new spin on things. Yeah, I'll help you find her"

"Do you know where she might be hiding?"

"Yes, she's in Essex's living quarters, but she's not alone. She's with a woman and a little girl."

Alex's mouth opened. "The woman and girl. Are they still alive?"

"Yeah, they've been here for a few days now. Do you know them?"

The sudden happiness nearly overwhelmed him, but Alex held it together. "They're our family. That bitch, Sloan, kidnapped them, and we thought they were dead."

Coburn frowned and looked Alex in the eyes. "Hey, listen, I didn't have anything to do with the kidnapping. I didn't even know the reason they're here until now. I just thought they were guests."

Alex saw the sincerity in Coburn's eyes. "It's okay, Jim. We know you had nothing to do with the kidnapping. Would you be able to help me get them out?"

"You bet I can. I know the code to get into his living quarters. You'll need a diversion, though. There are some guards patrolling around the main building. Hey, listen. Essex has a vault inside this hangar where he keeps prototypes of his inventions. If I report a break-in, the rest of the security force will be pulled from his living quarters to come here to investigate."

Okawna was as relieved as Alex to know Fala and Halona were still alive. "Does the vault have a steel door?"

"Yes."

"Good. I'll make it look like a robbery, so you don't get blamed for a false report."

Alex knew they were putting Coburn in an awkward predicament. Once his partner, Sam, realized Coburn was in on the theft, he would tell Essex, and there was no telling what would happen to him then.

Okawna had an idea. "Drive around the corner and radio your partner you're almost here, and to meet you outside. I'll take care of him so he won't know you're involved."

"You're not going to kill him, are you?"

Okawna held up a different pistol. "Nope. Tranquilizer darts."

"Works for me."

Coburn climbed back into his car and drove it around the corner of the hangar. A few moments later, Sam opened the door and stuck his head out to look around, and then grabbed the side of his neck when he felt a sting and slowly collapsed onto the asphalt. Alex ran around to the side of the building and waved Coburn back to the front, and once he parked and climbed out, the three men entered the hangar, dragging Sam with them.

Alex looked around the interior of the vast space and saw a strange-looking aircraft perched on the electro-magnetic launch railing. He just wished he had time to check it out.

Okawna got Coburn's attention. "Where's the vault?"

"Right. It's against the back wall."

Okawna grinned as he slid his backpack to the floor, reached inside, and brought out a roll of cream-colored cord. "Just show me where it is."

Coburn led them across the room to the concrete structure with a large steel door. "It's two inches thick. Can you blow a hole through that much metal?"

Okawna smirked at him. "This is not your normal detonation cord. It contains magnesium and aluminum powder, among other things, and it will melt through the steel in a matter of seconds."

Okawna finished sticking the clay-like material in an oval pattern on the steel door, then stepped back. When he pressed the igniter button on the end of a short fuse, glowing orange globules of melted metal dripped onto the concrete floor, and then a deep thud filled the room when the oval center crashed onto the ground.

Coburn grinned at Okawna. "Nice."

Out of curiosity, Alex and Okawna looked into the small room, and then stared at the models of interesting spaceships. There were also models of the living habits they saw in the hangar, then Alex turned to Okawna. "It's time to go."

"You don't have to tell me twice."

Alex knew if they burst into Essex's living quarters, Sloan could be armed. Maybe even Essex. The little man was always so jittery and paranoid they didn't want to risk getting into a gunfight, especially if Fala and Halona were close by. No, he wouldn't risk their lives again. "Hold on, Okawna. Jim, I have an idea. Rather than calling the break-in to the security dispatch, notify Essex first instead."

Okawna gave Alex a questioning stare. "I thought we wanted Essex in custody."

"We do, but if Jim calls this in to Essex first, I'm sure he and Sloan will come here to see what happened. If we get them away from the girls, we can rescue them without endangering their lives."

"Good point."

Coburn looked from Okawna to Alex. "One question. How are you planning to get out of here?"

Okawna smirked. "We were going to steal Essex's personal car and drive through the gate."

"That won't work. The guards know Essex, and they won't let you out. I have a better idea. I'll drive you through the gate in my patrol car and drop you off someplace, but I can't be gone too long or they'll get suspicious."

Alex was glad Coburn was on his side. "That'll work. I can arrange to be picked up when we're far enough away, so just drop us off and come back."

"Good. Once you've rescued the girls, hide somewhere outside the main building and I'll pick you up. I know the person on duty at the gate, and he'll wave me through without suspecting who is in my car."

Okawna put his hand on Coburn's shoulder. "Thanks. All right. Let's get started."

Alex and Okawna began jogging toward the main building, and Coburn waited for what he figured was enough time for them to get there, then called Essex.

***

Essex was in bed when he heard his phone ringing and slowly reached over to grab it. He looked at the screen and recognized the face, then pressed accept. "Coburn, this had better be important."

"We've had a break in at the electric launch hangar, Mister Essex."

Essex rolled off the bed and stood. "When?"

"I'm not sure, but recently."

"I'll be there in a few minutes. Don't touch anything. I want fingerprints."

"It may be too late for that, Sir. My fingerprints and Sam's are all over the place."

"I know that, you idiot! Just don't touch anything else! I'm on my way."

Essex slammed the phone down and hurried into the closet to change clothes then walked down the hall to one of his spare bedrooms. He threw open the door and flipped the light switch on.

When the door opened, Sloan rolled over and shaded her eyes against the light. "What's going on?"

"Someone broke into one of my hangars!"

Sloan rolled off the bed and stood in her panties and bra. "When? What happened?"

"I don't know, but we'd better go check it out."

Sloan pulled on her pants and slipped into her shoes. "It has to be Cave. Go find out what happened."

"Cave? Are you sure? He'd have no reason to break in to the electric launch hangar."

"No, but it could be a diversion. We still have hostages, remember? Plus, if it is him, I'm sure he'd be more willing to trade the device for the lives of the ones he loves once he realizes they aren't dead."

"He didn't agree before, so why should he this time?"

"Quit asking me stupid questions and go find out what happened. Now do as you're told."

"You're not my mother, so stop acting like it."

When Essex stormed out through the doorway, Sloan slid into her shirt and grabbed the pistol on the nightstand, ready to move to the front door, then had an idea. She slipped the gun into the back of her pants and headed down the hallway.

***

When Essex drove up and parked in front of the hangar, he recognized Coburn leaning against a patrol car, so climbed out to talk to him. "Show me what happened."

When Coburn noticed Sloan wasn't with Essex, his heart rate increased. He knew Alex and Okawna were walking into a trap, but at least the security force patrolling the main building were on their way here to the hanger. He stood and led Essex inside. "When I came to relieve Sam, it smelled like something was burning, then I found him unconscious on the floor, so I went over there to the vault room and saw the melted door. That's when I called you."

Essex hurried across the room and stared at the opening in the vault. "They must have brought a cutting torch."

When Essex went inside to look around, headlights from several security vehicles appeared through the front window, and Coburn ran out the door. "Secure the building!" He jumped into his patrol car and sped away toward Essex's living quarters, hoping he wasn't too late.

Chapter 36

HOSPITAL. NORTH BEND, OREGON:

Jerry stifled a groan as he sat up in the chair and stood to pull up his jeans. He looked at the television when the announcer introduced a meteorologist, then a young woman took over, talking about an unusual asteroid. When he saw the picture of a massive gold nugget, he stopped buttoning his shirt and grabbed the remote control off the bed to turn up the volume.

"Video clips of this ten-mile-diameter gold asteroid circulated on the Internet, where it was considered a hoax until verified by a reliable source at NASA's JPL in Pasadena, California."

"Are we going to get a better look at this gold nugget before it leaves our solar system?"

"Yes, its estimated trajectory will bring it within eight thousand miles of Earth once it passes Jupiter."

When a commercial appeared on the screen, Jerry pressed the off button and sat back down in the chair and bent down to tie his shoes, but grimaced in pain and eased back up. "This is going to be a long day."

Aaron stepped into the room from the hallway. "What was that?"

"Oh, never mind. I'm having difficulty bending down. Would you mind tying my shoes for me?"

Aaron knelt down and did as asked, then stood. "Have you got everything?"

Jerry got up and looked around. "Yep, that's it."

Jerry turned and headed out into the hallway with Aaron at his side. It took a few steps to loosen up his leg muscles, but soon his nephew had to keep up with him.

"I brought my truck so you don't have too much problem getting in."

"Thanks, Aaron. I appreciate it."

Aaron had parked close to the entrance and opened the door for his uncle. Once Jerry was comfortable, he climbed in and headed up to Humpback Harbor.

***

When Aaron drove his truck off the freeway, he had to stop before getting onto the two-lane road along the shoreline. He was about to turn right toward the marina and Jerry's home when his uncle put his hand on his arm. "What is it?"

"I'd like to see the campground."

Aaron hesitated, wondering how his uncle would react when he saw the damage. "You need to get home and rest."

"I'll rest when I'm dead."

"Don't talk like that. I nearly lost you."

"It'll take more than a ride to kill me, now take me to the campground."

Aaron turned left and headed south toward the campground, already dreading his uncle's reaction. A few minutes later, he stopped on the bridge overlooking the river.

Jerry eased himself out of the truck and then shuffled up to the railing. His heart broke as he stared out across what used to be his campground, when all that remained was the shower and restroom building, half buried in silt and debris. When he looked over the edge, remnants of his life's work were piled up against the pillars below him. He leaned back to steady himself, realizing everything he had so lovingly built was now only a memory, and tears rolled down his cheeks as he shuffled back to the vehicle.

When Jerry climbed in and shut the door, Aaron watched him wipe away the tears, knowing not to speak as he backed his truck off the bridge and headed for the marina. When he looked over at his uncle, Jerry appeared frail and withdrawn.

When Aaron parked his truck in the VIP spot near the boardwalk, Jerry noticed Curtis's sedan parked in the regular area behind his shop. He climbed out and stared down at the bare pilings dotting the marina, and in the distance, saw the rows of docks trailing from their buoys out in the harbor, and turned to Aaron, his heart bursting with pride. "You did a nice job. Thank you."

Jerry was about to walk along the boardwalk to the park when Brad drove up in his patrol car and climbed out, then he saw the concern in his nephew's eyes. "What's going on?"

"The sheriff is cruising along the shoreline with the other search and rescue boats. The entire western seaboard down to San Francisco has been torn up pretty badly, Jerry. FEMA is coordinating everything now, and they say this won't be the end of the destruction until the moon settles back into its normal orbit."

Jerry looked along the boardwalk at the seaweed and driftwood littering the once pristine waterfront. The shop owners and volunteers were cleaning up, and at the far end of the boardwalk, he noticed several people working in the park.

He strolled toward them, with Aaron and Brad at his side, receiving the occasional nod and thanks from the people he passed along the way. He also noticed the high-water marks one foot up the red brick foundations of the stores, eateries, and taverns. When they entered the park, he stopped and stared at the shattered remains of the gazebo, then looked at Aaron. "Was anyone else hurt when this happened?"

"No. It was empty, thanks to you, Jerry. You're lucky you weren't killed." He indicated the single section of mooring slip on top of the pile of broken boards. "We found you unconscious on the top of the dock, with a yellow rope wrapped around your rib cage. Did you wrap it around yourself before you slammed into the gazebo? Because it held you on top and saved your life."

Jerry stared off in thought for a moment. "I don't remember anything after the dock floated up over the piling."

Aaron stared out over the boat-less harbor. "I guess if this is going to keep happening, there's no reason to set up the mooring slips again. What are you going to do now, Jerry?"

He looked around. "That's a good question, but a better question is, how is this town going to survive without the marina and campground?"

Aaron realized Jerry was right and looked at his older brother. "You might think about applying for a job in another county."

"I was thinking of moving farther inland anyway, but I was going to wait until after you graduated from high school. But after seeing you in action organizing the removal of the mooring slips, I think you'll be fine without me. You can either come with me or stay with Jerry."

Jerry heard the roar of an engine, and went around the pile of debris, which had been the gazebo. When he reached the other side, he saw Curtis sitting behind the controls of a track hoe, getting ready to fill a dump truck.

Curtis noticed Jerry and his nephews looking over at him, so he shut off the engine and climbed down. He quickly took off his gloves and tossed them onto the seat, then hurried over to the Avery's, stopping in front of Jerry while holding out his hand. "I didn't get a chance to say thanks for everything you did."

Jerry accepted Curtis's offer. "I appreciate it, Tommy. I see you're not wasting any time."

"I held a quick meeting and we don't want the debris to reach Main Street, so we decided to start cleaning up before the next high tide."

"I didn't know you knew how to operate a track hoe."

"I'm not completely helpless, Jerry. I own a ranch, remember?"

"Fair enough."

"I'd better get back to work."

As Curtis turned and hurried back to his equipment, Jerry thought about Jadin's expression before she had left the hospital, wondering if perhaps the meteorologist was *ordered* to say the asteroid would miss the planet. It would explain her odd behavior just before she left, as though she would never see him again. He strolled to the railing on the other side of the gazebo and saw two of the steel posts and the handrail flattened against the concrete walkway.

Aaron noticed Jerry studying the railing and moved up beside him. "That's where you crashed through to the gazebo. You're a lucky man, Jerry."

"Maybe, but I don't rely on luck. It always seems to run out."

Aaron stared at his uncle. "We'll make it through this tough time. Things will eventually get back to normal, and I'll stay here and help you get things back up and running."

Jerry stared out across the harbor. "I hope we get a chance to do that."

Chapter 37

ESSEX'S FACILITY:

Sloan walked down the hallway and entered the other spare bedroom, where two bodies were lying on the bed. She turned on the lights and held a gun aimed at the woman and the little girl.

Fala woke up with Halona snuggled at her side. "What's going on?"

"It appears your boyfriend came to pay me a visit."

Fala sat up and looked into Sloan's eyes. "Alex is here?"

"Yes, possibly, and if you play your cards right, you and the brat could go home tonight. That's if your boyfriend cooperates. If he makes the wrong decision this time, I won't hesitate to kill you both in front of him. And then I'll kill him."

Sloan heard a tiny giggle and stared at the little rug rat, who was grinning at her. "What is so funny? I don't think your daughter understands the gravity of the situation."

Halona chuckled. "You have it backwards."

"What do you mean?"

"What you said. You have it backwards. You're not going to kill him. He's going to kill you."

Sloan's jaw dropped opened at the tenacity of the little shit. "I don't think so."

***

When Essex's car drove away, Alex hurried around the corner of the building to the door into his living quarters, with Okawna right behind him. "Stay here and cover me. I'll be out in a moment."

"Got it."

Alex entered the code Coburn had given him and stepped into the living room, listening for any noise. When heard the unmistakable sound of Halona's giggle, he sighed with relief. Thinking the coast was clear and Sloan had left with Essex, he tucked his pistol into its holster. "Fala? Halona? It's me, Alex."

Sloan grabbed Fala by the hair, yanking her off the bed and shoving the pistol against her head. "Don't say a word!" She noticed Fala's hands moving. "What was that? What are you doing?"

Fala held them up. "They itch when I get nervous, is all."

When Halona saw her mother's hand signals, she slid over the back edge of the bed as instructed. She was supposed to stay hidden, but she peeked over the bedspread.

Sloan heard footsteps in the living room, then another giggle from the girl. She kept the gun tight against Fala's head and moved to the side of the doorway, then waited for Alex.

Alex stopped at the junction in the hallway to look in both directions. "Where are you, Halona? If you can hear me, answer." He heard another giggle to his right. "Halona? It's me, Alex. Come on out, sweetheart."

Sloan glanced toward the girl who was hiding behind the bed, then yanked Fala's hair until she screamed before guiding her into the hallway. "Don't come any closer, Alex, or I'll put a bullet through her head." She watched Alex stopped in his tracks. "That's a good boy. Now, back away into the living room so I can see you."

"It's over, Sloan. Let them go."

"In case you haven't noticed, Alex, I have the upper hand here. I'm the one with the hostages, remember? Now move back to where I can see you."

Alex sighed and did as ordered. "Don't be ridiculous. You've seen too many stupid movies."

When Alex stopped in the middle of the living room, Sloan glanced around the corners before leaving the hallway. "Where's Okawna? You two are always joined at the hip. Don't tell me you came alone."

"He's outside."

Sloan cautiously moved into the living room and eased her way to the door. "I'm going to make this very simple for you, Alex. I want that device and I want it now. Or else your girlfriend dies. For real this time, right in front of you."

Alex considered his options, but Sloan was using Fala as a shield, so he could only hope Okawna would look through the window to see what was taking so long. "I'm begging you to rethink your decision about this device, Janice? It is the most powerful weapon ever discovered, and no one is safe from it. Not even you. Imagine that kind of power in the wrong hands, people with worse intentions than you. I can't let you have it. Now let them go and I won't have to kill you."

Sloan smirked at him. "Does it look like I care about the welfare of others, Alex, or the state of the whole planet? I just want my money. So forgive me if I turn down your offer, but I'd much rather sit tight until Essex returns with his mercenaries. Then I'll let them have their way with you until you give me that device. They'll be back any moment."

Alex knew he couldn't wait for that to happen and decided he needed Fala to move out of the way. The only problem was if he moved his head to give her a signal, Sloan would see it. A heavy thumping on the front door caused Sloan to look away, and Alex whipped his gun from the holster and focused it on Sloan's head. He jerked his head to one side for Fala to see, but she didn't seem to understand, so he did it again.

Fala stiffened when she saw Halona looking at her from the hallway, then she suddenly understood Alex's meaning. She brought her hands down so Halona could see her gestures, and when her daughter screamed, her maternal instinct kicked in, and a seething rage coursed through her body. She groaned against the pain in her scalp and twisted her head away from the gun as she tried to pull away from Sloan's grasp.

Sloan turned back in time to see Alex move closer to her. "You bastard!" When she felt Fala's hair being ripped from her hand, she pulled the trigger. A deafening explosion filled the room and she let go, then swung the gun around at Alex. The bullet from Alex's gun met her forehead, pitching her head backwards as brain matter splattered across the wall behind her. She collapsed onto the floor, slumped over in an unnatural position.

Alex rushed to Fala's side, kneeling to cradle her in his arms. "Are you hit?"

Fala stared up at Alex and yelled at the top of her voice. "What? I can't hear you! My ears are ringing!"

Alex pulled her close to his chest. "Thank God."

Okawna heard the gunshots and continued beating on the door, but it didn't open, so he used his pistol to shatter the front window and burst into the room. He saw Sloan on the ground, Alex cradling Fala, and Halona standing in the hallway in a state of shock, staring at the grisly scene. He rushed over and swept Halona up into his arms, covering her face while he carried her outside.

***

When Coburn pulled up in front of Essex's living quarters, he saw Okawna outside holding a young girl, and leapt out of the car. "I tried to get here as fast as I could to warn you Sloan wasn't with Essex. What happened?"

Okawna nodded into the living room. "Sloan is dead."

Coburn dashed inside, stepping over Sloan's body to reach Alex. "I'm sorry, but I didn't have any way to warn you. Is your lady friend all right?"

"Mostly, but she might have a ruptured eardrum."

Fala leaned back from Alex. "It's not ruptured, and the ringing is fading."

Alex leaned close to her ear. "Can you walk?"

"I think so."

She reached up and took Alex's hands as he stood, pulling her to her feet. When he tried to wrap his arms around her, she backed away and headed out the now open doorway.

Coburn looked toward the hangars, then grabbed Alex's arm. "We're running out of time. I've been gone too long and Essex will notice, so we have to leave before he alerts the front gate. If that happens, they won't hesitate to shoot."

"I promise to straighten this out with the local authorities as soon as I can."

"I know. I'll call this in when we approach the gate. Let's get you out of here while I still can."

Alex followed Coburn to the door, but before he stepped outside, he knelt down to search Sloan's pockets for the key to the gravity device. When he couldn't find it, he checked to see if it was around her neck, but it wasn't there either. He noticed an unusual outline underneath her shirt and ripped open her blouse. When he saw a more pronounced square outline under her bra, he reached in and pulled it out, then stood to put it in his pocket as he headed out the doorway.

***

Okawna was setting Halona in the back seat when he saw Fala walking toward the SUV, then looked inside. "Scoot over a little and make room for your mom."

Halona did just the opposite and scooted out of the vehicle with her arms out. "Mommy!"

Fala bent down and wrapped her arms around her daughter. "Are you okay?" She felt Halona nod against her shoulder and held her close as she stood. "It's over, baby. We're going to be okay."

Coburn looked around and then indicated the back seat. "Just lie down and don't be alarmed when you hear the siren."

When the girls were inside, Coburn closed the rear door while Okawna hurried around the SUV, opened the back hatch, and climbed in. Once Alex was in the passenger seat, he grabbed his radio. "This is Coburn. We've had a break-in at Essex's living quarters and the suspects escaped over the fence. I'm going after them, so open the gate for me." He turned on his siren as he sped away from the building and approached the gate. "Everyone stay down."

He drove them through the exit with no problem, and several minutes later, he pulled over next to a wide area of flat desert on the side of the road. "This is a good place for a helicopter to land, and no one from the facility will come looking for you out here."

When everyone climbed out and walked to the rear of the vehicle, Coburn grabbed a flashlight from the side compartment. "You can use this to signal your location. I'd better get back before I'm missed."

Okawna held out his hand. "I'm glad I didn't have to shoot you."

Coburn grabbed it. "Yeah, me too. My balls thank you as well."

Alex shook Coburn's hand. "I really appreciate your help."

"Yeah, well, I'm sure I'll get an ass-chewing from Essex, but it's worth it. Good luck."

As Coburn drove away, Alex called Ramey for a ride back to the base, giving him the GPS location from his phone. Next, he called Donner to explain what had happened. Fifteen minutes later, dust swirled up from the ground as a dull-gray helicopter dropped onto the desert. When they ran over and jumped inside, the bird quickly climbed back into the sky and swung around toward the base.

Ramey looked across at the woman and the little girl, then Alex sitting across from them. "What happened, Alex?"

"It's a long story, Commander. Let's just say we eliminated a threat and extracted some loved ones. "

Ramey leaned back. "Fair enough."

***

When they landed at the base, Alex saw Donner's jet on the tarmac, waiting for him and Okawna. As he watched him help Fala and Halona out of the helicopter, his heart broke over the misery he had caused them and turned to Ramey. "I'm hoping you can take care of Fala and her daughter until I can make arrangements to get them back home."

"Certainly, Alex."

Alex looked over at Fala hugging her cousin, and then when Okawna knelt down to hug Halona, Alex grabbed Fala gently around the sides of her face and kissed her passionately. "Head home and wait for me there. I have one more thing to do, and then I'm all yours."

Fala reached out, running her fingers through his hair. "No, Alex. This is goodbye."

"Fala, please don't start this again."

"I told you we are over, and I meant it. I can't compete with all this."

"You don't have to. I'll settle down and give you everything you want. I love you and I want to spend the rest of my life with you."

"But at what cost, Alex? You know as well as I do that you'll be miserable. The world needs you, Alex, to save it from itself. And even though I love you with every fiber of my being, I am willing to sacrifice my happiness so the world can have its hero."

"No. I won't lose you again."

As tears rolled down her cheeks, Fala stepped closer to Alex and kissed him gently. "Let me go, Alex. Please. You know I'm right."

Alex held tightly to her hands. "You know I love you, Fala. You will always have my heart."

"And you will always have mine."

Alex let her hands slip out of his, and then he slowly strolled towards the jet and entered the aircraft. The hatch closed behind him and he took his seat behind Okawna, and then looked out the window at Fala and Halona standing on the tarmac. As the plane taxied down the runway, he watched as the love of his life disappeared, and a tear slowly slid down his cheek.

***

When Essex parked in front of his building, he saw the door open and the window shattered, and cautiously entered. Bile rose in his throat when he saw the blood pool around Sloan's head and the semi-wet pieces of brain matter still peppered across the wall. When his stomach heaved, he turned and stepped back outside as a stream of vomit erupted from his mouth, splattering all over the concrete. He knew the local police would want an explanation, and he would be arrested, so the decision was made for him. He brought out his phone to call his attorney.

Chapter 38

GROOM LAKE:

David set his half-eaten sandwich on his plate, and then looked at the wall clock, which showed 9:52 PM, and there was still no word from Alex and Okawna. He just hoped they managed to get what they needed and looked across the table at Jadin. "I don't mind telling you, I'm a little nervous about testing the ship without Alex. If he's with us, I know he can help fix the situation if we get into trouble."

"I can tell you think highly of him. I feel the same way about my Uncle Jerry."

"How is he doing?"

She stared at the unfinished food on her plate. "Better. They released him from the hospital, and he'll be staying at our house while he recuperates. I don't know what he'll do now that no one can use his marina. My friend at JPL ran the numbers through the computer and it could take over a year for the moon to stabilize back to its original orbit. Even if we save the world from this asteroid, the tide is having such a devastating effect, in a few more weeks, it will completely redefine the coastlines. The world as we know it will be completely changed."

"The last I heard, California is losing massive chunks of shoreline each time the tide comes in."

"I know, and I feel so helpless. We have a spaceship with the most advanced technology humans can imagine, and we can't do anything about it."

They both turned when they heard the clatter of caster wheels in the main hallway leading into the hangar. They leapt out of their chairs and ran through the doorway, then caught up with Alex and Okawna, pushing the support frame holding two spacesuits and life support equipment toward the spacecraft.

When they reached the opening into the craft, Okawna and Jadin grabbed the rear end of the cart while Alex and David hoisted the front end over the rims of the airlock doors into the cargo hold. When the rear end was inside, they rolled it against a bulkhead.

Alex stepped on the lever to retract the wheels and then looked at his friends. "Okawna and I were talking, and if the space test goes well, we should keep going and complete the mission. The sooner we get this done, the better. What do you think?"

Jadin exhibited her usual enthusiasm. "I think that's a great idea!"

Okawna was worried. "Are you sure this is safe, David? I mean, neither of you have spacesuits if we lose pressure."

"Jadin and I are confident the ship is airtight, so we'll be all right."

Henry stepped into the cargo hold and looked around. "Is everything ready?"

Alex walked over and held out his hand. "We're all set, Doc. We'll see you when we get back."

Henry accepted the hand, but pulled Alex down for a hug. "I hope so, my friend." He did the same to the rest of the crew. "Good luck, for all our sakes."

When Henry stepped outside, Jadin closed the airlock doors and everyone went up to the control room. Alex stared out through the transparent outer wall and saw Henry standing next to the control for the massive hangar doors. When they opened, David eased the spacecraft out into a moonless sky. With his hand poised over the control panel, David smiled at his friends. "All right, buckle up, cause here we go."

Alex placed his hands on the window and stared down at the outline of the main runway, now quickly shrinking away below him. He thought about his experience in a similar craft a few years ago, which didn't go well, but with a little luck, this ride will have a much happier conclusion. He leaned against the back of one of the four chairs and stared behind the ship at the blue marble, growing smaller by the millisecond. If he failed to change the trajectory of the asteroid, every living thing on that distant world would be destroyed.

Okawna paced in front of the control console. "We're running out of time, David. Can't this thing go any faster?"

"I'm afraid not. This ship has two modes of operation. Normal space, with a maximum speed slightly slower than the asteroid, but still nearly eight-hundred-thousand-miles-per-hour, and faster than light speed, for covering great distances."

Jadin turned from looking at the stars around the distant gold dot to look at David. "That's impossible. Nothing can go faster than light."

"Not with any of our technology, but this spaceship can. The mirrored surface warps the light around the outside to create a field that also warps time and space around the ship. The ship isn't actually going faster than light, but the surrounding space is."

Alex listened intently, and a thought occurred to him, so he joined the others. "If this ship is slower than the asteroid, how are you planning to land on the surface?"

David looked down at the holographic monitor. "In seventeen minutes, I'll stop and reverse course at near maximum speed to let the asteroid catch up with us. Once we're on a parallel trajectory and speed, I'll ease us down onto the surface."

Jadin reached into a small cabinet, grabbed several small earpieces, and then gave one to Alex and Okawna. "I found these while we were waiting for you and the spacesuits to arrive. They must transmit and receive through the ship's intercom system, because I used one to talk to David from outside the ship."

Alex nodded and placed one in his ear. "At least we'll be able to communicate from the asteroid." When the conversation withered, Alex returned to staring behind them at the tiny blue dot against a star-filled background.

David held his finger over a colored touch pad. "All right, I'm reversing course now."

Alex watched the stars sweeping across his window as the spacecraft turned one-hundred-eighty-degrees. The ship suddenly stopped and Alex was thrown across the floor until he slammed into the wall, while Okawna crashed into the control console, and David and Jadin were compressed in their seats, then everything returned to normal.

David leapt out of his chair and knelt next to Okawna. "Are you hurt?"

Okawna sat up and David helped him stand. "I'm okay."

Jadin got up and saw Alex grimacing as he stood, and hurried over to help him. "Where does it hurt?"

"It's nothing. I'm fine. Is everyone okay?"

Okawna crossed his arms as he stared at David. "Who taught you how to fly?"

"Look, this is my first time in space, so give me a break."

"Well, any idiot knows you can't just slam on the brakes like that."

"That's not what I did. I haven't given it any power to reverse course, I just turned the ship around and it suddenly stopped"

Jadin checked the data on the monitor. "David's right. We should travel at the same speed and direction until he reverses course, so something's not right."

Okawna looked down at the floor, as if he could see into the cargo hold. "I bet it's that damned gravity device. I knew that thing was cursed."

David moved around and sat down in front of the control console. "Let me see if I can find out what happened. Just give me a second." He tapped some buttons while reading the data on the monitor. "It seems Okawna's right. There was a sudden change in the ship's inertial dampeners, and that's part of the gravity control system. It could just be a glitch. This thing crashed landed before we started trying to get it to work, so it's bound to have some quirks."

Alex massaged his elbow. "We don't have time to look into this much further. We're still alive and we're still moving, so we'll work that kink out when we get back home. Right now, reverse course and see what happens."

David waited until everyone was hanging on to the chairs, then entered the command and slowly brought the ship up to near maximum speed. "Everything appears to be functioning normally. Now all we can do is wait for the asteroid to catch up with us."

***

EIGHT HOURS LATER:

Jadin thought viewing the asteroid on a computer monitor was exciting, but now, with the gold and green rock only one-hundred-feet behind the ship, she realized just how massive it truly was. She at David and could tell he was having difficulty matching the spin of the asteroid, and after several attempts, he managed to get within one-hundred-feet, but the green and gold surface was still sweeping past his ship at six-miles-an-hour.

David looked at his friends, staring at the asteroid. "This is much harder than it looks, and I'm not sure what will happen when I try to land the ship. I'll try to ease us down, but you had better hang on to something."

Jadin had an idea. "Why don't we use this ship's gravity system to change its mass so it's not so difficult to control?"

"This whole concept is experimental, and I have no idea how the device will react. Even so, according to the logs about the experiment, we need to be at least four-thousand-yards from the asteroid when the gravity beam hits the ship in order to change its trajectory."

"I thought you said the device is off until you turn it on with the key."

"That's the theory, but I'd rather not take the chance. Just give me a moment to set us down on the surface."

"Hold on a minute, David," Alex interrupted. "You have a valid point about not knowing how the device will react, but you would still need to use this ship's gravity control to get off the asteroid. There has to be another option."

Okawna had an idea. "No problem. How about I just jump out onto the asteroid? I've jumped from a moving vehicle before, so how different could this be? I'll just tuck and roll when I hit the surface."

"It's different in space," said Jadin. "The laws of physics would make you bounce off the asteroid."

Alex had an idea. "I think I have something that would stop that from happening. It's a modification of how we're going to attach the device to the surface. Can you maintain this distance, David?"

"Sure. I can try to get you a little closer if you'd like."

"Let's not take the chance. I'll push off from the airlock."

"No," Okawna told him. "I'm sure you meant to say Okawna will push off from the airlock. Only one of us needs to do this, Alex, and you're injured. Besides, whoever stays here misses all the fun."

"The tether isn't long enough to reach the surface. You'd never be able to get back into the ship."

"Once I attach the device to the surface, I'll push off and you can come and get me." Alex was about to protest when Okawna smiled and put his hand on his friend's shoulder. "It's a walk in the park, or in this case, a walk on the asteroid. I'll be fine."

Alex knew it wouldn't be that simple and reluctantly agreed. "Let's go down and get you suited up."

Jadin followed them down into the cargo hold, and studied Alex's solution for attaching the device to the asteroid. Welded to a short steel rod, was an eleven-inch-square metal cage designed to hold the gravity generator. "Whatever gave you the idea of using VHB tape to secure the device to the asteroid?"

"A show called Modern Marvels. It's the strongest adhesive on the planet, and we're lucky the asteroid's surface is fairly smooth."

Okawna held up the roll of VHB tape. "So, what's your new plan to keep me from floating away? Stick this stuff to my feet?"

"Not unless you never want to move again. My plan is to put VHB tape on the bottom of the device, slide it into the cage, and have you shove it against the surface with the rod. The tape will hold it in place and you will be tethered to it so you won't bounce back into space. Toss me the roll of duct tape and I'll fasten the device permanently to the metal cage so it won't come free, then I'll attach your tether to it. Once the device is stuck to the asteroid, so are you."

Jadin reached out for the roll of duct tape in Okawna's hand. "I'll take care of it. Why don't you get undressed for the occasion?"

Okawna grinned as he gave it to her. "Nice pun."

Jadin became serious, and looked into his eyes. "This is a brave thing you're attempting."

"It's just another item to check off my bucket list."

Alex held the spacesuit open. "Are you sure you want to do this alone?"

"Of course. If something goes wrong, I'm counting on you to come and get me."

David's voice suddenly came from the intercom speaker. "Hey, I don't mean to rush you, but the closer this rock gets to Earth, the more difficult it will be to change its trajectory. We only have ninety minutes left before it's too late to make a difference."

"We're almost ready, David," Jadin answered.

Okawna stepped into the suit and felt the weight of the life support system on his back when Alex released the cable. When Alex stepped in front of him with the helmet, he smiled. "Don't forget to take some pictures for my scrapbook."

Alex tried not to let his anxiety show. "I will. Just be careful, okay?"

"You know me."

"Yeah. I do."

"See you when I get back."

Alex maneuvered the helmet over Okawna's head and slid the latch in place. "Radio check."

"Loud and clear."

"Read you the same. Here we go."

Alex guided him into the airlock, and when Jadin held out the cage, he attached Okawna's tether to the metal frame. He studied the duct tape to make sure it was secure, inserted the key into the device, and turned it on. When the three colored lights glowed, he slipped the rod into Okawna's hand. "I'm going to remove the protective film of the VHB tape, so don't let it touch anything."

"Got it."

Alex closed the sunshade on Okawna's visor, stepped around him and through the interior door, and then closed it to seal the airlock. Okawna pressed a blue-colored pad to equalize the pressure, and when it turned red, the exterior door slid open, and he looked across at the green and gold surface, slowly moving past the ship. When he pushed off, he realized something was wrong. "Oh, shit!"

When Alex heard Okawna, he ran up into the control room and saw the concerned expression in David's eyes, then spun around and stared through the window at his friend rushing toward the asteroid. "Why is he moving so fast?"

Jadin had followed Alex into the control room. "Oh, no! The asteroid's mass has significantly more gravity than we had expected."

Alex hurried across the room and put his face close to the transparent barrier, his body tensed in anticipation of what would happen to his friend. An instant later, he watched Okawna jab the device against the surface, crumple into a ball, and roll away from the device. He could only hope the VHB tape would hold everything to the surface as he watched the white tether line uncoil from Okawna's suit.

The line snapped taut for an instant, but the cage was ripped away from the device and Okawna continued tumbling across the surface. "No!" Alex roared, and slammed his fist against the barrier. Okawna lay sprawled on the dark green background, three-hundred-feet from the device. "Okawna! Talk to me, damn it!" Alex spun around to David. "I'm going out to get him."

David hated the idea of telling Alex he couldn't do it and gave Jadin a pleading expression for help. Jadin indicated she would and turned to face Alex. "No, you can't. I'm sorry. Even if there was a way to save him, we don't have enough time. This is the correct angle to change the trajectory, but once it rotates past us, we'll need to wait until it comes around again. And by then, it will be too late."

When he realized they were correct, Alex's hands clenched into fists in frustration and his elbow stung with pain. He turned back and looked out the window, staring at his friend. He noticed one of Okawna's legs move, then heard a moan through the ship's intercom. "Talk to me, Okawna." When Okawna rolled over onto his hands and knees, Alex breathed a sigh of relief. "I thought you were dead." He watched Okawna stand up.

"That was a ten-dollar ride. At least I'm not floating away."

Alex turned and smiled at his friends, who were doing the same. "I'll come get you."

"That's a negative, Alex."

Alex spun back to the barrier. "What do you mean? Don't be ridiculous."

"Getting here was the easy part, but I'll never be able to jump back into the ship. I barely rise above the surface when I move."

"I'll find a way to get you back."

"No, it will take too long. Just get away and move this damn asteroid so it doesn't totally ruin my day."

"He's right, Alex," said David. "Once we change its trajectory, we'll have time for a rescue mission."

Alex stared down at his friend, who waved up at him. "All right. Fine. I'll see you shortly."

He continued watching Okawna, who was shrinking to a small white smudge, as David backed the ship away from the green and gold surface. When the ship stopped, Alex looked over at David and received a nod he was ready, and turned back to the small white dot that was Okawna. "Here we go."

David released a deep sigh. "Okay. Three, two, one, on."

When nothing appeared to happen, Alex turned to David and saw his puzzled expression. "What's wrong?"

David pressed the amber pad several times, but nothing changed. "I don't understand. Why is it not working?"

Alex remembered an earlier conversation. "You said you couldn't shut it down from a distance the last time, because Sloan had turned it on manually. Maybe that changed its programming, and it will only operate in manual mode now." He turned to the window. "Did you hear my idea, Okawna?"

"Yeah, I'm on my way."

From their vantage point, they could only see the white smudge of Okawna's spacesuit, didn't seem to be moving, and Alex worried something had gone wrong. "Are you still there?"

"Yeah, I just arrived and the device. I didn't realize how far away it was. No wonder I blacked out." He knelt down beside the device. "Okay, I see the three touch pads, so which one do I push?"

"Essex said it was the top left pad."

"I don't trust him, do you?"

Alex hesitated. "No, but we don't have a choice. Once you push that button, you could be caught in the gravity field."

Okawna rolled off his knees and sat on his butt to look up at the ship. "It didn't kill Essex or Sloan, so just shut up and let me get on with it. All right, here we go. On my mark. Three, two, one, mark."

David noticed an eerie blue dot pulsating next to Okawna. "It's working, Alex. I can feel the drag on the ship. Okay, now it's my turn to set this bad boy on a new course. Three, two, one, on."

When nothing seemed to change, Alex spun back to David, who appeared to be straining to hold the amber button down while staring at the information on the monitor. "How are we doing?"

"It's not working, Alex. It has too much mass for the device to move enough to make a difference."

A brilliant explosion on the asteroid caused everyone to flinch, and then Alex spun around, staring at the charred remains of the gravity device. All that was left was a three-hundred-yard crater on the emerald and gold surface. His eyes searched the area near the crater, but saw no white smudge of Okawna's spacesuit. "Okawna, do you read me?" he listened to silence. "Okawna, are you there? Can you read me?" Still nothing. "OKAWNA!" he roared, and slammed his fist against the barrier. When he looked back, he saw the grief in David's eyes. "What happened?"

"I'm really sorry, Alex. I don't know what went wrong. Maybe we overloaded the system. The device was experimental, even to the original crew members, so maybe they didn't have time to work out all the problems. I just don't know."

Jadin looked away from the monitor. "I hate to be the bearer of bad news, but we weren't able to change the asteroid's trajectory enough. I'm afraid it's still going to hit the Earth."

Alex slammed his fist against the barrier again. "Okawna died for nothing!"

Alex stared forward at the beautiful blue planet, rapidly growing in size, while David kept the ship on a parallel course with the massive hunk of gold, now slowly moving past the window. In a few more minutes, he and his two friends would be the last living humans in the solar system. But what bothered him most was losing his best friend for a lost cause, and the suffering he had already put his loved ones through for no reason.

David decided to slow down and let the asteroid continue. At 800,000 miles-an-hour, his home would be destroyed in four minutes, and all he could do was watch the course of events from a distance. When he touched the pads to reduce their speed, nothing happened. He entered the command to reverse course, then felt the ship lurch, as if caught in a trap by the asteroid.

When he looked up, Alex and Jadin were staring at him. "Something's wrong. I can't break away."

Jadin hurried over to David's side and stared down at the symbols displayed on the small screen. "The asteroid's gravity is stronger than we thought."

Alex hurried over to join them, although he knew there wasn't much he could do to help. "Can we use this ship's engine to slow the asteroid down?"

David glanced at Jadin for an instant, and then nodded to Alex. "I suppose so, but it's still going to hit the planet."

"Would you rather sit by and do nothing?"

"Of course not, you know me better than that. Let's try it."

David gave the engine full reverse power, and the asteroid continued sliding past their view, only much slower than before. "I can feel the drag on the ship, but once we're behind it, we'll lose our grip completely."

Jadin turned to face him. "That's okay. At least we're trying."

Alex noticed Jadin move close to the invisible barrier and moved up beside her. "It's beautiful from out here, watching the Earth and moon doing their immortal dance with each other."

"I never thought it possible I would end up in outer space. I just wish the circumstances were different."

"I heard about the shift in the moon's orbit, but seeing it from out here, you can really tell how much closer it is to the planet."

"Yes, and it also increased in speed."

When the gold mass blocked their view, David waited until Alex and Jadin turned to look at him, then shrugged. "I think it's still working, but not for long. Our speed has slowed by one-hundred-thousand-miles-per-hour and it's still dropping, for what little good it will do."

A few moments later, the backside of the giant gold nugget slid past the ship, and then their speed dropped dramatically without the load. The asteroid raced away toward the planet and David reversed course, then increased their speed to catch up, even though he knew all they could do was watch the planet be destroyed.

Alex had trouble fathoming the incredible speed of the asteroid as it quickly shrank to the size of a basketball, with the Earth in its crosshairs. He felt incredibly helpless, not being able to change the outcome and having to watch it make an impact.

Jadin grabbed Alex's arm when she realized the moon's new orbit was moving it toward the asteroid. "Umm, are you seeing what I'm seeing?"

"Yes, I just hope the moon makes it in time."

Alex pushed his hands against the barrier, as if he could make the moon move faster by sheer willpower. The seconds ticked by as if hours, as the moon crept across the blue background. Inch by slow inch, the moon aligned on an intercept course with the approaching gold rock, and every muscle in Alex's body became tense in anticipation. "Come on!"

When the asteroid slammed into the moon at a shallow angle, a massive silver cloud of debris erupted from the surface, blocking their view of the asteroid for several seconds. Everyone held their breath, expecting to see a similar cloud of debris erupt from the planet, then Jadin was first to see through the cloud. "There it is!"

No one spoke as they stared at the asteroid, still moving on a collision course with the blue world. David changed their angle of approach for a better view of what was about to happen, when suddenly the giant gold nugget shot past the planet.

David leapt out of his chair. "It missed!"

Jadin wrapped her arms around Alex's neck, laughing and crying at once. Alex bent over and kissed her on the cheek and smiled, but when he looked out at the Earth, his smile slipped away when he thought about Okawna and turned to David. "We should get back to the base."

David stopped smiling, thinking the same thing as Alex. There was no reason to stay in space, and entered the command, then the ship changed direction.

***

Most of the concussion from the exploding gravity device was directed into space, but the rest slammed into Okawna, and he felt like a cannonball shot into space just before he blacked out. When he opened his eyes, a blue marble was floating among billions of white lights, and he realized he was alone in a vast expanse of emptiness.

"Hey, Alex, I could use a little help out here. Can anybody hear me? Hello? The scenery is nice, but I've had enough of this trip." For a moment, he thought it was just his imagination as the distant blue marble appeared to be growing larger by the minute, and then he realized he was headed straight for it. He wondered how it was possible and then remembered he was already racing through space on the asteroid at eight-hundred-thousand-miles-per-hour.

"Hey, Alex? If you can hear me, I would really prefer a different way of getting home." When no one responded, he decided to sit back and enjoy the view. A catchy song came to mind, so he began whistling.

***

Jadin tilted her head to one side. "I hear something."

Alex listened intently and heard a crackling sound from the intercom speaker. "Static?"

"No, there's a pattern to the noise. It almost sounds like, well, I'm not sure. Bad music, maybe?"

The static cleared and Alex smiled while he listened to Okawna whistling a song off-key. "Need a ride?"

The whistling abruptly stopped, and then Okawna's voice came through the intercom. "Hey, thanks for tuning in to the Okawna music station. Glad you could stop by. You *are* on the way to get me, right?"

"That's right. Too many complaints about the music you're playing, so we're coming to take you off the air."

David entered the coordinates, and then the ship immediately changed direction and headed away from the planet. "You're not too far away, Okawna, so I'll meet you halfway."

"That's a relief. I was on my way to a onetime engagement on this place called Earth. You might have heard about it. Of course, I'm not sure if it will be a lively audience."

Alex grinned. "You did it, my friend. It was surreal the way the events aligned to prevent the destruction of Earth. The last piece to the puzzle was slowing the asteroid enough to ricochet off the moon."

"Well, you just made my day even better. Hey, I see shimmering stars coming in my direction. Is that you? Because if it is, you're coming at me really fast, and. Oh, shit!"

Alex caught a fleeting glimpse of white when Okawna shot past the side of the ship just a few yards away. "Okawna?"

"Yeah, I'm still here. Damn, that was close. Seriously, David, who taught you how to fly? Listen, you might have forgotten that I'm moving in the opposite direction at thousands of miles-per-hour. So how about slowing down next time?"

"You could do a lot worse, Okawna. I'll swing around and approach you from behind, then try to match your speed."

Alex turned to look at David. "Can you maneuver enough to get him into the airlock?"

"Probably not, but I can get us alongside him, and you can jump out to grab him as we go past."

"What do you mean, go past him?"

"I can get close to his speed, but you can't imagine how difficult it will be to match it perfectly."

"All right. I'll suit up." He turned to Jadin. "Can you give me a hand? I may have a little problem with my elbow."

"Let's go below."

***

Okawna slid the sun shield up out of the way and watched his reflection slide along the side of the ship. "Hey, David, don't you think you should start slowing down?"

Alex stood in the open doorway of the airlock, waiting for Okawna to come into view. His plan was to jump out and grab him, but if he and Okawna were moving at different speeds, the odds would drop considerably. "How about it, David? Can you go any slower?"

"I can't see him from my vantage point, so tell me when we're close."

"Now would be a good time to start."

Alex wasn't prepared for the sudden change in speed and slammed into the side of the airlock, and then the opposite motion tossed him out into space, moving slightly faster than the ship. Okawna was just up ahead, but farther out than he hoped. In a few moments, his friend would drift behind him, and he would be forced to try again. The line jerked Alex back toward the airlock along the side of the ship, and he saw if he timed it right, he might push off and grab his friend as he passed by. He used the tension on the tether to align his feet toward the side of the ship and waited.

As Okawna drew near, Alex bent his knees, trying to get the most power out of the release as possible in space. "I'm almost even with you, buddy, so get ready to grab me when I do the same."

"I'm ready when you are. In case you haven't noticed, the Earth is getting bigger by the second, so don't miss."

"Here we go. Three, two, one. Now!"

Alex held the carabineer on the other end of the short safety line and pushed off, gliding out from the ship on an intercept course, hoping his judgment was correct. A moment later, he slammed into Okawna, fumbling for the clip on his harness. Pain shot through his arm when Okawna hit his elbow, but he gritted his teeth and pushed it from his mind. From the corner of his eye, he noticed the diminishing slack in the tether, and knew he was running out of time.

Okawna tried grabbing Alex's spacesuit, but he didn't have enough mobility to hang on. He wrapped his arms around one of Alex's arms and pulled him closer so he could attach the safety line. Alex stretched out, barely hooking the carabineer onto Okawna's harness when their motion was stopped by the short line and the reaction sent them both drifting back toward the ship.

Alex was facing away from the side of the spacecraft but knew what was about to happen. He grimaced when his backpack slammed into the side of the ship, then he bounced off, smacking into Okawna, driving them apart like pool balls. When they reached the end of the tether, they were jerked back toward the airlock.

Jadin stared through the window of the inside airlock door with her fists at her sides, frustrated there was nothing she could do to help them. If only she had a way to enter the airlock and drag them inside.

Okawna grabbed the short tether and pulled himself back to Alex. "I bet you didn't think something like this would happen when you woke up this morning." He noticed tiny ice crystals forming on the inside of Alex's visor. "Something is wrong with your life support system. We need to get you inside."

"I know. It's getting harder to breathe, but I have an idea."

"This should be interesting."

"Wrap your arms around the long tether and pull towards the opening. That should give you enough momentum to carry you back toward the airlock. I'll release the short tether connecting you to me, and you can slide along the long line and pull yourself inside."

"No way. You'll suffocate before you make it back to the ship. I have a better idea. Keep me attached and I'll drag us both back inside."

"You won't be able to hold tight enough with those gloves on."

"You let me worry about that."

Alex didn't argue, but it wasn't because he agreed, he just couldn't draw in enough air to speak. He was getting light-headed as he stared at the shadow of Okawna's spacesuit moving over his visor. Darkness appeared to be swirling down a tunnel in his peripheral vision, while he fumbled with the carabineer on his harness, then the tunnel collapsed.

Okawna slid along the line, waiting for the tug from the short tether, but it never came. "Damn it, Alex!" When he reached the open door, his glove became trapped between the ship and the line coming out from the airlock. He twisted around inside, barely managing to grab the handhold before he bounced back out through the opening. After attaching his short tether inside the airlock, he smiled. "All right. I'm inside, Alex. Are you ready to be rescued?" His smile slipped away. "Alex? Can you hear me?"

Okawna wrapped his free arm around the long line, pulled Alex toward the ship until his other hand came free, then dragged Alex faster to the airlock. Once he had him on the floor inside, he pressed the pad and the outside door closed, sealing the room. When the ship's artificial gravity came on, it caught him off guard and the sudden weight from his life support system drove him to the floor. He stared across at Alex's helmet beside him, but all he saw was the frost on the inside of the visor.

Jadin was staring through the window in the inside door of the airlock when the outer door closed. "We've got them, David! Get down here. I need your help."

She chewed on her lower lip as she waited for the airlock to pressurize. When the light turned green, she pressed the pad to open the inside door and knelt beside Alex. She couldn't see his face through the ice crystals, so she removed his helmet, and then saw his skin was pale, his lips were blue, and he didn't move. She had difficulty tilting his head back with his suit on, and when she tried breathing into his mouth, his passageway seemed blocked.

Okawna set his helmet to the side, then reached over and grabbed Jadin's arm. "Help me out of this suit so we can get him inside."

Jadin quickly released the straps on his backpack and then helped him stand up and slip out of the suit. David appeared, tossing the parts of Okawna's space gear into the cargo hold, and then they carried Alex out of the airlock.

Okawna started releasing the straps on Alex's backpack. "Breathe for him while I get him out of the rest of the suit."

Jadin didn't hesitate, knelt beside Alex, and began rescue breathing while Okawna slipped Alex's arms out of the suit, and with David's help, soon tossed everything out of the way. When Alex's complexion darkened, Jadin stopped assisting when he was breathing on his own.

Okawna smiled when Alex's eyes slowly opened. "Don't you ever do that again. I thought you were a goner."

Alex reached out and Okawna helped him to stand. "I guess my plan worked."

"That was stupid, Alex. I could have gotten you inside much quicker my way. We nearly lost you."

"I knew you had my back."

Okawna hugged him. "Always, brother."

Alex placed his hand on David's shoulder. "Take us home."

Everyone made their way back up to the control room and stared out through the front window, while David brought the ship relatively close to the planet above western North America. He slowed down to match the rotation and slowly descended into the atmosphere.

Chapter 40

GROOM LAKE:

David eased the spaceship into the hangar, where they saw a crowd of base personnel awaiting their arrival. Once the ship settled on the floor, the foursome walked down the stairs to the airlock, and when they stepped outside, the crowd applauded their accomplishment.

Henry hurried over to shake their hands. "You did it. How did you know to set the asteroid on a collision course with the moon, Alex?"

"It was pure luck, Doc."

"Director Donner would like you to call him right away."

"Of course he does."

"Now that we know this ship is capable of space travel, he would like to start a training program for NASA pilots."

Alex felt a hand on his shoulder and shook hands with one of the scientists. When he turned back, Henry was talking with an older woman, and he looked around at the grateful smiles from the base employees, feeling a sense of relief at the success of the mission.

Jadin felt a vibration from the phone in her pocket and brought it out to see who was calling, and recognized the number. "Hey, Patrick. Please tell me you have good news."

"I don't know how it happened, but the asteroid hit the moon and missed the planet."

"And?"

"Well, it knocked it closer to Earth and put it on a different orbital path."

"Damn! So the tidal effect is going to get even worse?"

"Actually, no. It was pushed so close to Earth so fast that our planet's gravity had a sling-shot effect. This will cause the moon's orbit to be more elliptical for several weeks until it settles back into its original pattern, but it will pass farther away, so lower tides for a few weeks. I don't know how it happened, but it looks like the asteroid corrected the moon problem."

Jadin heaved a sigh of relief. "That's great news. Thanks for letting me know."

Jadin saw Alex staring out through the window in the hangar door and went over to tell him the good news. "Things will be back to normal in a few weeks." When he continued looking across the desert, she put her hand on his arm. "I thought you would be happy we succeeded."

When he turned and looked at her, the sad expression in his eyes gave her the answer. "Just remember. Fala left you, not the other way around."

"Yeah, but I don't blame her." He indicated the spaceship. "This is who I am, and it's not what she needs."

When Alex turned back to the window, she wrapped her arm around his and stared across the desert with him. "I suppose you're right. As for me, I've been transferred to this top secret facility, and I'm looking forward to our next adventure."

***

MONTANA:

Donner's jet dropped Alex off at the airport in Bozeman, and would continue on to Oregon and Alaska to drop off Jadin and Okawna. After saying goodbye to his friends, Alex left the plane and entered the air terminal, then turned and stared back through the window as he watched the plane take off with his friends. This was the first time he'd been alone in a long time, and it felt awkward.

He grabbed his bag and carried it out to his SUV, tossing it onto the back seat before climbing in behind the steering wheel and starting the engine. After pulling out of the airport parking lot, he began a sad journey back to his ranch, where Barney would be the only one there to greet him. No giggling little girl begging him to carry her. No lovely woman with raven-colored hair to embrace him and kiss him hello. The house would be as lifeless and abandoned as he had left it.

Before, it was his sanctuary. A place to return to after his adventures and not be bothered by anyone, but over the past nine months, it had turned into a home filled with love and laughter, and it would never go back to the way it was. Now, it was a painful reminder of his life with Fala.

Rain splattered against the windshield, adding to his despondency, and even the thought of returning to his structured life as a teacher depressed him. As he listened to the rhythmic beat of the wipers sloshing across his windshield, he realized there was nothing left for him in Montana, and it was time for a change, a major change. He knew he would never be happy unless he was doing what he loved the most, and at that moment, he decided to move to Groom Lake and work full time with his friends. Fala was right, he was an adventure junkie, and he'd be miserable if it was any different. He smiled at the prospect of this new career and felt a surge of excitement. "I wonder if they'll let me bring my dog."

The end.

I hope you enjoyed Gravity, and I would appreciate it if you take a moment to write a short review.

Thank you for your time.

James M. Corkill

The next Alex Cave adventure.
PANDORA'S EYES

Chapter 1

GROOM LAKE, NEVADA:

Ex-CIA operative and geophysicist Alex Cave stepped into his friend's office. "What's going on, Doc?"

Doctor Henry Heinz, the base director, waved Alex over to a chair beside him to look at a monitor. "I received this recording from the International Space Station. It was taken after the launch of a new satellite called the SV1, for Space Vacuum One. It is supposed to be an efficient way to collect the orbiting space debris."

"Sounds like a good idea."

"Yes, but what they are using to do it got my attention."

Alex watched the recording, showing an eight foot long, octagonal cylinder with solar panels, floating among the stars, then a knot formed in his stomach when he saw the twenty foot long, torpedo-shaped device protruding from the center, and pointed to the monitor. "That looks like one of the alien weather control devices that nearly caused a new Ice Age, and I barely managed to get all four of them under control. Let's go, Doc. I need to make sure we're missing one."

They hurried down the hallway to the large commercial elevator, where Henry entered a code and stared into the retina scanner. The outside door opened, and then Alex grabbed the interior mesh door and slid it up. Once he and Henry stepped inside, Alex repeated the process to go down.

The elevator stopped at the lowest level, where Alex opened the doors and led the way along a wide corridor. When they reached the large door at the end, Henry entered a code and stared into a retina scanner again. The lock clicked and Alex shoved the door open, then rushed into the room and slid to a stop when he saw only one cylinder in the metal rack. "Damn it, Doc! This is supposed to be a secure facility. How can two of them be missing?"

"I will find out how someone managed to steal them. Your job is to get them back before he causes a global catastrophe."

Neither Alex nor Henry spoke until they entered the office, where Henry sat down and typed a command into his computer before looking at Alex while they waited. "You did not finish telling me about these devices."

"Oh, right. They were designed to attract pollutants from the atmosphere, but whoever is in control thinks it's going to attract the debris in space."

"I believe it is a good idea. All that rubble has to be tracked, and it has already caused millions of dollars in damage to several satellites, spacecraft, and even the International Space Station."

"You're right, Doc, if they know what they're doing. All the information about how they operate is on board our spaceship, so how could they possibly know what they're doing with that device without some kind of instruction manual? They don't realize they're meant to work in unison, all connected somehow."

Henry heard a beep and turned to the monitor. "One of our people here at the base signed for all the devices. Wait a minute. He quit eight months ago, right after the arrival date."

"That still doesn't explain how they know about its operating system."

Henry entered a command. "I had David make a copy, and I uploaded the information." When he saw the new data, he leaned back in his chair. "Someone hacked into my computer and made a copy of the data."

Alex stood and pulled his phone from his front pocket. "I'll call Martin right away."

On the first ring, the secretary for the Director of National Security answered. "This is Alex Cave. Is Director Donner available? Okay. Please have him call me right away." He looked at Henry. "He's in a meeting."

"I wish we had left them in the ocean, Alex. I have a very bad feeling about all this."

"We didn't have a choice, Doc. In order to get rid of the devices, they all must be together in one place."

Henry stared up at his friend. "Will you ever tell me your secret?"

"If what I suspect happens, I might need to tell all of you."

"Perhaps the Director could find out how they were stolen."

His phone rang, and Alex recognized the picture of the Director of National Security. "Hey, Martin. You're on speaker with the Doc."

"Hi, Alex. Are you getting settled in okay?"

"I'm getting there."

"What can I do for you?"

"Three of my devices never made it to the base, and their operation manual was copied. Now one of them is in orbit, called the SV1. Do you know anything about the company who owns it?"

"Yes, they're a reputable company with several military contracts. Have you ever heard of the DAR Corporation?"

Alex's posture stiffened when he thought about his unscrupulous dealings with the owner not too long ago. "I have. I thought they were demolition and reconstruction contractors."

"That's only a subsidiary of the main company. Their goal is to collect the billions of dollars' worth of precious metals from space. In fact, they're doing the first orbital test this afternoon, about 4:00 PM your time. The crew on the space station will send a live broadcast of the event."

"That's only six hours from now. You have to stop them, Martin. They have no idea how dangerous they could be."

"I believe you, Alex, and I'll do what I can, but one of these days, you had better tell me more about them."

"I know. In the meantime, could you send me all the data you have on DAR and the SV1?"

"I'll have my secretary send it to your private email account."

"Thanks, Martin."

Henry waited until Alex put his phone away. "Is there anything I can do to help?"

"Yes. Set up a remote video camera on that remaining device and monitor it during the test."

Henry thought about it for a moment. "If they are as dangerous as you claim, perhaps we should move it to the surface, away from the base."

"We're better off keeping it where it is. They were built to react with the environment, and there is less air in the vault."

"Very well."

"I'd better call Okawna. I hope he can have Bett pick me up in Seward." Alex selected the contact, then a moment later, he recognized the image of his best friend. "Hey, Okawna. Where are you right now?"

"I'm on the Mystic and we've just refueled in Seward. We're getting ready to head back out to resume the search for the last device. Why?"

"Don't leave."

"All right. How about a little more information?"

"Have you heard about the SV1?"

"No. Is there a problem?"

Alex told him about the missing devices and explained his concern. "The problem is the one in the water. When they activate the one in space, the one in the water will start freezing the ocean at an incredible rate, and you don't want the Mystic to be in the vicinity."

"How do you know about all this stuff, Alex? Oh, right. It's super top secret."

"I'm really sorry, my friend. If things develop like I think they will, I'll explain everything."

"Is there anything I can do to help?"

Alex thought about the *Mystic*'s helicopter pilot, Betty Mason, a feisty little woman married to Joshua, the ship's technical expert. "Is Bett on board?"

"Yeah, do you need a ride?"

"I do, but not from here. I'll meet you in Seward."

"Okay, I'll be waiting."

Alex put away his phone. "I need to borrow the jet. I'm meeting up with the *Mystic* in Seward, so I can keep an eye on what happens with the device in the Bering Sea when they activate the one in space."

"Yes, of course. Would you like to take David with you?"

"No, he should keep working on the cloaking system in spacecraft. Okawna and I can handle it."

"Of course. Keep in touch."

"I will."

***

EASTERN WASHINGTON. SV1 CONTROL CENTER:

Paul Carter was standing behind a young man, Scott Brackenbury, and a woman, Teresa Taylor, who were sitting in front of computer monitors. He looked at the large television mounted to the wall, showing a live image from SV1's on-board camera, and placed his hand on Scott's shoulder. "All right. Let's see what she can do."

Teresa turned to look at Paul. "You've decided the SV1 has a sex?"

"Fine. See what *it* can do. Are you happy now?"

She grinned. "Yes, thank you."

She turned to Scott, one of the engineers on the SV-1 project. "Ready when you are. Let's fire it up."

Scott placed his finger on the enter button of the keyboard and felt his heart rate increase. "Thrusters on standby. Sending command now."

Carter stared intently at the image from the camera showing the small end of a spinning, funnel-shaped distortion off the pointed end of the device. "Good work. Let's start with the harmonic resonance frequency to attract carbon atoms."

Scott entered the command into his computer. "All set."

Teresa studied the data on her monitor. "Verified. It's on."

The television showed a flash of reflected light, and then a slowly rotating silver object entered the distortion. "That looks like some kind of wrench."

Scott looked up from his monitor. "The field is holding. We've caught it!"

Teresa captured a still image of the wrench and did a recognition comparison. "It's one of the tools used by the Hubble telescope repair team."

Scott adjusted the camera for a wide angle view. "We're attracting more material, and at this rate, we should have this section cleared in a few hours."

A soft beeping came from the computer speaker and Scott saw a second resonate frequency, oscillating 180-degrees out from the one in use by SV1, then a moment later, it was gone. "That was strange."

***

NORTH OF DARRINGTON, WASHINGTON:

Rita Harrow stared up at the pewter-colored torpedo-looking device pointed up into space, then at the small monitor for the control computer. When the seconds vanishing on the digital clock reached zero, she pressed a key, and the device shut down and she looked over at Steve Preston, the owner of the DAR Corporation, and her lover. "The effect should be over."

Preston looked over at the tall woman with red hair. "Are you sure you have this thing under control? I mean, your first test altered the jet stream over the Northern Pacific Ocean, and now California is suffering a massive drought. Will it return to its original course?"

She crossed her arms over her chest and stared down at the ground. "I hope so. I didn't mean for that to happen."

"Are you ever going to tell me how you know so much about these devices?" He noticed the rage in her eyes when she looked up at him. He could tell whatever caused it was still bothering her.

Rita put her hands on her hips. "Why not? I was on a research ship called the *Mystic* off the coast of Washington, when a man named Alex Cave suddenly showed up and I was fired. I couldn't complete my mission, and it pissed me off. A friend did a background check on him, and it turns out, he's a close friend of Martin Donner, the Director of National Security."

Preston stared at her, waiting for her to finish. "And?"

"The *Mystic* belonged to millionaire Mike Tanner, who evidently became Cave's good friend. I figured my being fired meant they were up to something big, and I've been keeping track of Tanner's different ships to find out what it is. It turns out one of them recovered another device like this one and we took it. That's the one you have in orbit. One of our spies working at Groom Lake told us another one had suddenly arrived there, and a third one was being shipped from Adak Island in Alaska." She tilted her head toward the trailer. "You're looking at it."

"I see. How did you know what it does?"

"We managed to get our hands on the instruction manual."

"Don't tell me. Your spy at Area 51."

Rita didn't reply and pressed a button on the control panel, and then the twenty foot long torpedo-shaped device slowly dropped back down into the custom trailer. Another button closed the top, and then she shut the side door to the control panel and turned back to Preston. "I can hit anywhere at any time."

Preston stared back. "I'm not so sure."

"Now that we have one in orbit, I can hit with pinpoint accuracy." When his eyes remained uncertain, she turned back to the trailer. "Fine. Believe what you want."

Preston looked at his wristwatch. "I'd better get going. I need to be the first person to sign the contract to do the search and rescue, with a clause that says my company gets the contract for the cleanup. I'm going to make a fortune by controlling the weather and getting paid to clean up the mess I created. Isn't that a kick in the ass?"

"I know, and I get twenty-five percent."

Preston's smile faltered for a moment. "Even so, we're talking millions of dollars."

When Preston turned and climbed into his silver SUV and drove away, Rita stared after him for a few moments, wondering why he didn't kiss her before leaving. She hurried to the customized motorhome that towed the trailer, climbed inside, and then headed north toward US Interstate 5.

Award-winning author James M. Corkill is a Veteran, and retired Federal Firefighter from Washington State, USA. He was an electronic technician and studied mechanical engineering in his spare time before eventually becoming a firefighter for 32-years and retiring. He has since settled into the Appalachian Mountains of western North Carolina, and has a fantastic view from his writing desk.

He began writing in 1997, and was fortunate to meet a famous horror writer named Hugh B. Cave, who became his mentor. In 2002, he rushed to self-published a dozen copies of Dead Energy so his wife could see his book published before she was taken by cancer. When his soul mate was gone, he stopped writing and began drinking heavily.

His favorite quote. "When you wake up in the morning, you never know where the day will take you."

In 2013, he met a stranger who recognized his name and had enjoyed an old copy of Dead Energy, except for the ending. When she encouraged him to start writing again, he realized this chance meeting was just what he needed to hear at the right moment. He quit drinking and began the rewrite of Dead Energy into The Alex Cave Series, and thankful for that fateful encounter.

Other books by James M. Corkill
Dead Energy. The Alex Cave Series Book 1.
Cold Energy. The Alex Cave Series Book 2.
Red Energy. The Alex Cave Series Book 3.
Pandora's Eyes. The Alex Cave Series Book 5.
DNA. The Alex Cave Series Book 6.
Parallel. The Alex Cave Series Book 7.
Impact Yellowstone

Movie scripts available from the author.
You can contact him at. Jamesmcorkill@gmail.com